OLIVER R. FITZSIMMONS

NOTHING
LEFT BEHIND

Nothing Left Behind
© Oliver R. Fitzsimmons 2024

ISBN: 978-1-923289-22-2 (Paperback)

A catalogue record for this book is available from the National Library of Australia

Cover Design: Oliver R. Fitzsimmons and Clark & Mackay
Format and Typeset: Oliver R. Fitzsimmons and Clark & Mackay
Published by Oliver R. Fitzsimmons and Clark & Mackay

Proudly printed in Australia by Clark & Mackay

I owe thanks to my English teacher Mr Larkin for
encouraging my original interest in writing.

Thanks to my mother for doing the heavy
lifting in getting my work published.

And thanks to my editors, Michelle and Jason, who
polished this book into being its best possible version.

CONTENTS

Chapter One	Condemned	1
Chapter Two	Graduation	15
Chapter Three	The City Of Death	21
Chapter Four	An Odd Encounter	25
Chapter Five	The Path To Power	29
Chapter Six	Into The Abyss	39
Chapter Seven	Haven	45
Chapter Eight	The King	61
Chapter Nine	Escape	77
Chapter Ten	Deus Ex Machina	81

Chapter Eleven	Truth Is Pain	89
Chapter Twelve	Beast Of A Problem	95
Chapter Thirteen	People Of Faith	103
Chapter Fourteen	Lunacity	113
Chapter Fifteen	A Bright Greeting	119
Chapter Sixteen	Temptation	131
Chapter Seventeen	They Loved Cake	141
Chapter Eighteen	The Avarice Of Man	145
Chapter Nineteen	Addicted To Rageahol	149
Chapter Twenty	Obsessions	153
Chapter Twenty-One	God Loves Violence	159
Chapter Twenty-Two	Forlorn Frauds	165
Chapter Twenty-Three	The Heart Of Caligo	171
Chapter Twenty-Four	The Cost	185
Chapter Twenty-Five	The Birds!	197
Chapter Twenty-Six	Living Nightmare	207
Chapter Twenty-Seven	Running Before Time Runs Out	215
Chapter Twenty-Eight	Homecoming King	219

Chapter Twenty-Nine   The Ego Of Odin 223

Chapter Thirty   Blood Brothers......................... 233

Chapter Thirty-One   Battle Of The Gods.................. 241

Chapter Thirty-Two   Revenge.................................... 251

Chapter Thirty-Three   If It Worked The First Time ...259

Chapter Thirty-Four   Salvation.................................... 265

CHAPTER ONE

CONDEMNED

A young man despised the world in which he had the misfortune to live.

He hated his generic name and was bewildered by the names given to the children by the 'Seniors'—who, in his opinion, only had a loose grip on any art or literature.

John Smith was named after his father: John Salt, and his mother: Charlotte Smith, who had her name based on the label on a crate: *Granny Smith Apples*.

There were eighteen other 'John Smiths' in his village and forty-two other 'Johns'—each one's name was given odder origins than the last.

Everyone in the village was named after an oblique source.

The Seniors tossed documented knowledge at the children of the village, ordering them to teach themselves, expecting them to be utterly independent.

John, however, while being self-taught, had actually taught most of the children in his age group. Although not a genius, his intelligence exceeded any average, albeit he occasionally didn't distinguish the difference between fact and fiction.

Some educational input was made by the Seniors, and yet, most lessons consisted of listening about the *magic doom* that the world had long ago suffered, a disaster that arose from the consequences of divinity, ravaging the world they had been born to protect.

At seventeen years of age, John was bored of his sheltered existence in this enclosed *village*, which was, in reality, a collection of people living in a massive crater that had walls of shattered concrete blocks and rusted iron. The crater held around a hundred shacks to house a total of five hundred people; there was enough room to spare, but limited chance for privacy.

John and his only close friends—Walter 'Wally' Wyoming and Colonel 'Connie' King—had been companions for as long as any of them could remember; they were like brothers, except without the detriment of animosity.

The trio were all orphans, as their parents were assumed dead over a decade ago, after they had reportedly departed on an expedition to discover more survivors of what was referred to as 'Post-Apocalypolis' and had never returned.

John had little knowledge of parental affection: his mother had died shortly after giving birth to him, and the memories of his father were vague at best. He never knew the presence of a parent, and he didn't know how the absence had afflicted him.

The Seniors dwelt in a sizeable, presumably well-furnished metal tube dubbed the 'castle', despite it seeming more akin to a lone tower of steel with bent appendages. The village itself was named after a large fading inscription, the only figure still legible being an Arabic numeral for seven, thus the village was 'Seven', and the people were simply the 'Sevenites'.

It was early afternoon, and John and his comrades peered out from an alcove that had circular windows and was in a far-off section of the village; the semblance of a city neither of the boys had seen before could be seen, and beyond it was a collection of extensive hills, which appeared like the shoulders of sleeping giants. The city's status seemed to be in between formed and formless as, for any roof still standing, there was another that had caved in—it was as if the houses were teeth rotten from decay.

Opposite a collection of warehouses in the seeming centre of the city, four skyscrapers of variant heights overshadowed the ruins; the buildings were their own kind of corpses, as two had lost half of their shell, revealing a cross-section of steel beams.

'Upon that rock, I'll build my temple,' said Connie, his gaze fixed on the hills beyond the city of limbo.

'Hasn't someone already beaten you to it, bro?' said Wally.

'Not those ruins.' Connie rolled his eyes. 'The hills must hide some land worth exploring.'

'I wish I could share your optimism, Connie,' John—the youngest of the three—admitted, often speaking only after others.

'What? Don't you think there's something out there?' Connie asked.

John slouched in brief contemplation before he said, 'If there was anything worthwhile out there, it'd be gone now; the gods left us nothing.'

'No offence, but I hope you're wrong, bro.' Wally shook his head.

'Yeah, we don't know anything for certain,' said Connie. 'Besides, if there is nothing, we'll just build something up ourselves. Kind of my point.'

John chuckled. 'I hope to help somehow.'

'I'll hold you to that, buddy,' Wally replied. 'I guess we ought to be grateful the gods left us anything at all.'

John tutted.

After staring out into the ruins for an hour or two, the three friends progressed to a proverbial corner of the village, in which they sought further amusement.

The entertainment ultimately consisted of hours of rummaging through the mounds of cracked glass, broken metal, and twisted plastic that made up the village's floor in oft-vain attempts to discover something interesting that would take their minds away from the world.

John and his two friends continued to dig and softly claw into another pile of scrap, looking down to avoid staring at the counterfeit sky that was made of tarp and sickly eternal sunshine. John's eyes were pale grey, which reminded him of his boredom each time he saw them reflected from shards of glass.

Wally was the tallest of the friends; Wally's own opinion of displaying age and wisdom, aside from height, was the presence of facial hair, and he was proud of his sideburns.

Connie, like John, had grey-coloured eyes; however, his most notable attribute was his thick and wildly unkempt blonde hair, as he was the only blonde in the entire village.

John began his regular descent into melancholy until something in the rubble caught his eye, as well as the hawk-gaze of a supervising Senior. John gripped the item and lifted it out of its plastic prison. It was an odd object of metal.

John had learnt as many words as he could from reading the stories and dictionaries available in the crater's library. The carving *DESERT EAGLE* was spelt along the object's slide. He knew what a desert was, as it encompassed the outer rims of the limbo city, and he knew of birds, in theory, yet the object didn't share much similarity to an avian creature. It was an item unknown to him and most of his peers.

The Senior's arms uncrossed.

John tried to hold the barrel of the gun. 'It looks a bit like the village's seven sigil.'

The supervising Senior began to slowly descend towards the friends.

John turned the object in his hands until he held it by the handle. He noticed that his index finger slid into the loop that was home to the trigger.

Connie approached John. 'Hey—is that like a bit of a spade handle?'

John rotated his hand, examining the object from different viewpoints. 'I don't know ... it could be,' he replied.

'Since our birthdays are coming up,' said Wally, 'it'd be a cool trinket to show off to everyone.'

The Senior was now right next to John. 'It is nothing that falls within the concern of children.' His voice was raspy, hidden in the darkness of the Senior's hood. And then, as the Senior's skeletal hand started to reach towards John, Wally approached and slapped it away.

'With all due respect, *Master* Senior, don't talk to us like bloody kids,' spat Wally. 'We're passing childhood, and then there's only a few years before we're chosen for our adult paths, so shove off!'

The Senior's hand withdrew back into the shroud of his dark, roughly stitched robe. 'You are mere children.' He loomed over Wally. 'And *do not* address your Seniors in such a disrespectful manner.'

John ignored the growing disagreement—he was almost mesmerised by the Desert Eagle, an object unlike any tool he had seen before. After his pale eyes scrutinised the object's surface once again, he noticed how the trigger mechanism refused to budge when he squeezed it. He moved his gaze upon a small switch on the gun's side. He then used his free hand and moved the switch; it dragged along the Eagle's surface until it clicked.

Connie and Wally looked towards John; both appeared as puzzled by the noise as John.

John glanced at them both, then at the Senior. He swore he saw red eyes gleam from the Senior's shadow-filled hood.

The Senior's hands snaked from his robe sleeves, and he opened them to get John's attention. He slowly approached John. 'Okay, Smith. Put that weapon down, now.'

John was confused. 'Weapon?' He then stretched his arms as he stood back up, and in doing so, he unwittingly pulled the trigger mechanism.

The Desert Eagle shouted, merely coughing dust at Connie, and yet a cavity appeared in his chest. Blood leapt from the hole, spraying the ground and part of John's right arm.

Connie tried to mutter, but it was inaudible—only crimson fluid left his gaping mouth.

John dropped the gun in shock.

Connie tumbled to the ground as if his weight multiplied a hundredfold.

Wally took a few steps back, inaudibly mumbling in fright, tripping to fall; his mouth continued to flutter like a fish out of water, seemingly unaware he wasn't standing anymore. All he did then was watch, paralysed by fright and disbelief.

The Senior picked up the smoking pistol and deposited it into his robe. He grabbed the bleeding, gasping boy's leg and John's arm. Then he began to unceremoniously drag the boys out of the crevice of plastic bottles, windows, and earth.

John clenched his teeth so tight a slight trickle of blood ran from the corner of his now-parched mouth as he noticed that the Senior had brought them to the dirt-covered and wind-damaged Seniors' castle.

The Senior continued to drag the boys, pulling them up a wide and very long steel ramp that was once a wing. The end of the ramp was attached to the side of the large tube of the castle. A loud grinding noise assaulted their senses as a dull iron 'door' scraped along the tube until the sizeable hole it covered became clear.

The Senior pulled the whimpering Connie, whose breathing slowed to a crawl, into the opening, leaving John lying on the ramp to mutely stare at the ceiling's false sun.

John could hear the Senior's familiar raspy voice and then other harsher voices muffled from the enclave. He was then broken out of his daze by a light pattering sound. He saw his tears tapping the ramp as they fell from his cheeks, creating pools with Connie's blood that had remained. He felt something crack in his mind, yet it unleashed only an ache in his head, which did nothing to distract the ache in his heart.

The Senior, like a trapdoor spider, re-emerged from the large hole.

John felt a strong grip on his neck as he was forced up onto his feet.

The Senior pushed John into the opening.

'I'm s-s-sorry,' muttered the boy. He shuddered as the weathered door scraped along until it had swallowed them both. John became dizzy as blinding lights covered the area. His eyes adjusted to the light, and he noticed that the castle's interior looked like a cross-section of a multi-storey building.

Despite the damage and decay of the area, John could see that it was indeed richly furnished; the floor was covered in red, soft-looking carpet. He looked up and saw how the door mechanism clashed with the innards of the tube; the rusty and dusty look of it seemed to fill a large gap in the tube that may have been caused by a giant bite mark.

John glanced upon the surprisingly white walls; the walls behind him had an occasional circular window, and the walls that he could see in front of him curved away and were decorated with crooked picture frames nailed every so often. Most frames were empty, aside from specks of ash, although some still held faded portraits of business suit-clad men.

John felt as if his stomach and mind had leapt from his back, as he realised he'd been thrown down by the talon-like hands of the Senior. He peered up, seeing a long desk upon which material was hidden by a draping red tablecloth. Behind it, several Seniors were seated, with their attire slightly less tattered. John knew a few by name, but some he hadn't been introduced to before, including the black-cloaked one still pushing him around.

'My fellow saviours,' began the now-familiar raspy oration of 'Black-cloak', 'this child's fate is to be judged today! Through misfortune or malice, he has committed *murder*, which I have brought to your attention.'

John felt a wave of despair flush through him when he realised that he had somehow gravely wounded Connie— *Is he dead?* he wondered.

The centre Senior—wearing a gold cloak with red stitching that mimicked a circulatory system—shook his head. A deep voice then came from the dark between the gold as he said, 'This is unacceptable. If this boy remains in the village, others may, too, taint their hands with death.'

The other seated hoods murmured in agreement.

John began to struggle, though with a defeated effort.

A white-cloaked Senior, Lux, began to speak in a manner that would befit a baritone or an eloquent poet. 'Yet, Senior Masutā, this wretched child was and still is unaware of the proper use or even existence of negative technology. Should we have him slain for his ignorance?'

The cloaked entities muttered again.

'Um … hello?' John felt the Seniors' glares piercing his heart and soul. 'Do I need to be here for this?'

Soar, the deep-crimson-cloaked Senior, unleashed his gravelly voice. 'This boy is clearly disrespectful. However, it is obvious that he is no cold-blooded killer, and we should contemplate that he isn't a guilty murderer but a frightened infant. Therefore, we should show him some mercy.'

The Seniors all grumbled and groaned.

John tried again. 'I'm not a kid; I'm seventeen, you stupid old—'

A forceful stomp sounded from behind him, courtesy of the black-cloaked Senior.

The other Seniors murmured in disapproval of John's outburst.

The Senior named Masutā said directly to John, 'Close to adulthood, yet so far. It doesn't matter how old you are, Smith, the Law is delivered upon all equally in life. Although you may have forfeited *your* right to life by using negative technology'—he lifted the Desert Eagle pistol from the desk—'through our design, for your protection, you *are* a child in your knowledge and understanding of things. And you have been safer in ignorance. Safe until now, I confess.' He pressed a button on the gun's side and a rectangular prism slid out from its base with dust following. He threw the now-empty handgun towards John; it spun to a stop on the carpet before him. 'That thing is only an insignificant, infinitesimal part of the unaccountable amount of negative technology that nearly destroyed this planet, and it is the kind of chaos that we Seniors attempt to keep out of our last bastion of paradise.'

Black-cloak next to John lifted him to his feet and pushed him closer to the seated Seniors.

John's eyes became bloodshot as he couldn't muster any more tears, and his breathing slowed.

Lux stared intently at John. 'He is certainly no killer. He is not worth the effort of execution.'

Masutā declared, 'He may be pathetic and not worth the time it would take to carry out a complete trial to determine the manner of his demise, but he cannot be just tossed back into the village. No. We cannot risk the sanctity of the others with knowledge of the crime nor fate of young Smith.'

The black-cloaked Senior's grip tightened on John's neck, and through his peripheral vision, John witnessed that the Senior's eyes were glowing red again.

Black-cloak groaned before saying, with a rasp, 'Then what do we do with him?'

The other Seniors murmured in discussion.

'Well?' Black-cloak prompted. 'We can't keep him in the village, and it isn't justice to execute him! Then what can be done!?'

Soar lightly tapped the desk to indicate an idea. 'Banishment,' he said. He then stood and began to slowly walk around the table as he embellished. 'Banishment is really the only sensible punishment for this boy.' He gestured to John, ignoring the slight murmuring of the other Seniors. 'We cannot allow him to return to our society, and it would be unjust to end his brief life.'

Black-cloak released John.

'But,' John protested, 'don't I get a trial?' He was at a loss. 'Many textbooks mention something about "due process".'

Soar tutted. 'Smith, I thought you were smarter than that. This *is* your trial; how you behave is already influencing the outcome. Concepts such as "banishment" had been made obsolete in the past, but now, it is a sufficient punishment again.'

The black-cloaked Senior made an odd gasp, which developed into a taunting chuckle.

Masutā said over the rasping amusement, 'I think what our ... fellow saviour means is that by sending the boy into the wastes, you might as well kill him yourself. Life outside these walls cannot possibly be considered much of a life at all.'

John shivered as he contemplated the 'wastes'—the name the Seniors had given to all the desolation that was outside the walls of Seven.

The laughter died down as the black-cloaked Senior regained composure. 'Yes, by sending the child outside, you are condemning him to a fate far worse than any punishment that we or any of the citizens could deliver.'

Crimson-cloaked Soar grumbled, 'That would normally be true, but I think we should provide him with some of the low-tier negative technology that we have, and over the next few months, we could train him to survive.'

The other Seniors mumbled in disagreement.

'I said *some*—and of the lowest tier, my friends,' Soar continued. 'Without something, Senior Zero would be correct in assuming that John would die fairly quickly in the wastes.' He turned to meet John's gaze. 'And we should give him limited access to our archives of the world's True History.'

The rabble of the other Seniors became louder.

'Only to prepare him for the wastes and the potential dregs of humanity,' Soar concluded.

The Seniors mumbled until radiant Masutā said, 'Interesting proposition, Senior Soar. We shall discuss this. Take the boy to the cargo hold, Senior Zero.'

Zero grabbed John's arm in an iron-strong grip. 'As you will, Senior Masutā,' he said upon leaving to drag John down a steel-mesh staircase into a blue-light-filled room.

John began to giggle while attempting to stifle his laughter.

Zero groaned. 'What is so damn amusing to you?'

New tears emerged from John's grey eyes, but not from sadness. He attempted to speak, but he couldn't, as he couldn't contain his laughter. Finally, he sniffed, coughed, and answered, 'Well, it's just … um, I thought I had a dumb name, but *Zero*! I mean, really?'

Zero's talon-like hands shot up and gripped John's face. 'Listen, boy—we Seniors gained our current titles for the benefit of the citizens,' he declared. 'We have no conventional names, as we are no-one. We need to just *be*. To keep order in this society, we must forfeit true individuality.' Senior Zero released John.

'It's still stupid,' muttered John. He looked around the cargo hold, seeing torn straps, broken boxes, and cables that seemed to have wriggled out of the walls. He noticed that the area had all manner of objects, such as clothing, suitcases, and even a couple of skeletons of quadrupeds. 'You should clean this place up a bit.'

'Shut up,' Zero berated.

Soar then made his presence known by the clunk of his footsteps upon metal. He descended the stairs, reaching the waiting pair. He said to Zero, 'The decision is going to take some time, so Senior Masutā has ordered that you—since you have the most extensive … well, most *enthusiastic* knowledge of weaponry—edify John about the basic truth of negative technology.'

Zero grumbled, which Soar clearly took as an affirmative, leaving the two alone.

Zero then sighed and addressed John. 'Okay, well now … what did you learn as the reason for the entirety of global conflicts and the world's current state?'

John yawned. 'Yeah, yeah, we learnt how the world was ravaged over hundreds of battles between gods and demons, which with—'

A lifted shutter rumbled.

Zero twisted his own crackling wrist around then gestured at a collection of books, which had been hidden by the shutter. 'No, boy. "Counter-inventions".'

John said, 'Counter-inventions? That doesn't sound right.'

Zero answered, 'Counter-inventions gave birth to the world you now inhabit, although even such negative technology cannot be completely blamed for mankind's doom; it was humanity's inherent cruel and blood-thirsty nature to conquer … to kill … that led almost all humans to join the ranks of the dead. Without our guidance, it requires discipline to keep this instinct in check.' He hit a round red button on the wall, causing light to flush through the cargo hold, revealing it to be much deeper than the blue light had shown. 'Follow me.'

John mutely followed Senior Zero into a surprisingly wide and elongated hallway. At the far end, it was lined with a dozen bullseye targets. The walls were decorated with hundreds of metallic objects, and under them were boxes, some open and displaying small cylinder-like ammunition. John stared in awe, and then he scowled in disdain over some sharing basic similarities to the Desert Eagle.

Zero cracked the silence. 'This is an infinitesimal number of counter-inventions we've gathered for our records; they were extracted before any foolish hands, like yours, could reach them.'

John remained silent in shock.

Zero continued, 'However, seeing your current predicament, I see we weren't quite thorough enough in recovering the firearms.'

'They're not on fire,' commented John.

Zero ignored the observation. 'I will instruct you on how to use some of these weapons. It is an appropriate punishment: you will master the very tools that damned you to this situation. Seeing how the other Seniors wished for me to tell you about negative technology, I suppose you can take assurance in knowing that they have already decided on your banishment.' He slid out two leatherbound books from a high shelf that touched the ceiling. Zero shoved both books into John's hands, who lightly juggled them to keep from dropping them. 'It is just a matter of debating technicalities. Therefore, the Seniors, including me, will teach you the reality of the past and the wastes and train you so you can defend yourself against whatever you may face when you are banished. Now, let's begin …'

CHAPTER TWO

GRADUATION

The lessons were tedious, yet they were a different kind of monotony from his life prior; John felt that the alteration into a different rut was better than being trapped in the previous one, despite the agonising cost that led him into it. The absorption of new information helped distract him from his grief over the tragedy, which had become his freedom and prison.

John was informed of previously withheld details. This was a decision that had divided the Seniors; however, the initial debate had reached a near-unanimous declaration to enlighten John to give him the greatest chance of survival in the outside world.

Thus, among strange truths, he was taught that the medical injections that the villagers received upon their twelfth birthdays were not simply to stave off illness, but they were actually a concoction known as 'Huon'. While the only drawback for John was his strong fear of needles, the Huon concoction was otherwise harmless; it was the opposite of detrimental because it only delivered enhancements, such as increased strength and stamina, as well as improving a body's healing process, thereby enabling one to recover from wounds and injuries faster.

While John questioned the morality of this, he understood how being kept in the dark was preferable to being blinded by light. The Seniors' subtly enforced ignorance kept the majority of the populace complacent, and those with curiosity often opted to remain with the group rather than risk finding terrors that would disrupt the dull harmony.

After nearly four months of guidance from the Seniors while dwelling in the tower of what he now knew was the wreckage of a large aeroplane, away from the other citizens of Seven, John had learnt almost everything that the Seniors were willing to share and had mastered most of the weaponry in the cargo-hold vault, becoming an efficient marksman and close combatant. His study reached completion as he grew ready to depart into the real world.

Masutā assembled another Senior council, which John was brought to stand before by the talons of Zero.

It was the last of the summons.

Soar spoke in his gravelly voice. 'You have done well, Smith.'

The white-cloaked Senior, Lux, added, 'Yes, and it seems I was wrong in thinking that you were a pathetic child.'

John smiled. '

'You are now a … not-so-pathetic adult.'

John maintained his humble smile.

Soar stated, 'Whatever he is, he is certainly ready to face the wastes.'

The Seniors nodded in agreement.

Masutā's deep, authoritative voice then boomed, 'Quite prepared. John, you are ready, and we will provide you with a few items of negative technology to protect yourself with as you go forth into the unknown, as well as rations that should last a couple of months, during which you will need to find your own source of nourishment.'

Soar stood up and put his hand forward to grip John's in a handshake. 'We bid thee farewell, Smith. And be careful. Zero will show you to the exit of the enclave, the entry to the "wastes".'

Zero began to walk away and John followed suit, trailing Zero into a section of the Senior's castle that he had never been before. They reached the hollow end of the plane's tail, where a table had upon it an inventory that had been prepared for the departing boy.

John donned the 'armour': a metal-woven shirt, much like a vest, over his own, and a navy-blue overcoat with particularly deep pockets to complete the ensemble. In the right pocket was his nourishment of lambda pills and three one-litre bottles of water, and in the left was enough ammunition to feed his weapons to take on a small army.

John tucked tools into the vest's inner pouches: a handgun different enough from the Desert Eagle to not immediately provoke trauma, a switchblade knife, and a screwdriver ('Be prepared for anything,' he had been told by Zero on his first day of lessons). He filled the pockets of his pants with additional ammo, and on his right thigh, he attached a sheath to holster a titanium Bowie knife. Over his shoulders were two straps: one attached to a bolt-action hunting rifle, the other a medium assault rifle.

John patted himself down, musing over his opinion of his instruments of death—he felt conflicted about them; such things had ended the life of his best friend, yet his updated perspective on the state of the world made them seem more crucial than cruel. He appreciated the construction of the weaponry, but he loathed the imagination that could have conjured them; he experienced a feeling of grey befitting the hue of his eyes.

'Okay, boy,' said Zero, pressing a button on the wall, 'it is time.'

The wall at the farthest point of the plane, which appeared to be circular, clicked, and then it unveiled itself as a door, opening like a camera iris. A warm breeze entered the plane, caressing John's face; an unfamiliar experience, since Seven never had a gust breach its walls.

Adjusting his gloves, John began to walk down the extending silver ramp that appeared under the doorway. He heard the rough ground crunch as he stepped from the ramp's end.

Zero checked John's weaponry and then returned it to him.

John looked back for the first time at the exterior of his former home, realising its sheer scale. Its towering outer walls were ironclad and had various gaps that could be used as lookouts or turrets; some gaps he recognised because they were used by John and his friends to peek out at the land beyond them.

From his close proximity to it, the wall seemed to nearly scratch the eyes of the sky, and dozens of birds crowed around the roof's edge. The end of the village's castle protruded out of the wall halfway up. The wall seemed to grab it in a crude attempt of amalgamation as rusted iron clashed with the pale steel of the jumbo jet. The ramp had completely extended from the extremity of the protruding vessel, oddly rigid and stable.

'I guess I was, well, distracted by the accident,' said John, 'and preoccupied by the lessons … but can I now ask if Wally is all right? I haven't seen him or heard of him since the … well … the …' He gulped and composed himself. 'How can my judgement be confidential if he saw the truth?'

'Your stubborn associate was made amenable to the plan and agreed to not share what happened with anyone,' responded Zero. 'Don't concern yourself with him or anyone else; focus on your own welfare from now. You will need focus for survival and control.'

John pondered what Zero had shared, and he hoped that his sole remaining friend was well despite the trauma they both held. And then, realising that he was not going to get any further answers from Zero, John hopped back onto the ramp and extended his arm, offering a parting handshake. 'Thank you, Zero. I owe you thanks for your rare but true compassion.'

A grin gleamed within Zero's hood. 'That you do.'

The black-cloaked Senior then pushed John backwards; John almost fell, but he managed to keep standing. He stood again on the rough earth as the ramp slowly retracted into Seven, with Zero remaining on the end. John was certain that Zero's eyes glared red.

As the ramp gradually returned to its origin, Zero orated, 'But do not misinterpret the Senior Order's sense of justice for mere kindness.'

John cursed as the real sun peeked over the top of the wall, meeting his sight; he shielded his eyes, intent on watching Zero.

The raspy monologue continued, with an echo supporting its gravity, 'You are free from our responsibility, but we have cursed you with the truth and independence; a fate for which you should not be grateful.'

The silver ramp was almost retracted.

'Farewell, John Smith. For your own good, be slow to trust, and avoid those cursed hills.'

John felt a chill slide up his spine. For all his enthusiasm for new knowledge, he had not considered the cost for fear of grief and the unknown.

Facing a dark horizon that became clearer due to the light of the rising sun, John looked towards the lifting shadows, witnessing a view from outside the cradle of Seven's walls that was less inviting than he'd hoped. Cracked and ravaged roads streamed outwards from him, circumnavigating street blocks that held misshapen mounds of trash that he had presumed used to be people's homes.

Occasionally, a normal-looking house could be seen—well, one that looked like those he had seen pictures of in the books in the village—but the majority of them were in a state of disrepair, stripped of all their skin, revealing their fractured wooden or jagged metal skeletons.

Almost midway between a distant hill and Seven stood the four decrepit monoliths; the grey gothic-styled skyscrapers had most of their windows absent or cracked with broken sculptures protruding from their uneven surfaces. They seemed to be the tombstones of the former city.

The Seniors had told John that the ruined city was named—at least by them, because it was a name unlikely to have been its moniker during its prime—Necropolis.

CHAPTER THREE

THE CITY OF DEATH

John headed towards the horizon—he hoped that the cluster of grey hills hid some sense of civilisation behind them. In spite of, or perhaps because of, Zero's warning, John felt a compulsion to inspect the landmass of hills behind and beyond the city; therefore, he marched towards the hills.

Glass shards and dirt clods cracked and crunched beneath his boots as he traversed the city ruins. The wrinkled ground that surrounded him for miles was frequently broken into small tectonic plates that crushed against one another. Often, dry metal pipes protruded from the mounds and broken paths, seeming to be the dead, hollow veins of the Earth itself.

A cold breeze would periodically haunt John on his march; a scent of stale smoke and ash seemed to permeate each gust. His eyes threatened to tear in reaction, and so John was irked at each uninvited chill.

The sky was not blue, as John had hoped a wider vista would provide, but a dull red, while serpentine clouds slithered through the sky like twisted rainbows. The sky was simultaneously beautiful and frightening. There were promises of light blue beyond the hills reinforcing the sense of purpose, and John felt himself drawn towards them.

John panted as the sun gazed upon him from directly above, and he hurriedly drank from one of his water bottles to the point it was nearly dry. He opened a small case in his pocket. He retrieved one of his lambda pills—having been told that each pill would sate his hunger and thirst for approximately one day apiece—and then he swallowed it with the remainder of the near-empty bottle. He dropped the bottle while his entire body numbed and felt as if he might fall; however, his muscles tensed, causing him to stand up rigid.

John shook his head and limbs, returning to normal. He felt somewhat grateful that he had been given lambda supplements, as their predecessor was rumoured to have even stronger side effects. John had never actually seen a kappa pill, yet they were well known around his former home with a reverence and fear that one would associate with legendary artefacts.

The broken homes John walked by didn't brighten his pale-grey eyes; he saw human skeletons, often with flesh-turned-rock still clinging to them. The skeletons littered the area; some of them were frozen in unending displays of horror, gripping their skulls or clinging to their loved ones, while others were trapped in futile scrambles to escape, all of which for eternity. Depending upon the deceased, they were monuments either to love or to isolation.

John resisted the morbid temptation to kick the calcified corpses like clods of dirt and rock; the remains barely seemed human, so he pondered the morality of dismantling them. He opted to leave them as they were, moving onward if only to avoid ruminating on the ages of the deceased.

Through another vacant doorway, he was startled by the standing stone-like corpse of another lone figure. Despite his heightened heart rate, John similarly left the doorway deadman unbroken, at least by him.

The shadows of the four gothic towers covered much of the city in further darkness despite the midday sun. The jagged-edged buildings seemed to perform a silent song of woe —one that buried the city in eerie oblivion. John's crunching footsteps seemed eerily quieter than the silent hymn of the few structurally sound edifices.

As John walked through another destroyed house, he paused as a ray of light that pierced through the house's crevices illuminated a patch different than the rest. While the earth had been grey and dusty, John found an archipelago of life; feeble yet lively green grass defied the domain of death. He knelt down at the closest patch and then, removing a glove, he placed his bare hand across the blades of green; the soft strands gently tickled his palm.

If the overwhelming lifelessness of Necropolis could be challenged, even by a few parcels of lushness, then John felt that further life could exist beyond his small experience of the outside wastes. He resumed his route towards the growing grey hills, over the broken homes of the fallen.

CHAPTER FOUR

AN ODD ENCOUNTER

As John got closer to the hills, the signs that life ever existed faded as he walked over ruins that became less frequent, and all the exile could see from the ruins to the hills was a flat, bare desert—no movement aside from sand leaping up with light breezes that occasionally stroked the landscape.

John knelt, grabbing a handful of the earth. Standing up, he dropped the dust, watching it float then dissipate as the wind took flight. The sand was powdery but had seemingly endless tiny particles that shone like diamonds.

John's thoughts were interrupted by the sun smiling directly behind the hills; he continued but at a heightened pace.

When he heard a click under his boot, he froze.

All around him, embedded in the sand, were countless brightly shining metallic tubes, all of which were only a bit larger than a thimble, and each one was placed around holding their own metre-wide radius apart from one another.

John looked behind, seeing a gentle breeze shift and lift dust, and there were sand particles as red as the setting sun. Not knowing why, John didn't simply turn to flee back into the destroyed streets already trod—he broke into a sprint.

The metal tube he stood on leapt into the air and exploded.

John felt the heat from the burst landmine and then cursed loudly when he heard more of the tubes jump up behind him.

As he ran, he felt each subsequent blast getting closer to claim his life, shiny small particles greeting his peripherals.

The pariah prayed that the minefield was coming to an end.

As he reached the last row of visible mines, on a gamble, he threw his body forward, tumbling on the sand as he landed.

Small glistening dust specks danced through the air, descending next to the gasping outcast.

John sighed in relief that he had escaped the explosive minefield and hadn't been blown apart.

Suddenly, he heard a door open, close yet safely away from the minefield. He rolled onto his back and caught his breath, sitting upright.

A trapdoor in the sand revealed itself as it opened, and a small child emerged, ostensibly seven to nine years old. It was a scruffy boy wearing a dirtied white T-shirt and dusty faded-blue overalls with matching blue boots. He patted the dust out of his unkempt greyish hair as his eyes scrutinised John.

They stared at each other for an uncomfortable silent minute.

'Um … hello there,' John said in an attempt to commence conversation, 'little guy? What … um … what are you doing out—'

The small boy turned away to face the trapdoor. 'Hey, Leo, Mack, Howie! Get up here!' he ordered. 'We've got ourselves a guest that survived the boomfields!'

Three boys, similar in stature to the first, emerged like ants one by one from the trapdoor. They all wore the same attire as the first boy, the difference being the colour of their overalls and boots. Indigo, red, and orange. Aside from the boy in red, who had golden-blonde hair, the others also had silvery-grey hair.

The boy in blue turned again to face John. 'Welcome, and well done, my man!'

John lifted himself to his feet. He was slightly taken aback by these strange children. 'Who are you?'

The boy in orange responded merrily, 'We are the Teenage—ow!' He was silenced by a slap. Nonetheless, the boy in orange tried to continue. 'We are the Mighty—ow! All right, I'll shut up.'

The boy in blue smirked. 'We're a few strange things, but we're not those … Howie, you clod! I'm Richie.' He pointed to the boy in red. 'That's Mack.' Then to the boy in indigo. 'This here is Leo.' Then finally to the boy in orange. 'And this clown is Howie.'

'That's not nice,' sulked Howie.

Richie took a deep breath before declaring, 'Together, we are …' They all struck poses, to the befuddlement of John. 'The Killer Quartet!'

John stared silently at the boys. 'Okay, interesting …' he finally said. 'Are you going to try to kill me, then?' he enquired, raising his eyebrow.

The boys ceased their stance; the three who had emerged jumped back into their anthill.

'It's just a name, friend. Anyway, come on in.' Richie invited John with a wave of his hand. He then jumped into the open trapdoor.

John hesitantly stepped towards it, then he took the plummet himself.

CHAPTER FIVE

THE PATH TO POWER

Air hissed around John's ears as he fell through a metre-wide tunnel, its smooth metal sides subtly scraping the elbows of John's coat. Down and down, a freefall until the tunnel was no longer; its mouth was a part of the ceiling of a large cavern, which seemed to be hiding beneath the base of the desert mountain range.

A worrying distance of air was between John and the rocky cavern floor.

John braced himself for the pain of impact, futilely covering his face. When he hit the floor, it swallowed his legs as if it was made of gel; he removed his hands from his face and slowly opened his eyes.

Richie stood in front of John, now at eye level with the exile. 'Are you okay, my man?'

The floor under John slowly pushed him upwards to regain its original state. John looked down at Richie, then he nodded meekly.

The cavern was much wider than it was deep; the ceiling was covered with stalactites while the floor was uneven with bumps and stalagmites close to the walls. On the opposite side of the cavern was a pair of shiny lift doors, above which a dimly lit red dome watched over the chamber.

In the middle of the cavern, Mack, Leo, and Howie were already seated around a table that appeared to have formed out of the floor, as did the seats that they sat upon.

'What the hell is with this floor?' John asked, still scanning all around the cavern. He tapped his foot, discovering the floor to be static and firm.

Richie stared at the floor. 'Oh yeah, right—that would seem a bit weird to an "outsider".' The boy's eyes looked back towards John. 'This cavern has some sensor things all around, which can predict the velocity of a visitor's arrival then shift the molecules of the expected impact area to make a soft landing. It's possible 'cos the cave, and a lot of the soil outside, as well, contain lots and lots of nanites.'

'What-ites?'

The boy in indigo overalls answered, 'Nanoscopic sentient mechanical symbiotes … AKA nanomachines, AKA nanites, AKA bugs, although no-one uses that last one. Their functions are plentiful. Incidentally, it's what makes up the entirety of our bodies.'

'Mechanical? So, you kids are all machines?'

'In a manner of speaking. We are synthetic organic entities—*sorges*, for short,' Richie's portmanteau echoed 'forges' of old. 'But you can use *android* for any of us, if you'd prefer. Except for our buddy Mack there; he's purely a fleshy human like you.'

The boy in red overalls waved shyly.

'He was left in our care a long time back.'

'So, what now?' asked John. 'Why did you bring me into this … cave?'

'We are your orientation party! And then we will have an actual meeting with one of the Uplifted,' Richie said.

'When in Haven, my man … I'm sorry, I forgot to ask, what's your name?'

'John Smith.'

'John Smith? That's a pretty popular name,' murmured Howie.

'Yeah, yeah—I know how damn common my name is,' John grumbled. 'Anyway, what happens now?'

'Well, *John*, normal protocol is that when a "candidate" arrives, such as yourself, they are detected,' said Richie, 'and an Uplifted comes from Haven to escort the new candidates into the facility there.'

'What's the point in that?' asked John. 'I spent my life stuck in one place; why would I want to be trapped in another?'

'You wouldn't be "trapped",' said Richie. 'Besides, Haven lives up to its name; it's a paradise through and through. You can just relax, or you get to discover your true potential.'

'Right,' said John, unconvinced. 'So, when will one of these "Uplifted" come to sell me the real pitch?'

'Straight away,' said Richie, but then his enthusiasm vanished with a resigned sigh. 'At least, that's how it's supposed to work. I'm sorry to say, for the last bunch of years, none of the Uplifted arrive in person anymore, so we now provide the backup option.'

'Which is?' asked John.

'Well, if you're interested, you have to go into Haven by yourself, taking the long way: the path on the hill,' Richie said. 'Over the hill, you go to the top entrance … in the middle of the facility … over one of the scary, long platforms.'

'Is it even safe that way?' asked John.

Howie jumped onto John's back, causing John to fall to his knees from the excessive weight of the dense android. He then slid off John, crouching next to him. 'We don't know. 'Cos our programming prevents us from entering Haven's boundary,' said Howie. 'So, if we peek or disobey the Uplifted in any way, we could go *ka-boom*! Like that.'

'Really?' asked John.

'Probably.' Howie shrugged.

Mack shifted slightly as he appeared to be uncomfortable on the cavern floor, and then he began to slink towards the cavern wall.

John noticed the frightened boy. 'What's wrong …? Wait! What do you know?' he demanded.

Mack mumbled, sitting back down next to the rock table. 'I was curious about what happened when the candidates went into Haven through the top way,' he said softly. 'The last two guys from a coupl'a months ago …' He sniffed. 'The guys who kept sayin' they were on some "special mission".'

'Ha! I remember those guys!' said Howie. 'They were armed to the teeth, but they were like *"no kid, it's not cool; it's evil to fight worse evil"*, and some crap like that.'

Leo smacked the back of Howie's head.

'Yep, we remember, buddy,' said Richie. 'That was, like, ten weeks ago. What happened to them?'

'Well, I followed them to see … It was … bad,' said Mack. 'After they went into the entrance, they started yelling … I dunno what they were saying—they were too far away. Then they started to run away.' Mack sniffed again, another failed attempt to stop himself from crying. 'One guy … he was slower than the other. Looked like the floor tried to eat him.' Mack was becoming more visibly upset. 'The other guy … he went back to help his friend and … and …'

'What happened?' urged John.

'Then all these grabby things came out of the entrance and took his friend,' Mack uttered, and then his tears broke the invisible barrier that contained them. 'He ran, then more things came for him. Something wrapped around him but … but he kept running. He kept on trying to help his friend, even—though he was gone, he kept trying. That's when … when he lost his legs. He tried to crawl, but he was dragged back … Then … I ran away …'

'Why didn't you tell us sooner, Mack?' asked Richie.

'I wanted to but … I thought, I hoped it was a nightmare. But if it wasn't, I was afraid.' Mack spoke quietly through his tears. 'I thought if the Uplifted were listening—I … I thought if I told you, you'd be blown up.'

'I suppose it's a moot point now,' said John, 'but did those guys tell you where they came from?'

'Afraid not, my man,' said Richie while patting Mack's back. 'They weren't interested in chatting much, just wanted to know the way inside.'

Mack rolled onto his side so that he faced the cavern wall, and his comrades and John uncomfortably yet respectfully averted their gazes as he quietly sobbed. The cavern, aside from Mack's sadness, remained silent.

The fog of quietness broke as the trapdoor entry to the cavern creaked open, and, from the sound of his grumbling, a man entered through it.

A figure dressed in a black cloak and a dark coat, wearing a dark-blue balaclava, was at the opening in the cavern roof. 'Yo, K-Killers!' a slurred harsh voice reverberated through the entry pipe. 'Killer Quarter … Quaver … You guys. Are you home? Damned if I know where else you'd be.' The figure stumbled and fell into the cavern, hitting the floor, which almost completely buried him to lessen the impact of his face-first fall; a satchel he carried fell out of the smooth tube mouth and hit him. The man attempted to stand but lost his footing and tumbled. The flexible floor noticeably struggled to keep its shape as he kept falling onto it.

With a fierce fury in his normally dull-grey eyes, John stomped towards the fallen person. He gripped the man, lifting him up; grey eyes met bright-green ones.

'Oh, well, thanks … ah, what are you doin—' the man's attempted gratitude was silenced as he was forced against a cavern wall.

John held the figured pinned against the wall. 'Hey, Richie!' he barked, 'who the hell is this? This one of those supposed uplifted?'

Richie ran up to John, and then he broke John's grip on the dark figure. Leo and Howie also jogged to join John and the wheezing, inclined man.

'Relax, John! It's only Murray,' said Richie. 'He's a friend of ours. He comes by once in a while, and he's the one that brings food for us.'

'Food for the human kid, you mean?' asked John.

'Nope, food for us all,' responded Richie.

'What?' asked the bemused exile.

'Well, scrap metal, anything, really,' replied Richie. 'Used to sustain our bodies by internal nanite processors, which are partly fuelled by—'

'Blood!' interjected Howie, flaring his canine teeth.

'Blood?' asked John.

'Actually, we drink blood that has been already extracted,' explained Leo. 'We only *really* need it once every two months or so; the blood is processed in our internal harvesters to act as fuel. It lasts longer in us than it does for you humans.'

'Speaking of,' mumbled Murray as he stumbled towards his burgundy satchel. 'I've got … I've got—' he slurred. 'Got more stuff in my sack!' He chuckled loudly, although it quickly turned into a cough. Murray opened his satchel, causing Howie and Richie to rush to him excitedly like children on Christmas, if such a thing ever existed.

John doubted there could have ever been such a thing as gaining gifts for another's birthday, granted he hadn't actually ever received presents for his own—excluding occasional mandatory vaccinations.

Within the satchel were containers—some held meat, others held warped fruits—as well as a dozen glass bottles: four filled with water, the rest with blood.

Murray retrieved a flask from his coat, and then he gulped its contents like his life depended on it. As he pocketed the flask, he pulled out a glass bottle that had a brown paper bag clinging to its lower half. He essentially inhaled the alcohol and then tossed the empty bottle onto the cavern floor. 'Wh-what do … do you kids say?' he stammered.

'Thank you, Murray,' the android boys replied in unison.

John was dumbstruck by the instantaneous change in atmosphere.

Murray stumbled past John and the artificial trio towards the rock table.

'Okay, well, sorry about roughing you up,' said John.

'Don't worry 'bout it,' slurred Murray. 'That's how most, most people say hello to me.'

'Uh-huh … So, who the hell are you?' demanded John.

'Didn't ya hear … what's-his-name?' Murray drunkenly responded. 'I'm Merv … Ray … Murray!' He slowly tilted until he was lying on the rock table, snoring.

John faced Richie, who was slurping blood out of a bottle.

Richie stopped drinking. 'Yes?' he said, wiping blood from his upper lip.

John shook off his disgust. 'Who is this Murray guy?'

'Murray. He's one of the few people who refused to remain in Haven, John,' Richie bluntly stated.

'Okay, that's not what I was asking,' John replied. 'I mean, who is *he* to be able to drop in here like it's not a big deal?'

'Well, you'd laugh at me,' said Richie, with apparent honesty, 'but I suppose you could say he's been like a dad for us. He arrived in a group, but then Murray and some other dude left to search for other settlements. Murray continued to drop by regularly. We guess that along the way they found a storage facility, because around two years after his first departure, Murray returned with food and drinks for us, and also for Mack, when he was left with us. He's a tad brutish, but he has a good heart.'

'If you needed food,' said John, 'how did you survive before Murray's deliveries?'

'Oh, the Uplifted sent us periodic supplies,' said Richie. 'But one day, they suddenly stopped, and we were left on emergency power; Murray saved us!'

John scratched his head. 'Was he …' He pointed at Murray. 'Was he always like this?'

Murray breathed boisterously in his slumber; Howie slid up to him and prodded the sleeping man's face. Howie was flung back as Murray's swung arm forced him. However, the inebriate didn't awaken; instead of snoring, he just mumbled with each breath.

Richie looked at Murray and then back at John. 'No, not always,' he said. 'At that storage place, I'm fairly certain he found a lot of booze, because from one day, he seems to be drinking something. Didn't slow him down, though!'

'Uh-huh,' John muttered; his curiosity had been piqued. 'You said there was another "dude"; when did Murray and his friends come here?'

Howie made Murray swat at non-existent bugs by repeatedly poking Murray's balaclava-covered face.

'Around eleven years ago,' said Howie.

John became motionless.

'That's right, John, eleven years ago,' said Richie.

'So, the rest of his friends entered Haven?'

'Oh yeah, now I remember!' said Howie. 'One guy in the group was the last John we met before you.'

John felt tense but shook it away. He marched towards Murray and lifted the man, forcing him to stand.

'I'm up, I'm up,' muttered Murray, holding his head and groaning.

John grasped Murray's coat collar. 'Are you a Sevenite?'

Murray stumbled slightly. 'What?' he mumbled.

John released Murray, forcing him back into a seated position. 'Are you from the village known as Seven?'

Murray grimaced. 'Yes, I was,' he replied. 'A long time ago.'

John lifted Murray to stand again. 'Did you know my father?' he demanded.

'I don't know who *you* are,' responded Murray, 'but I got this feeling of déjà vu with you … you do look familiar.' He pushed John with so much force that John fell back towards the other side of the cavern. Murray then stumbled forwards, and John marched forwards; they met in the middle of the cavern.

'I am John Smith,' the exile said. 'Do you know my dad? His name was John Salt.'

Murray turned away and resumed his seat on the rock table. 'Yes, I-I know, I mean I knew both of your parents … John and Charlotte.'

John slowly approached Murray. 'Is my father in Haven?'

'I … I don't know where he is.'

'All of Murray's party, except himself and some Scarface dude, stayed at Haven, John,' interjected Richie. 'If you think your dad was in that group, then it is likely he would be living among the Uplifted.'

John walked over to Mack, and then he grasped the boy's arm and pulled him out of his fetal position. He dragged Mack to the centre of the cavern and lifted him to his feet. 'I'm going into Haven,' he declared. 'And … Mack, is it? You're going to help me get in there.'

'What! All you have to do is go up the hill,' said Mack with exasperation. 'Why do you need help for that?'

'Richie said these Uplifted haven't been here in person for a long time, so I guess something questionable happened in Haven,' John explained. 'If it's dangerous, I just need someone to watch my back. Apparently, the "robot trio" can't go over the hill without being shut down or blown up, and I'm sure as hell that Murray can't tell up from down.'

Murray spluttered, 'N-no! Don't take the boy. Did Seven have a dramatic drop in smarts over the years? There's no point going into that place. Let me explain, please …' His sudden stress caused him to hyperventilate, and then he collapsed onto the floor.

'My point exactly,' said John. 'So, Richie, can I borrow one of your quartet?'

Richie grinned kindly; his fellow androids stood by his side. 'Well, if your dad's in Haven after all, eleven years is long enough time for a family reunion,' he responded. 'It is our priority to assist any "candidates" who have shown potential, even if minuscule—minuscule in a good way—to get to Haven! And besides, Mack can enter Haven, so he can help you.'

Mack whimpered; Howie and Leo, standing on either side of him, each grabbed an arm.

'You'll be fine,' said Howie with a reassuring smile. 'Chillax.'

'We'll be waiting for your return, buddy,' said Leo, patting Mack's back.

'Yeah, the Uplifted were cool,' said Howie. 'Last time we saw them, anyway. A bit up themselves, but basically harmless.'

'But it's impossible,' said Mack.

'Hey, buddy, I just learnt that androids are real,' said John. 'So, what is "impossible" can't be certain. I need you to watch my back, but don't worry, because I'll watch yours.'

Mack smiled, although he was still unstable and trembling, and a frown appeared to be fighting for control of his face.

CHAPTER SIX

INTO THE ABYSS

John stared up at the cavern ceiling, examining the entry tube's opening above. Stalactites seemed like digits around the palm that held the aperture. 'How do we … you know, get out of here?' he asked.

'Oh, that's easy, John,' replied Richie. 'Just stand under the hole and say "exit".'

John stared at the android for a moment, and then he repeated the word to the ceiling. A vacuum sucked John up through the tube, and the air hissed around his ears as he was pulled upwards. He was shot up until finally his head slammed into the shut trapdoor, flinging it open and allowing the rest of his body to be spat out of the ground.

John was tossed into the air, and then natural gravity caught up to slam him onto the desert sand. He moaned as he gripped his aching head. John was then greeted by the misery of the wastes: the minefield hidden in the dancing sand, one of the various sites of ruins, and almost beyond his sight, between the visage of decaying towers, a view of his old fortress home.

Out of the open trapdoor, Richie, Howie, Leo, and Mack lifted themselves out of the cavern's top entry.

'I forgot to mention the ladder function that can be activated when you're nearly at the top,' said Richie. 'Sorry about that.'

John didn't respond to the late and useless warning. He then turned to examine the hills, which were much closer. As he began his march towards an arch at the foot of the hills, he noticed an engraving along the arch read DIRECT YOUR MIND AND GRATITUDE TO US WHO RAISED YOU UP FROM THE EARTH. 'I doubt I'll learn about humility here,' he muttered.

Under the arch began a path that seemed to be scratched into the hill's side, slithering to the top like a trail left by a giant serpent.

Mack breathed deeply—his eyes, once shaded with anxiety, seemed more resolute—and then he ran to catch up to John.

'Later! Come back soon!' the androids called after the humans before leaping back into their dwelling.

Howie stayed on the surface. 'Bring us back something nice!' he yelled before Richie pulled him into the trapdoor.

When John and Mack reached the path, their steps no longer sank into soft, silvery sand; the path appeared to be a mosaic of stone bricks, but it was actually made from metal. Their steps clunked each time on the hard path.

As they reached the halfway point of the path, John experienced a growing feeling of entrapment. On either side of the path, rocks appeared out of the hill, which seemed to take the form of an enormous hand, its fingers almost capturing the path and the young travellers.

John sighed in relief when they finally reached the top of the hill.

At the end of the patchwork path was another arch, but it was almost three times larger. John's breath froze as his gaze was forced upon the great valley that the hill range surrounded. The valley seemed like it could have been an eye of the Earth itself. Yet the valley's size was not the most overwhelming element to John, but rather the city inside of it: Haven.

The entire interior of the valley was covered in platinum-shining metal. The bottom of the valley was littered with towering spires and skyscraper-like structures; all were connected by elevated covered walkways that spider-webbed throughout. At the valley's centre was a colossal spherical construction with antennas protruding from all over its surface. It stole a third of the valley's total volume.

Bordering the roundish building were other spherical constructions, although they were significantly smaller than the central sphere. The smaller spheres appeared like bubbling water attempting to climb up their superior neighbour. The massive central orb had four cylindrical towers that reached the hill's height. On the top of the towers an edifice sat, connecting them together. It was a dodecahedron-shaped building. Six walkways extended from points around the dodecahedron, all equally distanced apart.

One of the walkways connected to the path that John and Mack had just ascended. They cautiously stepped onto the smooth silver walkway and exhaled in relief as the crater remained silent. When they began their first steps along the walkway, they cursed in surprise; their left sides were being pulled forward while their right sides moved backward. They hopped onto the walkway's left side as it slid towards the oddly shaped entrance of Haven; the right side crawled back towards the hill.

'Oh, okay. It's just like an escalator.' John sighed.

'What's an eggs-ater?' asked Mack.

'Escalator. We're on one.' John sat down on the seamless horizontal escalator. 'There's no point wasting our energy by walking all night,' he said as Mack sat down with him.

The stars were unseeable, as the light that filled the city robbed their place in the night sky.

'So … do you belong to the Uplifted or your android buddies?' a curious John asked.

'You coulda' asked on the way up here, you know,' Mack retorted.

'Well … Sorry, my mind was elsewhere,' John admitted. 'But don't deflect; you're not an android, not an Uplifted, so why were you staying in that cavern?'

'Don't want to talk about it.'

John raised an eyebrow. 'If you're worried about me spreading your secrets, trust me, I'll keep it to myself. So, come on, why were you with Richie and the others?'

'My mum was from Haven,' Mack said solemnly.

'Your mother was from Haven?' asked John. 'Then what happened to your mother after she left you?'

Mack's expression grew dour.

John broke the quietness. 'Why hasn't she ever visited you?'

'Because …' snapped Mack, 'because she left me in that cavern … the night she went far away from Haven.'

'How do you know that for certain?' John asked. 'We could find her in Haven.'

'No, we won't,' Mack said. 'A long while back, I asked Richie about my parents. He told me that he never met my dad, but my mum said he was gone too.'

'Gone?' asked John. 'As in dead, gone?'

'I dunno … Richie said my mum wasn't too clear on what had happened,' said Mack. 'She only shared a small amount and told them to share the info in sections, and only to me.' The small boy fell silent, gazing at the starless abyss of the evening.

'The androids are programmed to obey?' John asked.

'I don't know if it was like that,' said Mack. 'I've never seen the Uplifted, but you saw how Howie, Leo, and Richie are—they don't listen unless they want to.'

'Seems dangerous to create something powerful,' muttered John, 'without being sure they can be controlled.' Some lessons from the Seniors echoed in John's mind.

'Maybe dangerous,' said Mack, 'but they were also kind to me, so I don't think they had a problem with Mum's orders about me.'

'So? What were your mum's orders?' John implored.

Mack faced John again. 'Leo said she actually begged them,' he replied. 'Begged them to tell anyone that came after her that she was never there. And begged them to lie, say that I was a wandering orphan and they adopted me to train as another one of the Uplifted's messengers.'

'So, if the Uplifted are just *people* from Haven,' said John, 'was your mum always one of them, or was she an outsider like Murray and his friends?'

'Oh … um … I asked Richie that. And he said he recognised her from the large group of candidates … the same group that Murray was in.'

'The one Murray was in,' John reiterated. 'The same group as my dad?'

'Yeah, guess so.'

'Well, that's a pretty cool coincidence,' John said. 'Your mum might've known my parents when they still lived in Seven.'

'I dunno; does it really matter?' Mack retorted. 'I asked Murray if he knew my mum; he just told me that the group "wasn't exactly close-knit". But he did say he remembered a pregnant lady, and that was all he knew.'

'That was your mum?' John assumed. 'We'll find her, Mack, I'm sure of it.'

'Maybe. Maybe you're right, but I don't really want to see her.' Mack yawned. 'I don't care anymore. Richie and the guys and Murray were the ones that took care of me. They were there from the start …' His eyelids began to droop; he then quickly fell asleep.

John stared at the planet's rocky satellite; its pale surface mimicking his eyes.

CHAPTER SEVEN

HAVEN

The sun peeked over the hill from which John and Mack had climbed. The moon still stood defiantly, albeit fading slowly as the day commenced. They had reached the platform that encompassed the dodecahedral structure, which held the top entrance into Haven. John dragged along Mack, who was still half-asleep, in through a large arched doorway.

Inside the relatively small building, eight equally sized walls surrounded them; opposite them, a wall also held a large arched doorway. On each of the walls to the left were a pair of platinum lift doors yet, on the mid-right wall, only a plain wooden door guarded a passageway. The ceiling was perfectly round, with lights along its circumference. The building's interior was made of a strange dark-blue metal. Next to each door was a black dome the size of an enclosed fist embedded in the wall.

While John knocked on the lift doors, Mack tried to turn the wooden door's handle, but it refused to move.

John approached one of the black domes and tapped it. He then leant closer to the vertical dome. 'Anyone there?' he enquired.

The black dome he addressed turned a bright red, and then a white-lined red circle lit up in the centre of the dome.

'Yes,' a dark, solemn voice answered. 'Welcome to Valhalla, the sanctuary of gods.'

Mack walked up next to John to examine the red 'eye'.

The pair stared intently at the red robotic eye, which scrutinised them, too.

'Gods live here? What about the Uplifted?' John asked the eye. 'And I thought this place was called Haven?'

'Reality hasn't been fortuitous for me in that respect,' the eye replied. 'I am the monitor of this superstructure, to ensure it remains functional, including security against invaders.'

With a gruesome memory in his mind, Mack's fists began to shake angrily. 'Why did you do it?' he demanded.

The red eye focused on the quivering boy. 'What?' the dark voice intoned.

Mack stood totally still. 'You nearly killed those guys from a coupl'a months ago!' he yelled. 'Why? Why did you do it?'

'Cease your self-righteous whining, kid, and calm down,' the eye's voice replied. 'Any mutilation was not of my doing.'

Mack looked stunned as he simply stood silently.

'You said you're in charge of this place, of "Valhalla's" functions,' John said in Mack's stead. 'So, how couldn't it have been you that crippled them?'

The voice sighed. 'Usually, I am permitted command,' it responded. 'However, on the time of approximately eight weeks ago, those individuals called upon the current lord of this facility by his true name. Therefore, he took personal control of the external security momentarily.'

'So, you're *not* in full control then,' John observed.

'No, but I used to be,' the voice replied with sadness that was still tinged with anger. 'I was the caretaker of Haven. My name is Doctor Adam Factorem, and that was the case until the current master usurped my role and opted to rename this place "Valhalla". I am not a computer system nor am I exactly human anymore.'

The boys tilted their heads in puzzlement.

'Listen—it is irrelevant,' Factorem's voice said. 'I am kept alive to continue running this facility and to assist in his … experiments.'

'Whatever. Can you please just let us in?' John asked. 'I'm looking for my dad, and Mack wants to find out why his mum left Haven, or Valhalla, or whatever this place is called, and if he can find her.'

'Departed Haven? That's a rare occurrence,' said Factorem's voice. 'The last person who departed—albeit *escaped* would be a more apt term—fled shortly after the king took control; eight years or so gone by. My, how the time erodes like everything else … But I digress; that woman was always a self-centred sort.'

'*Hey*! That's my mum you're talking about!' Mack shouted.

'Well, I sincerely apologise,' the voice retorted. 'But listen, infant, if I heard your friend right, she did abandon *you* as well as this place, so you shouldn't be concerned about her.'

'No, he can't do that,' said John. 'He wants to know about his parents, just the same as anyone else; besides, he's owed some answers. Now, listen—let us in. I must find my dad, and we must find out anything to show where Mack's mum went.'

'You *must*? Don't you have anything else important to do?'

'Not anymore.'

The red eye turned black like its fellow domes. 'Very well. I will take you to the king,' said Factorem's voice. 'You might be able to sway Valhalla's ruler to enlighten you as to where your family members are; however, assuming you wish to survive this encounter, you need to hear what I have to say.'

The wooden door behind them clicked open.

Under its proverbial breath, the voice muttered, 'You prideful brat.'

Through the doorway, which a simple piece of wood blocked, they were greeted by the top of a wide spiral staircase. It appeared to descend the curved interior, with its end beyond sight.

The boys began to descend the stairs, slightly blinded by the brightness of the white steps and wall. Every so often, the wall had a black dome embedded in it. As the pair passed them by, the domes came to life with a red light.

The voice coughed. 'You must be wondering why you have to use the stairs,' it said. 'It is because the lifts would immediately notify the king of your presence here, and even though you wish to speak with him, it would be unwise to give him early knowledge of your presence. This way, there is only a … forty-seven percent chance he will discover your arrival.'

'Why would that be bad?' John asked.

'Well, the king was responsible for changing this facility into *Valhalla*, not to mention the mutilation that the child saw the other month, so you tell me, child,' Factorem responded. 'Even when he's not angry, the king is a deeply disturbed individual; an incredibly dangerous one as well.'

The duo's steps echoed from the stairs all around them.

'He is in almost total control of this facility's internal mechanisms,' the voice continued, 'which he manipulates to sustain his twisted experiments. He even stole my previous projects—harmless innovations, yet he twisted them into his own personal weapons.'

The whiteness of the area was occasionally reddened, as if it were blushing in shame, due to the light of the crimson eye.

'If the king of Valhalla is such a bastard, why not replace him?' John asked.

The dark voice sighed. 'Didn't you hear me? The king has absolute control of the facility,' it replied. 'Regardless, even if I could regain power, he programmed a security protocol that prevents me from using the system to attack him; and he has his treacherous grasp over the supreme command module.'

The steps of the boys continued to ring around them.

John peered over the inside railing; he cursed silently as he realised that they hadn't even reached the one-quarter mark. 'Is there a way for us to get down there faster?' he asked.

Factorem murmured, thinking aloud. 'Yes. Yes, I believe there is.'

The stairs retracted, turning the spiral staircase into a spiral slide.

John and Mack screamed as they slid further and further down the spiral. While they were rapidly reaching the bottom, John sweated as he imagined the pain from the impact against the first object they hit.

The walls nearest the bottom became malleable and, almost like water, spilled onto the slide around them, carefully wrapping around the boys. The melted wall gradually slowed them down until they reached a complete stop at the bottom of the staircase. The white wall lifted them to their feet, and then it withdrew back into its original state. The staircase clicked, and the slide returned to being steps.

John breathed heavily, attempting to calm down. He eventually became less anxious. The bottom of the staircase was an opening into a large hallway. Like the staircase, the hall was blindingly white. The robotic dome eyes were present every few metres along the walls, next to various hollow doorways. A black-domed eye next to the boys shone red.

'Why the hell did you do that?' John asked. 'Also, how?'

Factorem gave no response, so John and Mack both sighed as they started to walk down the corridor.

Each doorway was a passage into rooms that were all similar in design. In each room, the far wall had a double-sized bed, which was formed from the room itself.

On the wall above the bed, another blackened dome eye sat. It began to glow red. 'Excuse my delay,' Factorem's voice finally responded. 'I was just trying to think of a way to explain the mechanics of the stairs in a manner that you could comprehend; it takes significant effort to even simplify the data.'

John approached the red eye. 'Well?' he asked.

The voice coughed. 'This entire facility is infused with countless amounts of nanoscopic sentient symbiotic machines, which are more commonly known as nanites,' it explained. 'Nanites are embedded in almost every cubic nanometre of Valhalla's very structure and can be manipulated to alter their surrounding environment, as well as multiple other functions that can essentially bend reality itself … at least, whilst within these halls with such a prevalent volume.'

John and Mack left the room, returning to their path down the white corridor.

'Bend reality … how?' John asked.

Their footsteps echoed through the lonely corridor.

'Well, for example, I am able to communicate with you through the nanites, as they can emulate basic vocal cords for speech anywhere,' Factorem replied, 'and display holographic imagery. I can even activate an interactive and self-aware program of a dearly departed colleague of mine.'

Next to the boys, a ghostly apparition flickered, and then it gained a tangible form of a middle-aged man who had short yet rough dark-brown hair that had a few grey strands, and he wore oval-framed glasses and a flowing white lab coat that made him hard to differentiate from the hallway.

John and Mack jumped back in shock; the blue-tinged hologram bowed.

'*Guten Tag, Kinder.* I am Doctor Alistair Toat,' he said in a slight smug manner.

John spluttered in surprise but composed himself quickly.

'This is the downloaded personality of that colleague; nevertheless, he is ultimately the same person,' Factorem explained.

Toat grinned and gestured down the corridor to encourage John and Mack to keep going. As they walked, Toat walked alongside them, but his footsteps caused no noise.

'I can even manipulate gravity,' said Factorem. 'At least within this super structure.'

'Now that is definitely impossible,' John argued.

'Oh, really?' said Toat. 'When did you start walking on the ceiling?'

'I'm not—' John's objection was silenced as he realised that above him and Mack was Toat, who was upside down; the many doorways through the hall were now inverted as well. 'What the …?' he stammered. 'When did you …?'

John and Mack fell upwards, slamming back into the original floor. They groaned while on their backs.

John noticed that all the blackened domes glowed with the now-familiar red eye.

'Gravity is simply magnetism …' Factorem's voice sighed. 'You can see that I am capable of so much, but my influence has been stifled by the king,' the voice said. 'I can change the nanites into any form that I can imagine. However, the king can also manipulate the nanites, which he, for the most part, uses for his sadistic experiments and self-serving enhancements.'

John thought back to his education, or rather, updated education in the castle of Seven. The Seniors had seemed so forthcoming upon deconstructing the grand fiction they had used to keep the citizens free from the guilt of being human and the revelations about the true dangers that had ravaged the world. John began to fear that he had been deceived again, if not merely by omission; the black-robed Zero had been blunt, yet it could have been another misdirection.

'Due to the king's treachery, he holds greater control than I.' Factorem's voice seemed sorrowful. 'Thereby, my defiance would be temporary, but his vengeance is endless. Thus, in opposition to him, I am ultimately powerless.'

John and Mack strained back up onto their feet.

Toat leant on John. 'It is such magnificent technology, don't you think?' he said, his Germanic accent evident. 'The nanites can consume their surroundings and instantaneously replicate or replace it to become much stronger and better. Or use it to increase their own numbers, forging them into any form they are commanded.'

'Who are you, really?' John asked. 'Why tell us all this … stuff?'

'Indeed, of possible questions, those are among the ones I am obliged to answer,' the voice responded. 'As I said, I am Doctor Adam Factorem; the greatest scientist the world has ever known. I was the overseer of Haven, as I said before. However, I did not tell you that it was through my own errors the current king became master of the renamed Valhalla.'

They reached the end of the white corridor. Now before them was an intersection of hallways. The hallway that the white corridor led into was dark and threatening, like a starless night. The left direction abruptly ended at a pair of lift doors. The right direction couldn't be determined well, as it curved away; its end was out of sight.

The two boys and the hologram stood motionless.

'How is it your fault?' John finally asked.

A red eye came alight immediately in front of them. 'Well, he arrived at Haven in a group of around … I think ten,' the voice responded from the eye. 'He was the most depressed … none were particularly mirthful, but he stood out even among a sombre group. He reminded me of myself when I was young and full of potential, without direction. But he had such a magnificent mind, one unlike any I've known since my late wife.'

Upon the utterance of a compliment to the king, Mack's awe appeared to have shifted, and his expression shadowed once again.

John pondered the identity of the one who Factorem loathed yet was now in command of the vast silver structure. A tinge crawled through the back of his mind—a subtle sense of dread that he couldn't clearly understand; the last true sense of fear had been a month prior, upon his unintentional slaying of his friend, Connie. Yet this fear was different, and John couldn't ascertain whether it was around the dangerous king or something deeper.

'I was looking for a successor, or at least someone living, who could decrease the burden of Haven—a million lives and countless experiments splitting my mind into endless threads of assistance. Anyway, I thought that if someone had guided me during my darkest days, I would have made fewer mistakes. So, I shared our knowledge of the advanced sciences we have developed to help him move on from his past and push him into our future, to guide him to be a teacher for others once I stood down.'

There was a black dome above the lift doors and more periodically along the dark-blue corridor; they all glowed with the glowing red eye with a distinct white ring as a pupil. 'That lift only leads back up to the entry point,' Factorem said. 'Turn right; it leads to the king.'

The trio followed the red eye's directions, turning right, beginning their tread through the seemingly endless dark-blue corridor.

'As I was saying,' Factorem continued, 'I instructed him of the full functions and capabilities of Haven and the research it contained. I lament my foolishness; I should have realised sooner.' It sounded weary. 'He shouldn't have been trusted. I should've realised that fact when he made a cruel twist on my own terminology.'

Mack gripped John's arm and grimaced. 'I don't think Mum simply fled this place ... maybe I was abandoned as a distraction?' he whispered.

John contemplated his clear anxiety. He wanted to support Mack in any way he could; he shared his sense of dread but was able to set his own aside by focusing. John placed a hand on Mack's shoulder to encourage him to continue processing his more juvenile emotions.

'I think going in further and questioning this king is a really bad idea ... worse than I first thought ...'

John tried to appear confident. 'Look, let's just see what he has to say; we both need answers, *and* we have each other. I won't leave you, Mack, I promise.'

Mack bit his bottom lip and nodded.

Oblivious to or ignoring the disruption, Factorem droned on, 'I believed that it would be empowering for the people, both born here and from afar, to become known as the "Uplifted" ... One could surmise that the change in title to *gods* was a linear decision, yet one that I should have heeded as a warning, which I later realised. Even before him, there was a downside in being the Uplifted, since it made many of the residents grow egotistical, each believing themself to be superior to anyone else in the whole world.'

John and Mack's footsteps started to clang; John realised that the smooth floor that they had been walking on had ended and they were standing on a metal grate. A foul stench wafted through the grate, and it made their eyes water.

'Returning to our hellish realities.' Toat chuckled.

They turned their gazes down. Through the grate was a pit, and at the bottom of the pit, a hideous creature snarled. The creature was essentially a blob, three times larger than an average adult human. Its throbbing light-green flesh had sparse patches of straight wiry hair.

It had several gaping mouths around its being, all filled with rows of razor-sharp teeth and grotesque lumpy tongues flopping side to side. It had no legs, instead dragging itself around the pit by using claws that lined its lower side. It had no arms but had several long flailing tentacles; at the end of each seemed to be four long fingers. Around the creature were small piles of bones and mangled organs.

Mack fell to his knees, retching at the sight of such a creature.

John knelt and assisted Mack to his feet. He walked the stumbling boy towards the return of the solid floor. Mack breathed slowly and shuddered.

'What the hell is that thing?' John exclaimed.

'That is one of Herr King's experiments,' said Toat. 'Although, it's kind of funny, because in a way that is one of his least morally questionable experiments.'

'But what *was* it?' John demanded.

'It's one of the king's chimeras,' Factorem answered. 'Building zero-three of Haven was … I suppose you could say an ark—'

'But really, it was a glorified refrigerator,' interjected Toat. 'A collection of zygotes for the future purpose of a zoo.'

'Yes. Thank you, Alistair,' Factorem said, clearly irked. 'Anyway, contained within the Ark were hundreds of different animal species being held for safety … however, the king's first attempts at biotechnology changed that. The king's first experiments of his own were mainly focused on genetic manipulation and splicing; he wanted to create the strongest and smartest animals to prove himself "a god", or some such absurdity.'

Without ego or pride, John had considered himself above average, yet his confidence dipped upon learning there were intellects capable of creating life. The mechanical achievement of nanites had already intimidated him, and thus the biological mastery further perturbed him. He swallowed these feelings to focus on the active situation.

'So, he gradually took sample after sample from zero-three. He pulped and sifted their genetic material, combining the DNA of various creatures into disgusting amalgamations to create new species entirely … Mercifully, most of the specimens died. That chimera in the pit is one of ninety that survived; I'm not certain myself how many of the others are still alive. If not a god, the king proved that he was certainly capable of distorting nature. Such a waste of a remarkable mind.'

With a look of repulsion, Mack spat onto the floor.

The group of two humans and one hologram continued down the long dark corridor; they eventually reached a position where the right side of the wall was made of glass. They stopped to look through the glass; Toat flickered and vanished.

An eye of Doctor Factorem on the left wall lit up. Under the red eye, a thumb-sized cube extended. John grabbed it and slowly pulled it from the wall. A small swarm of glistening nanites followed the cube, and then they formed into a thin chain attached to it, effectively making the cube a part of a necklace.

'This will be of crucial assistance,' said Factorem. 'It is Doctor Alistair Toat's core processor. His presence and knowledge will appear whenever you command it to, and on occasion, despite your commands. Yet you will need it.'

John donned the neck chain and then tucked it into the front of his shirt so it was out of sight.

Through the glass wall on the right, the interior of the central spherical structure of Valhalla was visible. The sight made John question reality again. An enormous smooth pyramid utilised the base of the sphere's insides, and like a mirror image, another smooth pyramid protruded from the ceiling.

The tips of each pyramid met in an orb that was of considerably smaller size in comparison, yet still it seemed the most dominant. Slowly rotating around the orb were five massive rings, thereby making it appear akin to a solar system.

The installation was made of the same dark-blue material as the corridor that contained John and Mack. An eerie blue glow emanated from the centre orb, despite it being pure white.

'That is my antimatter generator,' Factorem explained. 'In part, due to the advancement of nanotechnology, we were able to dissect atoms without causing them to disintegrate or explode disastrously.'

The two guests were awe-struck by the generator.

Factorem continued, 'By dissecting and examining the basest states of atoms, we were able to comprehend negative matter. This antimatter is all around us; however, it was impossible to bring it into this reality. At least, it was impossible, until the advent of nanotechnology. A method was discovered to pull antimatter that exists on an alternate plane of reality into this world. My generator's main function is to convert antimatter into positive energy; perpetually harnessed energy that is used to power this facility ...'

The existing awe elevated in John; it was another revelation. And it appeared to bring about wonderment in Mack, as reverence flickered across his face.

'Yet, any antimatter that is channelled can be very unstable or even destructive when it is mistreated. An explosion caused by antimatter won't stop until it has been totally cancelled out; that is, if it has consumed enough matter of this universe to become a neutral equation.' Factorem's red eye looked down in a manner that appeared to reflect regret. 'The king is close to discovering how to completely harness the power of antimatter for his own whims,' he said. 'He will be able to unleash raw, destructive potential, yet he lacks consideration of consequence.'

The pair resumed their path down the corridor.

After several minutes down the hallway, both sides of the corridor were opaque again.

'What are your names, boys?' asked Factorem.

'Oh, I'm John and this is Mack,' the exile replied.

'I can tell from Mack's attire that he lives with a group of sorges,' said Factorem, 'but you, John, tell me … are you from Seven?'

John stood still, stunned. 'How did you know that?' he exclaimed.

'My scanners can analyse one's organic material,' responded Factorem. 'Within you, they detect Huon fluid assimilated into your system, and Seven is the only settlement that I'm certain of having Huon, thus a logical deduction. Be careful, John, the king will be interested in that substance flowing through your veins.'

The boys continued their walk down the corridor. It was now evident that the corridor had become larger than before, as if they had travelled through the body of a snake and now had escaped its mouth, and they had begun going through a tunnel that the snake itself was following. The hallway was still the same dull dark blue, and along the floor, against the walls, were sphere-like objects that were large enough to hold grown adults.

John gasped as he realised that each spheroid held a person who was grasping their knees in the fetal position. A glowing dark-green sphere clung to their torsos, or vice versa. Each person was dressed in a silk-like white robe into which golden stitching had been sewn. The stitching created numerous decorative patterns, some floral, some tribal, and some even appearing to emulate astronomical signs.

On top of each person's pod was a tangle of wires, which ran up a coil and disappeared into the ceiling.

John approached one of the pods; the person inside displayed no signs of life other than a look of distress distorting their expression. 'What … What the hell are these things?' he stammered. 'Who are these people?'

A robotic wall-eye glowed red. 'They are … well, they *were* the Uplifted,' Factorem responded. 'These pods were designed so that one could regenerate their cells. Doing so maintains what I suppose you could say is "immortality".'

'Immortality?' spluttered John while restarting his pace.

'Well, not true immortality; there is no such thing,' Factorem explained. 'A human is still a human, no matter what they call themselves. The pods don't provide immortality in a *traditional* sense. But they do provide one with a lifespan that surpasses even the most naturally longevous individual.' Doctor Factorem sighed wearily. 'At least, rejuvenation is the intended design of the pods … When the king discovered the existence of these pods, he showed great enthusiasm. However, when he took control of Haven, I realised his enthusiasm was not from appreciating scientific achievements, but from his plotting. He renamed his new peers "gods" but did this to them.'

The pods were frequent along the hall until they reached an intersection.

John and Mack stared at another red robotic eye.

'Head to the right, that's the passage to the king's chambers,' the eye said.

The boys turned right to find more pods lined against the walls, with more downtrodden Uplifted entombed within them.

'Jo-John,' Mack stammered.

'What's up?'

'Can't we go back?' asked Mack. 'Can we leave before it's too late?'

John paused in his step. 'We're here for answers,' he said, 'and the world can be dangerous, but don't worry, we'll be fine.'

'How can you know that?' said Mack. 'Haven't you been listening? This king sounds terrifying.'

John knelt to Mack and whispered, 'It might just be some exaggeration. I mean, this disembodied voice used to be in charge. Nobody likes being dethroned.'

'I would not underestimate the king,' intoned Factorem. 'I won't dissuade a confrontation; however, neither will I send you to him without awareness.'

The side of John's mouth stretched in a moment of irritation, both due to the unseen scientist's apparent omniscience and John's attempt to instil confidence in Mack being undermined, despite it being a falsehood he was simultaneously telling himself.

CHAPTER EIGHT

THE KING

John broke through the cold silence. 'I've been wondering. Well … Doctor Factorem, why do you keep referring to this usurping leader as the *king*? You clearly don't recognise his authority, so why the royal title?'

Factorem groaned. 'I refuse to use the name he adopted,' he replied. 'The king renamed this place and chose his new moniker to mock me! He abhors hearing his true, original name, so if I utter it, he programmed a failsafe that would torture my every nerve ending if I said it.' Factorem's voice managed to turn even darker. 'I see potential in you; potential that you'll be able to end his tyranny. He may lower his guard when facing young humans, so that's the time to take him down. You must destroy him for the sake of all.'

'Destroy? You mean murder?' stammered John. He was starting to get the feeling that his trip to Haven to find out more about his father was creating moral challenges that he hadn't anticipated.

'Have you not been paying attention to anything I've shared?' Factorem asked.

'But I'm just a kid,' John protested.

'Are you?' said Factorem. 'Or are you on the cusp of being an adult?'

'Well, *on the cusp* only means … on the cusp,' retorted John, beginning to feel an ache beneath his forehead. 'Besides, I'm not a killer. And how will killing some king help me find my dad, or Mack his mum?'

'As you have witnessed, the Uplifted are now being held as prisoners,' said Factorem. 'When free, among the multitude, there is a chance of finding the information you seek.'

'But is murder the only option?' said John, his headache worsening. 'I don't want to kill.'

'I am sorry. Soon, you will have no choice,' Factorem's voice said. 'Now, I will have to decrease communication. You are getting too close to the king for me to communicate with you without his notice anymore.'

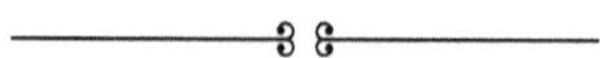

John and Mack walked for what seemed like hours until they finally reached the end of the large corridor. A grandiose doorway took up the space available; it held a pair of doors. The double doors clashed with the corridor, as they appeared to be wooden. The wood had images carved into its body, depicting violent fire and majestic and horrifying creatures. At the centre of the doors was an angelic figure outstretched with beams of light stemming from its body.

John and Mack each grasped a golden handle that each door held closed together. They pushed inward. The doorway opened while the wooden door's hinges creaked as if it were in pain.

They entered a huge hall; it appeared to be the interior of a dome that hugged a top section of the central sphere of Valhalla, almost like a giant eye of the structure itself. The hall had three entrances, each with similarly designed wooden doors.

On the wall, which held the solitary entry that the duo had used, there were three levels of pods, holding more of the Uplifted. On and along the opposite wall was a cluttered laboratory with many pipes, tubes, glass cups, and miscellaneous liquids, among other unidentifiable gadgets.

Around the hall floor were several surgical tables, some of which were occupied by corpse-like individuals strapped down. Thin pipes originating from the floor had their tips dug into the head and arms of the captive people.

The floor itself had hundreds, possibly thousands, of thick wires and thin cables snaked across the surface. Each worm-like wire slithered to the very centre of the hall. Here, the wires and cables bundled together, causing a form that appeared to be a throne, which was elevated on a platform made of other cables.

John and Mack silently gasped when they saw a seated figure on the throne; it appeared to be sleeping. The figure was, or at least had been, a man. Its attire was dark-red boots and almost robe-like white pants. It was shirtless, revealing the figure's abundantly muscled form.

It was bulky, with thick veins pulsating under its skin's surface. Its skin was a dull grey while its veins were a dark green. Parts of its skeletal structure were visible; the edges of its ribs and shoulder blades pierced through the dull grey flesh, exposing its bone structure to be at least partially metallic.

Its arms clearly displayed cybernetic modifications protruding from the grey skin.

It lacked eyebrows, but it did have silvery, shoulder-length hair, slicked back. Thin cables from the ceiling punctured the figure's head, chest, and behind its large frame.

'Hey, have you got a weapon for me,' Mack whispered.

John reached into his vest and pulled out a pistol. 'This shouldn't be too heavy for you, and you could handle the recoil,' he whispered while handing Mack the handgun.

Mack aimed at the figure.

'Wait for my lead, Mack,' John hissed.

Mack, however, fired the gun; the shot echoed around the hall, but neither the figure nor anything was hit. A small puff of smoke weakly hovered and then dissipated closely in front of the figure.

John swung out his medium assault rifle from his back, and aimed his eye down the sight, unsteady due to struggling to find an unobstructed target.

Mack fired again, and again, and again. The subsequent shots revealed what was stopping the bullets dead: small bolts of lightning jumped from every direction, desperately yet successfully intercepting the bullets' paths.

The figure's eyes shot open; its left eye was pale blue with a thin vertical pupil akin to a cat or serpent while its right appeared to be a compact version of Doctor Factorem's red eyes. The cables in the figure's skin detached and then swiftly retracted into the ceiling. The figure grinned, showing sharp, jagged teeth. It lifted its right hand, and instantly, the door behind its right leapt open. A large cluster of cables shot out of the doorway as if it were a cobra preparing to strike its prey.

The cables wrapped around Mack and began to pull him into their den. The small boy screamed while he fired repeatedly at the mass tangle of cables. A few loose strands dropped off the cluster; however, they didn't hamper it in the slightest. The handgun clip ran empty; Mack tossed it at the cables but to no avail.

A tentacle-like branch sprung off the main entity, gripping and ripping John's machinegun from his grasp, snapping it like an insignificant twig.

John tried to pursue the cable tendril mass that had captured Mack only to discover he couldn't budge. His legs up to his knees had been enveloped by thin cables that had grown out of the floor.

Mack's cries for help stopped when he disappeared into the doorway from which the synthetic tentacles had originated. A net of cables filled and blocked the doorway.

John felt the wiry cables move, and he was dragged to the foot of the throne, whereupon the muscular creature looked down on him. 'You fiend!' John yelled. 'What have you done with Mack?'

The creature displayed his shark smile. 'I assume you mean that *child*,' he said in a soft yet harsh voice. 'Do not worry, I will not hurt him … yet. He is no use to me now, but in a few years … he will become like my servants.' The figure pointed to the pods. 'Oh, how rude of me, I should introduce myself,' the grey man continued. 'These pathetic whelps were known as the Uplifted, but I allowed them to be my fellow gods. As I decreed this place Valhalla, I decreed myself: Odin.'

John attempted to lunge at him, but the cables' hold was too tight, completely restricting any mobility.

Odin smirked. 'Adam! Adam, why did you not tell me we have guests?' he asked.

'I do apologise, sir.' Factorem's dark voice surrounded them. 'I did not notice them entering.'

'I know you're lying, Adam,' stated Odin serenely. 'But do not worry. You know I would never kill you, the great Doctor Factorem. I owe my life to you.' Odin pointed at John. 'Child, your little friend will be useful in a few years' time, but you … You will be useful … now.'

'Why?' demanded John. 'Are you gonna put me in a ball like the others? You parasitic bastard.'

Odin chuckled softly, pointing at the people bound by the surgical tables. His cybernetic eye glowed brighter. 'No. Not the pods, child,' he said. 'I do believe that you are from my old home, since the scanners have revealed that you have Huon flowing through your veins, just as all those older than twelve at Seven have … as, too, those gentlemen had, before they became a meal on my dinner tables.'

John glanced at the human shells being held prisoners, then back at Odin, whose grin grew. 'What about those two that came here two months ago?' John demanded.

'Oh, you knew of my earlier guests?' Odin asked. 'One of them, Alex, I think his name was, he's right over there.'

On one of the surgical tables, an individual lay twitching uncomfortably and moaning weakly, but he still had vastly more life and colour left than his fellow imprisoned neighbours.

'And the other … he's a special child,' stated Odin. 'Colonel was his name, and I knew him when I lived in Seven.'

John froze in shock. 'Colonel?' he said. 'Connie's alive! H-how?'

Odin chuckled. 'So, you also knew him? That boy is special—so much strength and vigour, and exceptional genes; as if a little chest wound could kill him,' he proclaimed. 'His endurance, however, is also what made the Seniors decide on his fate: to become their weapon. But now, he is currently in the process of being reborn, to be *my* weapon instead.'

'You monster!' spat John. 'Don't you realise what pain he's been through already?'

Odin chuckled again, although slightly darker. 'I know exactly what he has been through, child,' said the king of Valhalla. 'Only mild persuasion drove him to tell me the tragedy of when his best friend, considered a brother, accidentally shot him, which gave those miserable old Seniors the opportunity to turn him into their little science experiment; they implanted cybernetics into not just his heart where he was injured but throughout his whole body. They made him into their "pet assassin"—another spineless attempt on my life; me, a god—but now he belongs to me.'

John felt weakened by the reminder that it was his fault that Connie had suffered so greatly. 'Why don't you just end his suffering?' he asked. 'Let him go or just kill him to end his misery.'

Odin grinned. 'How morbid. There's no need to do that,' he said. 'I may need him. You see, I have devised a much better way to acquire more Huon. I'm sure the Seniors told you of the enhancing properties of the substance.'

John haltingly nodded.

Odin continued. 'Thanks to Doctor Factorem, I realised why the Seniors use so little of it for each injection. I learnt that the more of that wonderful nectar that's inside someone's system, the more their stamina increases, and the stronger, more resilient, and more intelligent they'll become.'

John then stammered, 'Is that what happened to the people on the surgical tables … you sucked the Huon out of … out of the bodies and injected it into yourself?'

'That's right. What a clever child,' Odin said. 'With the Huon from Sevenites and the energy I consume from all of my *divine* minions, I am rightfully Valhalla's true one and only god—the god above all the gods!'

John tried to struggle free; however, more wires slithered out of the floor, enwrapping his torso. 'Why? Why do all this?' he demanded with difficulty. 'Doctor Factorem told me you were once an ordinary man; why did you turn yourself into a freak?'

Odin slowly approached John, towering over him. 'That *ordinary man* was a pathetic piece of trash, no better than you, child,' he responded. 'He couldn't even protect his own wretched hide …. Eleven years ago, had you asked me why I would choose to become stronger through the suffering of others, I would have said as a means to an end: revenge …. But as the years went by, as I lost my human weaknesses, as I became a god, I cared less about the ties to the feeble wretch that I used to be.'

'If you're gonna rant at me,' John said with a sigh, 'just kill me now. I don't want to hear any more of your insanity.'

Odin leant forward, meeting John's direct gaze. 'Now, I could say I'm doing it for justice … but I'd just be lying,' he seethed. 'I am beyond simplistic notions of justice. What interests me is the vast supply of Huon that I *know* the Seniors have hidden under Seven; I plan to use it in my divine stratagem to recreate this worthless planet into a paradise. I will be the saviour that the Seniors failed to be.'

John looked from one side of the chamber to the other, finding no clear escape available; he tried yet failed to be stoic as Odin turned to face him again. John's heart raced and his mouth dried, the throbbing in his mind exacerbating the torment.

'When I succeed, I will complete my ascension into the role of supreme deity: I will achieve true immortality!' Odin ranted. 'In the past, I was forced to be just like any other subservient pawn, but soon I will be worshipped; I will be adored …' Odin gazed up before eying down John again. 'And, you know what, child? I admire your spirit for coming in here and standing your ground; unlike the other rats, when they realised the futility of their actions, they quickly resorted to begging for their lives. My momentous triumph will be achieved in a matter of days … I admire your courage, so I shall grant you the privilege of witnessing that before you die.'

John's blood felt even colder; his elevated heart rate seemingly carried the chill throughout his body.

'After I take all that Huon and the Senior Order's own "negative technology", I won't need to feed from this worthless rabble anymore. Therefore, you, mortal, you will have the privilege of observing my triumph over those decrepit Seniors as I take their precious Huon and everything they hold so dear!' Odin smirked proudly; his sharp teeth sent shivers down John's spine.

'But … but if you're a god now, why would you want to ravage an entire settlement for more power you don't need?' John asked. 'Why don't you stop? The Sevenites have nothing to do with the Seniors' actions, so you don't need to punish any of them.'

Odin tightened his fist and delivered a punch to John's forehead.

John cursed loudly from pain and the realisation that blood had begun to trickle down his face.

'I may be a god now, but I want to become greater than that!' Odin thundered. 'I'm sure you've seen it yourself; the

Seniors are a corrupt mob of selfish, self-righteous bastards! I despise my former self, but I at least owe him some form of retribution. The Seniors will watch like the cowards they are as I tear their world apart! They will obey my will, rather than force me to bow down to theirs ever again. They will lose their citizens, just as I lost everyone I ever cared about!'

John stopped swearing and spat out blood that had leaked down into his mouth. 'What? What do mean everyone you cared about?' he asked.

Odin recomposed himself, stepped back away from John and resumed his seat on his mangled throne. 'What do I mean? Obviously, I mean just what I said,' Odin replied with a hiss. 'It may be difficult to believe, yet I once had a content, if sickeningly mediocre, life. Until one day.' He appeared solemn. 'One day, I watched a child become twisted into a mindless creature—a creature that destroyed my life and the lives of many others. I was powerless to stop it …. A Senior watched as helplessly as I. But he and even the insane child aren't truly responsible … the real monster was the progeny of my best friend; he caused the chaos and got away with it.'

John dwelled upon why he hadn't known of this information, presuming any of it was based in reality. The Seniors had constructed a myth to keep the evils of the outside away, yet could they have created lies closer to home?

'That *"poor innocent" accidentally* poisoned a child and thereby poisoned every life around him.' A green vein along Odin's temple throbbed. 'When I was a mere human, I … I was too weak to convince everyone to rebel against the Seniors' decrees. Because of that spawn's actions, the Seniors forced every adult witness into exile.'

John tensed anxiously while Odin's other veins seemed to pulsate.

'Too old for the memory wipe? Unlikely. The Seniors merely favour punishment over justice. Before our banishment, the Seniors spent a month updating us about reality and sharing platitudes for survival,' Odin said. 'Trust your instincts? How pointless. Even up until we were cast out into the wastes, I begged them to see the truth, but all we received for countering a Senior's word was more of their nonsense.' Odin ascended the small metallic staircase and then resumed his seat upon his throne of tangled cables. 'In the end, we were resigned to the Seniors' commands; but they did provide at least some useful advice, which was to travel to the hills. Hence, we reached this treasure trove of knowledge and technology. Valhalla's former ruler was more generous than I am about accepting uninvited strangers, so there was no minefield, which I'm impressed you survived,' he said. 'Upon my own arrival, these so-called Uplifted, the inhabitants of Haven, acted amiably, but they refused to honour my plea to hold the Seniors accountable; their welcome was another bitter insult.'

John thought of the story within Seven of a group that had disappeared during an expedition. He wondered if their reason for leaving was actually the one he had believed to be true; he feared the fate of his father had already been taken into Odin's hands. John despaired that he hadn't been an exception to exile but rather part of a pattern, although his fear of the towering grey 'god' hung heavier in his mind.

'The Uplifted all acted friendly and feigned interest in our stories, but I saw through them—not that there was much of a disguise to hide their smug condescension. Not the good doctor, however.' Odin chuckled. 'Adam understood my sadness. He took me under his brilliant wing. I think he truly believed that his tutelage would inspire me to come to terms with my grief and overcome it, isn't that right, Adam?'

Factorem merely mumbled incoherently in response.

'You *were* right, Adam … in some respect. I was inspired to surpass my faults into greatness. I suffered, but my suffering was only a minor step towards my glory! The Seniors preached about the damage caused by negative technology, but I soon understood that they only wanted to prevent us from gaining power over them. Only the weak and ignorant can truly be treated like mindless slaves …. I can at least understand their logic.' Odin leant against his right fist, his elbow on the ostensible arm of his mechanical throne. 'The Seniors learnt of my plans here, and like the predictable fools they are, they have been sending assassins to murder me, although half of those toothless killers weren't completely informed. And the Seniors believed that I wouldn't raise my hand against weak, would-be killers, even if they were privy to my past persona, or even if they were other survivors of the massacre, like young Alex and Colonel.'

John recalled Alex, who was someone he wasn't close to but remembered being one of his peers he had assisted in education. However, with some remorse, John found he didn't care about Alex, at least in comparison to his suddenly resurrected friend, Connie; the increasingly distracting pulse of pain in his head further disrupted any hope he had of processing the emotions, let alone in a dangerous scenario.

'Alex's only value to me was his status as a Sevenite, with the Huon inside of him, but Colonel … that kid is another story. He was able to adapt to more advanced implants than should be survivable.' Odin now leant on to his left palm, with his left elbow resting on an arm of the throne. 'Through all their righteous rambling, the Seniors are just as willing to use counter-inventions as those they condemn. And because of Colonel, they have sown the last seed of their inevitable destruction!'

John coughed as blood from his forehead continued to sneak into his mouth. 'But this violence you plan—it isn't going to help,' he stammered. 'It won't honour the dead; it will disgrace their memo—!' His words were replaced by cries of pain as the cables around his body tightened.

Odin stood up, striking the throne arms. 'How *dare* you! Don't preach pacifism at me, wretch!' he roared, his red eye glowing brighter. 'Did you not agree to Adam's failed plot to kill me? And I may not be human anymore, yet I loved my family and friends; my triumph will celebrate them, not bury them like the Seniors want! I am above human weakness, yet it still burns how John was like a brother to me, and his betrayal hurt me more than anything his destructive child or the Seniors ever did! As a final insult, he lacked the courage to merely remain with us to rebuild something, as he cowered off into the wastes.'

The cables loosened, allowing John to breathe, although he could only manage to gasp. 'John? John Salt … was your friend?' asked the son of the man in question.

'Yes, but he was so full of treachery that even when I was his friend, I doubt he really ever considered me as one.'

'Where is he … now?'

'As I told you, he fled,' said Odin. 'Unfortunately, before I had remade this place into my Valhalla, thus he escaped judgement yet again. I don't know where he is now, but I no longer care … Why do you care?'

John felt reluctant to answer honestly, and yet he saw no other option forward; his mind wouldn't, or couldn't, find any path that wasn't revealing the truth. 'Because I'm his son.' The boy trembled. 'I'm John Smith.'

Odin's face displayed a stony look, befitting his grey complexion; he began to walk back down to John, heavy footsteps reverberating louder than prior paces.

With each step taken, John felt the cables around his torso tightening.

Odin's fury seemed to emanate from him. He clenched his fists and then began to furiously pummel John; each strike hitting harder. Then he stopped to glare with absolute contempt at the boy.

The look on Odin's face was familiar to John from further back than he could coherently remember. The pain that tortured John's senses was familiar as well; however, the last time he felt pain with such severity, it was not of the flesh but of the heart and mind.

Something in John's mind began to break from its bonds; he was struck by an overwhelming headache that hurt much more than the thrashing. In his brain, the pain and fear cracked a shell that held evil memories in his mind. He wept suffocatingly, his sorrow echoing throughout the cavernous hall, but then, he just fell silent. John felt himself plummet back to his childhood, becoming a powerless, speechless and immobile observer of his six-year-old self ....

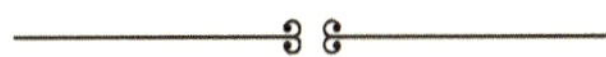

Child John was crouched in the rubble, using bricks as play vehicles. Young Colonel and young Walter were playing with him, as well as another child, who had blonde hair like Colonel.

The children were in a shallow pit, and in the surrounding area, other children were at play in their own selective groups. John's father was also there, along with his friends' parents and relatives, including a handsome blonde man with rich green eyes, as well as other adults whose faces were blurred in memory's degradation. All the adults were supervising their own descendants and relations.

Atop the edge of the flattish pit stood the shaggy, black-robed Zero, overlooking the recreation.

Child John reached into the pocket of his tattered garment; his small hand emerged with a smaller case. The younger version of the exile turned to the child with blonde hair. 'Hey, Tommy.'

Tommy looked up from his glass castle.

'I got some of my daddy's magic beans. Wanna' try one?' Child John asked.

Tommy wore a look of uncertainty.

Child John continued, 'The beans are the thingies that give superpowers. Don't you wanna be super?'

However, seventeen-year-old John remembered that he had sneaked into his father's room and taken his kappa pills because he was curious about their purported 'enhancing' effects, but he was too scared to sample the pills himself.

John's memory became blurred, as if something in his head was trying to stop the event from returning to his conscious thoughts. His recall refocused ....

Child John was in the centre of the pit where a bloody massacre had occurred, with dead and injured all around. John's father had received a vertical slash that cut from the edge of his right eye down his right cheek, ending at his jaw.

Tommy was covered with dripping blood. He tackled Child John.

The boys struggled and fought until Child John kicked Tommy off him; he quickly crawled to his toy bricks and then grasped one of them.

Child John swung back to face Tommy and began to desperately pummel the other child's head. After hearing a crunch, he stopped and stood, dropping the blood-covered brick. He saw his former friend's caved-in skull and the look of despair now permanently cast in his lifeless gaze. Child John looked up and met the eyes of Theodore King, father to both Tommy and Connie.

King's eyes were flowing with tears of sadness and rage and holding a scowl similar to Odin's stern visage although, unlike the god, he had two light-blue eyes and messy blonde hair. 'You ... you wretched runt!' King reached into his rough coat pocket and pulled out a dirty silver knife as large as his forearm.

Zero sprinted into the pit.

John Salt jumped in front of his son as King stabbed.

John Salt gasped as cold steel stabbed beside his right scapula; the blade's tip erupted as a crimson point appeared near his right shoulder, narrowly missing his offspring.

Zero reached King and then punched his throat and ripped the knife from his hand; the bloody blade bounced onto the rubble where it was swallowed by remnants of a dead world.

King collapsed onto his knees in front of the black-cloaked Senior.

John Salt fell back away from his offspring, gripping his knife wound; the laceration across his cheek seemed exacerbated by a rigid expression of pain ....

John's memory flickered, like a dying light bulb that refused to submit to the darkness ....

The remembrance became tangible once again, enabling Child John to witness the crimson Senior, Soar, dragging John Salt and Theodore King up the slight slope. John Salt trudged along, becoming faint due to blood loss; King struggled fervently. 'The truth? The truth? You know damn well what happened!' King yelled.

Soar kicked King's knee.

'Say something, John!' King shouted with venom. 'You know damn well that your son did this! For god's sake, John, you can save us all from banishment and bring that boy to justice!'

John Salt muttered for King to be quiet.

Soar and his prisoners were out of the pit.

'You miserable little monster!' King shouted at John. 'You worthless rat; I'll get you for this! I will slaughter you!'

John's memory blanked until he witnessed his recollection's end.

Zero walked slowly towards Child John; he knelt next to him. Zero retrieved a syringe from his cloak and pierced Child John's neck, injecting a bright blue liquid. The chaotic remains faded into blackness.

CHAPTER NINE

ESCAPE

Seventeen-year-old John felt himself rocket out of his broken remembrance, hearing, seeing, and feeling nothing—until he reopened his eyes. John was still in Odin's clutches, within a great dark hall, ensnared by cold metal wires, and not a second had passed. 'You … you're Connie's father?' John said.

Odin's red eye shone bright, stabbing a chilling darkness through John's mind.

'Aren't you Theodore King? Oh god, I killed Tom—'

Odin covered a hand over John's mouth; the grey-skinned man chuckled through clenched teeth. 'You're the one who set me upon my path to greatness, and for that I am grateful,' he announced. 'So, I will spare you your pathetic life. But … I still owe a debt to my old self … despite being purged of all weaknesses that once restrained me. I won't kill you … but I'm going to make you wish that I had!'

The cables around John tightened so much that his skin was cut; small trickles of blood slid down the serpentine constrictions.

Odin clenched his fists, crackling his knuckles, and then his frenzied attack recommenced.

John's eyes welled up with tears as his nose was hit and cracked. His breathing became wheezy as the cables tightened further, and his ribs cracked under the stress of pressure and punch. He wept as the pain intensified, and then he screamed as he felt his broken ribs puncture his skin and scrape his lungs. He gurgled when blood erupted out of his mouth.

Odin grinned as he continued the brutally merciless beating.

John's vision became blurred due to the mixture of pain, tears, and blood.

Odin struck the left side of John's face with so much force that John's jaw unhinged. He then briefly stopped the torment to show his palms to John. His palms seemed to be entirely metal, melded with his grey skin; at the centre of his right palm, small conical spikes grew instantly and then retracted. Odin used this palm and grasped John's left arm.

John screamed as best he could with a broken jaw as the spikes stabbed through his coat into his arm.

Odin chuckled as he twisted his spiked palm, causing the cuts on his captive's arm to grow wider.

John felt the warmth of electricity being generated from the spikes, and he cried when they burnt his flesh throughout his whole body.

Odin speedily dragged his hand down John's left arm, tearing his coat sleeve to shreds and leaving weeping lacerations. He then clenched his fist, drawing it back.

John winced, expecting another hit; however, he didn't feel more of the beating. Thinking he had died, he instead opened his eyes.

Odin's arms and legs were constricted in a section of the ceiling that appeared to have moulded into a thick worm that encompassed his limbs. 'Adam! What do you think you're doing?' he roared.

'Saving the boy's life,' Factorem replied.

'Ah … yes, I got carried away again,' said Odin. 'I need to save this child. I do not want his torment to end so quickly; thank you, Adam—'

'*No!*' yelled Factorem. 'I am saving the man who is going to stop your madness! John, what're you waiting for? Use your damn knife! Cut yourself loose!'

John looked at his Bowie blade still in its scabbard and unsheathed it. Then, using his uncut right arm, he sliced the cables that bound him.

'No, you don't!' Odin yelled. His red right eye glowed, and a mesh of cables blocked the exit.

John slashed through the cables with the knife like a machete cutting wild jungle vines. Wires shot out of the floor and grabbed John's right leg. They squeezed while John cut at them. He screamed when his leg bones crunched, and then he finally quelled the wires and began to run away, limping.

'You might escape now, but I'll find you again no matter how far you run!' roared Odin. 'As soon as my plan is complete, I will focus the entirety of my existence on hunting you down! You think this was pain? When I find you … I will teach you about pain! I will dismember your body and feed you your entrails! I will—'

The threats continued but became inaudible as John got further away. He coughed and wheezed through the pain, which intensified with each hop. 'Ali-hair!' he spluttered. He then dragged the strap of his rifle over his head, discarding the weight of the weapon.

The cube around his neck shone, and the hologram of Doctor Alistair Toat appeared. 'Activate protocol Elabor-Null-Drei!' he ordered.

A large cocoon formed out of the floor and enveloped John, cradling him securely. He felt as if he were falling, except that gravity had gone sideways at high speed. He was carried in the cocoon back from whence he had walked through the facility.

John's terror grew as he flew past the metal grate of the pit where the hideous chimera blob lay. It squealed wildly as John's blood rained down upon it; its gaping mouths greedily catching the crimson liquid. John sharply turned a corner where the cocoon carefully placed him in front of the lift doors at the end of the first corridor through which he had traversed. It dinged amiably; its doors opened. A black dome on the lift interior wall lit up red.

'Perhaps I overestimated you,' said Factorem. 'Nevertheless, if you survive, I implore you to return … I-I can't hold back the king forever.'

John fell into the lift; the doors closed. He felt his body rise, but his stomach dropped. He wept from the physical agony as well as the mental anguish over hints of childhood trauma and the guilt of leaving Mack behind.

'John, don't worry about your little friend,' said Factorem. 'I doubt the child will be within his notice, yet I will still prevent Odin from lashing out at him … when you return, be prepared …' His voice managed to fluctuate to an even darker tone. 'To kill that traitor.'

The lift dinged.

John heaved himself up and limped out. He was back in the dodecahedral structure around the entrances of Valhalla.

'Go to the right, John,' said Factorem. 'The way you came from is on the only moving pathway. Farewell, and please return soon.'

John wheezed as he limped out of the oddly shaped structure. The sun's rays glistened from the pools of blood forming around him. He collapsed onto the only moving pathway, which carried him in the direction of the android boys' cavern. John then passed out.

CHAPTER TEN

Deus Ex Machina

John groaned when he was awoken by the rustling of his reddened grey coat-tails being pushed against the slight elevation at the end of the shining escalator. Using his right hand, he pulled himself onto the stone-looking metal pathway.

Due to the limitations of only two adequate limbs, John struggled to stand. He cursed as he placed too much pressure on his fractured right leg. He gripped his burnt bleeding left arm through his shredded sleeve and began his limping descent along the path scarred into the dead hill.

John winced as he felt his ribs pinching further through his flesh. Every several steps, he coughed, blood spewing out each time. He then sighed somewhat in relief as he reached the arch at the end of the path, at the bottom of the hill.

John half-limped, half-dragged himself along the path; he swore loudly in his head. He fell onto his knees and then collapsed onto his face into the soft yet scratching sand. A trapdoor creaked open nearby.

Blue-overalled Richie emerged. 'What in the hell!' he exclaimed. 'Leo, your sensors were right; someone's here!'

Leo and Howie followed their leader out of the cavern. They lifted the wounded exile and carefully carried him to the trapdoor.

Richie dropped into the cavern. 'Okay, now carefully lower him,' he ordered.

Leo and Howie, the latter too obviously absent-minded, dropped John; he plummeted into the cave.

Richie caught him, but this gesture caused John's back to bend; he slumped in Richie's arms, attempting to cry vulgarities.

Howie called out an apology as he and Leo entered the cavern; the trapdoor closed after they did.

Richie carried John and then placed him on the rock table.

John's eyes searched around at the commotion, and he finally settled a little knowing he was somewhere safe, although his howling body made it seem like danger still had him in its hold.

Murray was lying on a bed-shaped rock along the cavern wall, breathing loudly.

'Murray! Get up and help us!' Richie cried out.

Murray groaned, and then he dragged himself to a seated position. He stood up and rubbed his eyes sleepily. 'Yeah, I'm up,' he said. 'Whaddya' want?' Murray then turned towards John. 'My Saint Francis, what the hell happened to him?'

The androids didn't respond, since they were huddled around John, so Murray merely crouched next to them. He lightly tapped the dark-silver cube that was hanging over John's bloodied shirt, and then they all jumped back in surprise as a man-sized hologram materialised instantly next to them.

'You are Sorge fifty-one Alpha, Beta, Gamma, are you not?' Toat hurriedly asked.

The robotic trio nodded while Murray crawled back to his bed.

Toat then commanded, 'One of you: take my processor core and connect it to your central processing unit.'

Leo picked up the cube; the neck chain retracted into the shiny object.

'Be careful, Leo,' Richie warned.

Leo pushed the cube into his left temple; it entered as if it were a stone into water. Toat's hologram disappeared; Leo tensed, and then his eyes flashed blue. 'This boy is only still alive because of the Huon in his system.' Leo spoke with Toat's voice. 'So, we must hurry. Give me your hands.'

Richie and Howie began to unscrew their wrists.

'Not literally!' yelled Leo-Toat. 'Well, literally, but still connected to your bodies.'

The unpossessed androids nodded, and each grabbed a hand of the possessed one. They twitched; their arms bulged briefly then returned to normal. They began to loosen their grips.

'Wait,' ordered Leo-Toat. 'Okay, you can let go now.'

Howie and Richie released their hold and began to shake their arms as if they were aflame.

Leo-Toat held out his open hands; on each palm, a bright silver ball rotated. 'Commence Deus Ex Machina procedure,' he said. He pushed his hands together and the orbs merged, making a light-blue sphere double the size of the individual orbs. Leo-Toat muttered a hundred phrases in an instant and then pushed the orb onto John's chest. The sphere disappeared into John's torso.

'What was that?' asked Richie.

Leo blinked, and then his eyes returned to normal. The small cube slid out of Leo's left temple. He grabbed it and then placed it on the rock table next to John.

The hologram reappeared. 'I borrowed some of your nanites,' Toat answered. 'And I gave them a new priority program to become symbiotic with Herr Smith.'

Richie struck through the hologram. 'You could have warned us!'

'I thought it would be more amusing to see your *adorable*, shocked faces,' Toat replied.

Richie opened his mouth, ready to seemingly criticise the holographic personality; however, he was interrupted by John screaming.

John's back arched, and he lurched upwards, arms extended back. He fell back, pounding the rock table with his fists and feet. An odd blue aura generated from his skin. As it faded, he went limp. He then screamed again; he felt his bones crack and realign into place and reconnect; his cuts and lacerations sealed, becoming slightly steaming scars, which then faded. He gasped as if starved for oxygen, then sat upright, breathing heavily. John examined his hands and arms in disbelief.

'Now,' said Toat, 'he is fixed. Not only that, but he can also manipulate nanites, just like Odin, although with a much lesser efficacy, and only the nanites of his own body.'

'Wait,' Murray said while approaching the hologram, 'did you say, *Odin*?'

'*Ja*, I did. Now let me finish, please,' Toat replied. 'I have also programmed the nanites to strengthen John's very being. They will be able to regenerate his body from any damage caused. They live symbiotically within him; they can function like stem cells, repairing or replacing any damaged cells. Since the nanites absorbed the Huon in his blood, they can heal him moderately faster than they normally would.'

John turned himself, sitting on the edge of the rock table. His thoughts scrambled in a mashed jumble.

'Good to have you back, John,' Richie said with a friendly smile.

John shook his head to break the stupor. 'Dammit! I must rescue Mack!' he exclaimed before trying to stand, but Murray pushed him back down.

'You met Odin and just left Mack in there with him?' Murray said in an oddly sober tone. 'Odin was the psycho that Lucy said she ran away from.'

John stared stunned at the hooded man.

'Lucy, huh? That name sounds familiar,' Howie mused aloud. 'Oh, yeah! That was the human who left Mack with us.'

'Mack's mother ...? I still need to help him find her, after I get him,' John said. 'Murray, Mack told me you knew his mum—did you know Odin as well? Is he Theodore King?'

Murray turned away, refusing to reply.

John grunted in annoyance; he stood up and then began to march towards the ladder that reached up to the cavern's trapdoor.

'Wait!' ordered Toat.

John stopped and slowly walked back to Toat.

'If you listened to anything I said,' continued the hologram, 'then you would have heard me say: you can manipulate the nanites *like* Odin; however, he is still far more powerful than you. And there is something else you should know: if you allow yourself to be helpless in a near-death situation again, your nanites will take total control of you. Due to the basic programming necessary from the limited time I had available, they will do anything to protect their host, even if that means turning it into their puppet.'

John swore and then kicked the ground in frustration.

'If you are worried about your little friend, don't be,' Toat said calmly. 'When Doctor Factorem isn't being tortured for dissidence again, he will be able to prevent Odin from hurting your friend too greatly.'

'How is that supposed to make me *not* worry?' demanded John.

Toat needlessly scratched his forehead. 'Well, I thought you would gain some solace in the knowledge that the boy will remain unharmed for a time.'

'I don't care if it's a long time,' fumed John. 'I forced him to come with me into bloody Valhalla, so I have to get him out!'

Murray sighed and then placed a hand on John's shoulder. 'He's right, kid,' said the sober drunk. 'You can't rush back in there unprepared.'

'But Connie—' John struggled to think clearly against the propulsion of panic. 'He's alive, but Odin has Connie, too.'

Murray's eyes seem to flare. 'What'd I just say?' His calmness seemed restored. 'You can't rush back in. Now, did you find out anything about his power? Lucy told me he uses a lot of Huon, is that right?

'Well, he does need it to sustain the full potential of his strength,' interjected Toat. 'His strength is also augmented by most of his body being reinforced or replaced by cybernetics and nanites, although the remainder of his flesh is wholly dependent on Huon, which is why he has planned to attack Seven, no matter what else he claimed.'

John picked up Toat's cube-mind; two thin silver chains grew out of the cube's sides, joining each other to form a neck chain again.

'I think I know where to get a weapon that can possibly beat Odin,' said Murray.

'Where?'

'You'll see.'

John sighed, placing the cube neck chain over his own neck. Since he was no longer on the brink of death, he realised the poor condition of his attire. His coat was tattered, as well as being darkened and still damp from blood. He emptied its lower, relatively undamaged pockets; the small boxes of bullets rattled and the bottled water sloshed as he dropped them onto the rock table. He took off his coat, sloppily dropping it onto the cavern floor, and it became a pile that resembled a bloody rock.

John's vest and trousers were a little torn, but he deemed them to be adequate. His shirt was ruffled, and the left sleeve was ripped into ribbons; John tore off the damaged sleeve, leaving him with a half-shirt. He removed his semi-gloves and irritably tossed them onto the bloody pile.

The androids had gone to the cavern's other side, where they were playing some kind of card game.

Murray tapped John's shoulder; he placed his black coat into John's arms. 'Wear this,' he plainly instructed.

John mumbled his appreciation while he navigated his arms into the coat. It clinked. John reached into the pockets and began to casually pull out bottles of whiskey, vodka, and beer, and then place them onto the rock table.

Murray pulled back the hood of his black cloak, revealing his dark-blue balaclava; it had two eye holes and an opening for his bearded chin and lower face. Without his coat on, Murray's belt was visible; it was completely gold. It had multiple small holsters that housed bullets around the belt; on its left side, a larger holster held a six-shot magnum revolver handgun.

John examined his new coat rather admirably. 'So, what is this special weapon, Murray?' he asked. 'Is it some kind of EMP generator that can short-circuit Odin's nanites?'

'Well, if it is, it won't work,' interrupted Toat.

'What do you mean?'

'Well, it's true that an electromagnetic pulse can disable or even destroy machines dependent on a power source,' advised Toat. 'As such, the nanites made in Haven are not immune but are extremely resistant to an EMP's effects. Therefore, if your weapon's function is to create an EMP, then you will have to think of something else because it won't work long enough to matter.'

'Don't worry, the weapon doesn't do that,' stated Murray.

'Then what is it?' asked John as Toat vanished.

'You'll see,' responded Murray.

John groaned, annoyed.

'All right, I'll at least tell you where we can get this weapon from,' Murray relinquished. 'It's at the same place I get all my supplies. It's a place out in the wastes that is a massive shopping complex.'

'How long will it take to get there?' asked John.

'Hmmm … I believe I don't know.'

'You don't know!'

'Well, I never timed it, and I don't have a clear-cut concept of time, anymore,' retorted Murray. 'I guess, I dunno … a day, two?'

'Crap …' said John. 'We'd better get moving then.'

'Adios, amigos!' Murray called to the three androids. 'We'll see you next … when we see you. Wish us luck!'

The androids simply mumbled encouragement, as they were engrossed in their card game.

John sent a meek farewell to the distracted androids as well.

Murray was then sucked up into the entrance tube to the surface, and John followed suit.

CHAPTER ELEVEN

TRUTH IS PAIN

John pulled himself out of the cavern opening, slamming the trapdoor behind him. The shifting sands hid it almost immediately.

Murray had already begun following a path; it was a route that was perpendicular to the minefield and the base of the hill range.

John jogged to catch up to Murray, his steps instantly covered by soft, sparkling sand. 'Wait up,' he called, albeit unnecessarily, as he felt stronger than ever before in his short life. John caught up with Murray and began to walk alongside him.

'Don't talk to me,' said Murray. 'I tried to tell you not to go into damned Valhalla, but you didn't listen.'

'You passed out before you finished explaining why we shouldn't.'

'Shut up.'

'Odin told me he hadn't seen my dad, at least after he took over,' said John. 'So, that leads me to believe that you went with him into the wastes. So, where is my dad now?'

'I … I don't know, Junior,' responded Murray. 'We were separated a while ago … I don't know where he is … I'm sorry.'

'Damn it … then tell me, Murray, I heard you say that you knew Mack's mother, Lucy,' said John. 'And Mack told me that she was one of your group of outcasts as well.'

'What's your point?' grumbled Murray.

'I believe you can help me fix some gaps in my memory.'

Murray stopped walking. 'You really don't want to know.'

'I already know that it was my fault that Tommy died, but I can't clearly remember why … or what happened exactly,' John said with a frown. 'All I can see are … glimpses, but I can't connect my memories together.'

Murray sighed. 'Well, fine, I'll tell you what I saw before Tommy went crazy. You were a stupid, disobedient kid,' he said. 'Us adults didn't keep a close eye on you; in that moment, you gave Tommy a kappa pill, which I'm sure the Seniors told you were extremely dangerous to those who haven't been processed with Huon yet.' Murray stroked his beard, in clear contemplation of a severed subject. 'Excluding the children who, like you, had their memories suppressed, there were twenty-seven survivors of the massacre when that kappa pill drove Tommy insane and violent, and all of them were sent into exile to prevent ruining the "purity" of Seven.' Murray slumped for a moment. 'Your dad, and Ted, and me … we were best friends all our lives. But after supporting your lie, older John was despised by all the outcasts; I was the exception. Unlike everyone else, we knew, and I think the Senior knew, too: you were just a naïve kid and truly didn't want others to suffer.'

'My lie?' asked John.

'Oh, I'm sorry,' said Murray. 'I figured you realised. After Tommy's death, you claimed your father and Ted were the ones who gave him the kappa pill.'

John's despair was thrashing against the prison walls in his psyche; he wouldn't let it escape with the sand in the breeze.

'But, like I said, it wasn't your fault; you were a kid who was curious and then panicked,' said Murray. 'Even so, I'm sorry to say, my sister, Lucy—she hated you most of all. Not because she thought you were guilty, but because she was pregnant when we were tossed out of Seven.'

For John, the pain that had seemingly been due to suppressed memories had begun to fade, but it was replaced by a deeper sorrow that weighed heavier than he had thought possible. He battled the realisation that he had uprooted Mack's life before he was even born and had done it again with the unprepared exploration of Valhalla.

'Lucy couldn't believe that all the witnesses were made into exiles because of a kid's mistake … her misery and Ted's anger started to fester within the whole group before our banishment; that didn't change, even at Haven …. So, eventually, your dad chose to leave Haven, and I tagged along.' Murray bent down and stuck a hand into his left boot, retrieving yet another flask.

'I'd thought you'd had enough by now,' John muttered silently.

'What?'

'You heard me,' John replied. 'Why are you always drunk?'

'When was I drunk?'

'Back in the cavern.'

'I wasn't drunk,' said Murray. 'I'd been carrying that bag of stuff nonstop for three days. I was just bloody tired.'

'Whatever,' said John. 'Anyway, where is this "shopping complex"?'

'Ummm … somewhere over the minefield,' Murray answered.

John coughed in shock. 'O-over the minefield!'

'What? Did you expect it to be right next door to Valhalla?'

'How do we get through the minefield without a bunch of explosions.'

'Chill out, kid,' said Murray. 'Do you really think that I'd be going back and forth all these years without a way?'

'All right, fair enough.' John pondered in silence momentarily. 'Murray, you said that Lucy ran away from Valhalla to escape Odin,' he said. 'And Odin told me he was in the same group of exiles as my father … so … he's truly Colonel's father, Theodore King, isn't he?'

'Geez, it's like seeing your parents again. Your dad always wanted to know everything, too, and your mother always wanted to help with someone's problems,' mused Murray before taking a slow breath. 'Yep, Odin used to be Theodore King: father of Colonel and Tommy King. Tommy murdered those people … including his mother, and then you killed Tommy in self-defence, and then the witnesses were banished. After all that, Ted didn't have anyone he considered to be family left.'

John's mouth was agape, and yet he had nothing to say; silence reigned. The only exception was the crunch and squeak of the sand when stepped upon. 'But what about Connie—'

The two pariahs stopped when they heard a clunk.

John looked down, moving the sand with the sole of his boots; a metal trapdoor was revealed. He looked to his right; the section of the hills that surrounded Valhalla was steep—so steep that it would be impossible to climb.

The hologram of Doctor Alistair Toat flickered to life next to them.

'In case you were wondering: your saviour and guide is still here,' said Toat, walking along with them. 'And some advice: avoid stepping on metal hatches like those.'

'Why?' John asked.

Toat shifted his glasses further up his nose. 'Well, the very first, original leader of Haven encouraged freedom for his citizens, so he created certain exit points: if they wished to leave, they could. However, now the hatches contain sensors in the plates that enable Odin to locate any heat signatures around Valhalla's perimeter.'

'Well, thanks for the warning,' said John. 'But how do you know so much about this place? Did you design it yourself or something?'

'I do not have any records on whether I did or didn't. Frankly, I don't care,' responded Toat. 'I am an invention of the individual Alistair Toat. I only know who he was, plus most forms and functions of technology in existence; that's what I am. That's who I am.' Toat vanished, receding into the small cube that hung around John's neck.

'He's very… very strange,' mused Murray.

John felt odd agreeing with the observation, yet he found the conclusion not entirely conclusive. The disembodied Toat hadn't only saved his life, but the replicated intelligence had elevated John into being something greater. 'Wait,' said John, 'to finish my question.'

Murray turned aside to face him. 'About?'

'Connie!' said John with more insistence than intended. 'Didn't Ted King—or damn Odin—care about Connie?'

'I don't know, kid.' Murray sighed. 'Maybe, and maybe you've realised that losing family can break a man, and a person like Ted … there's no heart left.'

Instead of dwelling too absolutely on the rediscovered ocean of grief, John tried to estimate how his heightened form could allow him to atone in some way. He set aside, or rather pushed down, his misery, and he hoped that his ostensible mechanical evolution, along with the secret weapon spoken of by Murray, could allow him to stop Odin—formerly Theodore King—and at the minimum rescue Mack and perhaps save Connie, though that endeavour seemed less plausible. John tried to consider the goals noble, though he couldn't deny a slight selfish motive in trying to undo the damage he had caused to alleviate his own sense of guilt.

CHAPTER TWELVE

Beast of a Problem

As the sun retreated behind the hills, half of the sky already bowed to the will of a starry night. The odour of iron and ash wafted from the minefield, hidden in the evening breeze.

'Okay, we're here,' said Murray.

John looked around; the hills behind him were much more akin to those above the android kids' lair—they also had a stone-like metallic pathway etched into them. He scratched his head. 'Where?'

Murray pulled up his left sleeve, uncovering a silver watch-like object around his wrist.

'Where did you get that?' demanded Toat as his blue-tinged image lit up.

'Eleven years ago, when me and the others arrived at Haven,' responded Murray, 'John chose to leave because he didn't want to burden the others with his presence and the memories it would bring. I decided to go with him because I didn't want my best friend to be alone. An Uplifted called something like Athena wanted to give us something to help, so she gave both of us a Jackal device.' Murray tapped the watch, and a holographic keyboard appeared, hovering above his wrist.

A computerised monotone voice spoke. 'Hello. Thank you for using the Jackal multi-purpose tool. If you wish to hear my complete functions, please press one. If you already know, then please proceed.'

Murray pressed a sequence of keys. 'Athena warned us that they might "hurt a little bit" when put on,' he reminisced. 'The little Jackal bastards drove spikes into our wrists. I don't know whether the spikes are supposed to secure the device or prevent someone from taking it, but it hurt. A lot!'

'*Ja*, well,' said Toat, 'they are designed to be used by the Uplifted if they desired to explore the outside world, and they had a much higher tolerance for most things, including annoying pricks.'

John heard Murray curse Toat and his possible ancestry under his breath.

Murray finished typing; the computerised voice hummed and then intoned, 'Activating safe path through blast zone … closest sector … detected. Program: steel step executing.' The keyboard vanished; a green light shot into the minefield.

The ground began to shake, and John nearly lost his footing, causing him to swear in surprise. The minefield next to them grumbled, as if a giant was awakening from a deep slumber beneath. Five rectangular columns emerged from the sands of the minefield, and then additional pillars burst up until fifty columns had surfaced; each standing a metre high, and each having a several-metre gap between them and their peers.

At the top of each column, a thick shining cloud of nanites gathered, hissing and clicking. They pooled themselves together until each column had a silvery drawbridge atop it. The platforms slowly lowered, reaching their neighbouring column. The platforms melded together, forming an unbroken bridge; it was completely ignored by the mines. A ramp extended from the end of the bridge closest to the humans and the hologram.

Murray clapped his hands once. 'Pretty cool, eh?' he said. 'Athena told John and me about this trick a while back; it was originally to deal with flooding, apparently. She also told us the best direction to head for was this way.' Murray resumed his casual pace, his steps now clunking due to the metal surface of the bridge, which, despite its inherent smoothness, was not remotely slippery.

John stood still, like a tree rooted into the ground. He broke his stupor by shaking his head and then jogged to catch up to Murray.

Toat accompanied John, gliding silently through the air next to him. He crossed his arms. 'So … you are the one who keeps using the steel step.'

Murray turned to face the hologram. 'Yeah, what of it?'

Toat shook his head, and then replied, 'Well, for years now, Odin has been sending his chimeras to deal with a "pest" problem. How did you keep surviving the monsters?'

Murray stroked his beard, and then he grumbled. 'When I'm going to the lads, I kill the creatures with my gun, "Callahan", but … most of the time, when I'm leaving, I … out … run … them.'

'Wh-what?' Toat stammered. 'And you named your gun?'

'Well, bullets aren't limitless, and most of the creatures aren't really that fast … definitely weren't too smart, and no I didn't name my gun, it's just what its box said,' Murray responded. 'So, that was Odin sending those things up here?'

John froze as he heard a metallic trapdoor being thrown open; he looked back—despite the setting sun, visibility was rather clear. Then he saw the now-open trapdoor near the hill.

A loud growl roared out, which turned into a high-pitched squeal.

Murray also stopped, joining John's stare at the open hole.

A large beast emerged from the trapdoor; it cracked the hole wider to accommodate its size. It crawled onto the sand and stood on its hind legs. It was twice as tall as John when upright. Except for half of its head and its belly, it was covered in thick brown fur. At the base of its hind legs were hooves. Its bare flesh was fat and light red. Its face had a snout; mucus was slowly dripping from it. Its mouth took up almost the whole width of its head. An under-bite held two thick tusks. Its eyes, ears, and hands were human-oid, although at the end of its long fingers were razor-sharp claws. The monstrosity growled and then squealed again.

'What the hell is that thing?' cried John while slowly stepping backwards.

Murray followed suit. 'It looks like a half-man and half-bear,' he said before squinting. 'And half-pig!'

Toat rubbed his face in annoyance. 'It's a Hunter-class chimera,' he explained. 'I have records of what kinds of chimeras Odin has sent over the years, so beware; I know this one is a lot faster, a lot stronger, and a lot harder to kill than the chimeras you faced in the past.' As Toat began to vanish, he suggested, 'I think you should run *now*.'

John and Murray looked at each other; they broke into a sprint, fleeing the Hunter.

The Hunter growled and squealed and began to hurriedly stomp after them, its hooves creating a loud clang as they pounded on the bridge. It was gradually closing the gap between itself and the travellers.

John yelled, 'Murray, you said you could kill these monsters!'

'Yep, thanks to ol' Callahan here.' Murray affectionately patted the magnum on his belt.

'So, use the damn thing!' John shouted.

Murray unholstered his magnum; he fired two shots in quick succession at the Hunter. The view of the chimera was blocked by a pair of simultaneous explosions. Murray slowed while John skidded to a halt.

'What the hell?' John exclaimed.

Murray chuckled, spinning the magnum around his index finger. 'You can't survive in the wastes with just any old gear, Johnny-boy.' He gripped the gun tightly. 'I use explosive shells!'

'Are … are you crazy?' John stammered. 'If a normal gun backfires, it's not good, but with that one … you'd be blown to pieces!'

Murray chuckled again. 'Chill. It's a helluva lot more reliable than most guns and bullets.'

John gazed back down the bridge. Thick smoke from the blasts just began to drift away. 'Crap,' he grumbled when he saw the smoke clear.

The Hunter was now on all fours, breathing. It stood up on its hind legs again; aside from a few scorch marks on its abdomen and slightly smouldering fur, it was unharmed.

Murray fired two more shots at the Hunter; explosions erupted on its chest and head. The heat from the flames licked John's cheeks before receding. The smoke faded into the night sky, and yet the Hunter still stood, although one of its tusks cracked; half of a tusk fell to its hooves. The Hunter looked at the broken tusk and then back up at the travellers. A scowl appeared on its face, its eyes turned entirely black, and it growled furiously.

John and Murray once again sprinted away, their melodic foot clunks clashing with the chimera's erratic hoof clangs.

As he ran, Murray fired over his shoulder. A blast on the Hunter's legs caused it to stumble and roll forwards like a hairy boulder.

The Hunter squealed, and then it jumped up to immediately continue its fevered pursuit.

Murray shot at the beast, but it raised a clawed hand, blocking the path of the bullet.

An explosion materialised on the creature's palm, but it merely shook it off while maintaining its pace. The Hunter slashed at the pair.

John cursed when he felt the tips of its claws swipe at the air behind his neck.

Murray swung open his pistol's cylinder; the empty bullet casings fell out behind him. He pulled out a new bullet from his belt and slid it into a chamber. 'J-Junior!' he gasped. 'We … we have … to stop! I can't get … get a good … aim … while this chimera thing is … at our … throats!'

'Dammit!' exclaimed John. 'Okay, but try shooting its eyes this time!' He stopped, ducked, and rammed into the Hunter's legs.

The creature squealed in surprise, and then it growled as it fell.

John swerved around the falling monster and then jumped onto its back; he unsheathed his Bowie blade. He stabbed at the creature's back, but its thick hide only bent and wasn't punctured by the strikes.

The Hunter tried to claw at John but was just barely out of reach.

Murray finished filling his revolver's chambers; he flicked his wrist to close the cylinder.

John sheathed his knife and released his hold on the creature's neck. As he landed on the bridge, he leapt towards Murray, to avoid the Hunter's back-swipe.

As the Hunter turned towards the travellers, Murray fired two shots. Both bullets pushed into the Hunter's right eye; the black gooey eye caused the bullets to remain static. Murray fired twice again; the third and fourth bullets collided with their fellows, forcing them to puncture the Hunter's eye.

The Hunter squealed angrily and gripped its head in pain. Before it could completely cover its head, the bullets erupted. Fire ripped through the Hunter's skull; its final squeal was cut short as its head was consumed by an inferno. The explosion jumped out, quickly turning into dark smoke that seemed invisible as it rose into the night.

Out of the smoke, the Hunter fell to its knees before tumbling onto its side. Its headless neck spewed out a torrent of bubbling green blood.

John unleashed a heavy sigh.

'Well … let's keep going,' Murray said nonchalantly.

'W-wait,' stammered John. 'How did you become such a good shot?'

'Practice, Johnny, my boy,' replied Murray. 'Now come on.' He returned to his casual pace down the bridge.

John followed. 'The chimeras aren't always that strong. Are they?' he asked.

Murray stroked his beard. 'Nope,' he casually responded. 'That's the toughest one I've ever seen.' He emptied the hollow casings from the magnum revolver's cylinder and replaced them with unused ones; he then holstered the weapon.

'Alistair,' said John. 'You called that chimera a Hunter-class. How did you know that?'

Toat's hologram appeared next to them.

'You should really pay more attention, *Kind*,' Toat said while adjusting his glasses. 'Doctor Factorem told you: we had to help Odin in his … interesting … experiments. Therefore, I know exactly what each chimera is or was, and you know, it's a real credit to you, Herr Smith. Odin must be so riled by your visit that he is sending out his most dangerous creatures to deal with anything that the sensors identify.'

'Wow, I'm honoured,' John said monotonously.

'*Ja*, well, you should ask for help next time, as I can access many mechanisms, and could have done this—' Toat snapped his fingers; the section of bridge under the Hunter's corpse retracted instantly and the body fell. There were several clicks, then a thick column of flame erupted in its place. The blaze was snuffed out as the section of bridge returned.

'Why couldn't you have done that earlier?' asked John through gritted teeth.

'Well, the creature could have brought you down with it,' responded Toat. Then he smugly added, 'Besides, no-one asked.' He vanished.

John muttered insults under his breath.

'Don't worry, kid,' Murray said before gulping down the contents of a flask that seemed to have appeared out of nowhere. 'From all that … that running, we're more than halfway across the steel step bridge.'

CHAPTER THIRTEEN

PEOPLE OF FAITH

After uncounted minutes of *clink-clunk*, the men were greeted with the barely audible shift of sand as they descended from the ramp at the bridge's end. Murray tapped his wrist-fixed Jackal device and quickly typed into the holographic keyboard that appeared. The keyboard then disappeared into the Jackal; a computerised voice intoned, 'Command accepted. De-activating steel step.'

A green light shone on the bridge. The bridge path became a silver mist, which was sucked into the tops of the columns that they had rested on. The columns dived back into the sand, leaving no evidence that they were ever present.

John mused to himself, 'Why can't it emerge as fast as that?'

'So, Johnny, how do you feel?' asked Murray.

'Umm, fine, I guess.'

'Well, I'm friggin' tired,' said Murray. 'You might not have to rest after that super fun walk-chase, but I do. Good night.' He pulled his hood over his head and then shaped a pillow out of sand. He lay down, but then he sat up, lifting his hood a bit. 'What does the moon look like now?'

'What?'

'The big white thing in the sky.'

'I know what it is.' John sighed. 'But what does it matter?'

'There is a shortcut to the shopping complex, the … uh … Caligo's Plaza,' said Murray. 'It cuts a day off the trek, but it's only safe depending on the moon. So, what's it like?'

'It's full.'

'Good.' Murray smiled. 'That means we can safely go through Lunacity.'

'Which is?'John's question remained unanswered, as Murray had drifted under slumber's restful spell. The young man sighed, returning his gaze to the sky—a larger vista than any he had gleaned from Seven.

Unlike the predominantly grainy status of the sands between Seven, Necropolis, and Valhalla, the earth nearby was more akin to a vast unreflective mirror; the glass was cracked beyond pattern or reason. It was relatively solid as John pressed his boot heel on a part that fused with the sandy edge near the minefield. It cracked like thin ice, except there was no water beneath it, only more glassy ground.

There was a fine layer of dust clouding the view of every surface; whether it was native dirt or had been carried by the tempestuous winds was unclear.

John sighed. He sat on a relatively flat boulder next to Murray and stared at the vast desert in front of them beyond the smooth, cracked flats; it was far less flat than its perpendicular neighbour, as it was sculpted with numerous dunes of shifting sand. He resumed his admiration of the starry cosmos that filled the night.

John found it odd how the moon was marred with more crevices and craters than he had seen in his old astronomy book; he buried his puzzlement along with the many other questions he felt would never be resolved.

John watched on as day gradually retook its place from the night; he pondered his absence of fatigue but opted to appreciate the rising light instead.

When the sun pierced his eyelids, Murray yawned widely, stretching his arms as he stood up. He gestured for John to follow him.

'Did you sleep well?' enquired John, slightly bitterly.

'What … oh … yeah, it was okay,' replied Murray. 'Now come on, still a far … ish … way to go.' He looked keenly at John. 'Wait. What is it, Johnny?'

John pointed to a tall figure that was a dozen metres behind Murray who turned and furrowed his brow.

The figure was a tall, muscular man clad in black vestments that had a slight vertical gap through the front displaying, around his waist, a thin, radiant yellow sash, with one length of it flowing down next to the opening of his outer coat. Around his neck was a long strand of minuscule black and white beads, at the end of which was a small golden crucifix. His hair was unkempt and grey. With eyes that were fierce and shared the hue and ferocity of an ocean, there were few wrinkles or any significant signs of tiredness. Barely visible through his coat and under the sash were the hilts of two swords: one was the thin white elongation of a samurai katana; one was the golden cruciform of a Templar sword. The scabbards remained hidden by his long coat.

'Who are you?' John demanded while taking a step back.

'I am a servant of God; humble Saul is my name,' he responded, his voice having an indeterminable accent yet evidently Celtic in origin.

'You serve Odin?' John asked, flinching with alertness.

'I know not this Odin,' Saul replied, allowing John to feel less tension. 'But the matter at hand is a question: are either of you men followers of Lunatology?'

'Um … no,' John replied, half-laughing. 'Why? Are you recruiting for it?'

'I simply have an opportunity to offer anyone who follows it.'

'Well, the moon is full,' said Murray, 'which means the "Loonies" will be on their best behaviour; we're actually heading through their city, if you wanna follow us.'

'Much obliged,' said Saul. 'What are strangers in the desert but potential brothers?'

'Wait,' John said, only loud enough for Murray's ear. 'Is this a good idea? He seems kind of dangerous.'

'Don't worry so much, Johnny,' Murray replied with a light slap on John's shoulders. 'More the merrier; 'sides, that ghost … wait … hologram fellow gave you some major upgrades—even if there's a problem, we'll be fine.'

'If you say so.' John was tense, but he tried to return the strange man's friendly smile.

Saul then said, 'Thank you, kindly. In the names of the Mother in Heaven and the Mother on Earth, let us depart.'

John and Murray—and further back, their 'new friend', Saul—began a crunching march over the glassy fields.

John pondered aloud, 'What is Lunatology?'

'Huh? Oh yeah, well, we call them the "Loonies" or the "Lunatics",' said Murray. 'They can be a nasty bunch. Sometimes they act all friendly and nice, but the next day, a different group of them will try an' kill you, all depending on the phase of the moon.'

'So, why do you want to do business with some group like that?' John asked Saul.

He replied with a smile, 'I'm on the Great Crusade, which involves, let's say, negotiating with any deviant faiths.'

'Okay,' John muttered, avoiding further eye contact with Saul's oceanic gaze.

After hours of walking, with occasional bursts of wind throwing sand into their faces and scratching their eyes, John saw that the ground ahead was solid. Ruins of city blocks stretched from the horizon to their feet. Aside from the passable condition of the roads, the city displayed no indication that it ever was one. The interlacing streets hugged barren city blocks that held only rugged rough mounds of rock.

Murray went to the nearest boulders and sat down. 'I need to take five, okay?' he said.

John nodded, and the strange man mimicked Murray, sitting down next to him but leaving a metre of space between them.

'Tell me about good ol' Teddy,' Murray asked.

'I think you'd probably know more about him than I would,' John muttered while avoiding eye contact, finding it uncomfortable with anyone, he realised.

'Yes and no,' explained Murray. 'I knew Theodore—good old Ted—but I don't personally know him as *Odin*.'

'I … don't think you want to know,' John said. 'Also, do you really want to share dirt with a stranger? No offence intended, sir.'

'Oh, don't mind me, brothers,' Saul said. He pulled a leatherbound book from within his coat, opening it to golden-edged pages, whereupon his vision was occupied with the text.

'So, go on, kid,' encouraged Murray.

'It isn't pleasant, Murray.'

Murray chuckled. 'Yeah, Lucy said something similar,' he said. 'She told me that the man we knew died with Tommy … she told me Odin is a real monster, like the fairytales the Seniors told us were history … and right before Odin conquered Haven, turned it into his Valhalla, he shared his scheme with her: with stolen wisdom and strength from the Uplifted, he'd unleash his revenge upon the Seniors and any Sevenite in the way. His plan was already in motion, so she couldn't do anything to stop him directly. That's why she ran away, Junior. Nearly a decade ago, I saw my little sister again. Luckily, on one of my visits to Richie and the boys, she met me in the cavern.' Murray paused momentarily to drink from a bottle he pulled from his sleeve.

John felt a tangential query arise in his head until he had to express it. 'Why was Lucy so special that Odin would share his scheme with her?' he asked. 'Odin isn't Mack's father too, is he?'

'That's disgusting, Johnny,' replied Murray. 'Nightmare to even imagine.'

'Sorry,' said John with a shrug. 'It just doesn't make sense that she escaped.'

'I was told that near the beginning of his rule, he had only imprisoned the Uplifted,' Murray explained. 'He then would enter hibernation cycles, which was when the previous chief or whatever, Factorem, would have slightly more control. Not enough to take back power from Odin, but enough to allow someone to escape.'

'I did see something similar,' noted John. 'So, what else did Lucy say?'

'Anyway, Lucy said she held no love for the Seniors but didn't wish them death, and she definitely didn't want all Sevenites to suffer for our banishment,' Murray recalled. 'She knew of Odin's experiments in attempting to siphon Huon from others, and then she even saw the first of his biological experiments and was worried for the safety of her child, so she put her son under the care of Richie and the other androids; hiding him in plain sight.'

John, barely getting a hold of his guilt due to what he had done directly, was finding himself feeling more remorseful for the actions his mistakes had inspired in Odin. John recalled the transient visual of the pre-'deified' man of Theodore; he pondered if the man would have always turned to a path of cruelty and immorality, or if it was John's naïve choice as a child that turned peace into slaughter.

The rage emanating from both Theodore's matching eyes and Odin's artificial heterochromatic eyes had a terrifying effect, much like staring into a cyclone; thus, perhaps the man had only changed in shape, but never in spirit. Whether Odin had been vile from the beginning or if he had been twisted by trauma, John couldn't help but carry a stinging sense of responsibility.

'Lucy said she was sorry for siding against John and me—like it really mattered … So, I promised I would visit Mack as he grew up but never tell him that I was his uncle in case Odin caught me; but as long as I'm free, I would keep an eye on him all the same.' Murray finished the bottle's liquid, and then he tossed it onto the street; it bounced and clinked then rolled into a gutter. 'The morning we were ready to head off to Caligo's Plaza, Lucy was already gone, without Mack. And I never saw her again. But for eight years, Mack has been kept safe with those lads, hiding right under Odin's nose. Safe, until, you know.'

'Not only Mack … Odin has Connie now,' John said.

'Who? Oh, right, Odin's eldest son,' said Murray. 'I'm sorry; Odin probably doesn't care about his old life anymore, so I think Colonel might be dead—'

'No, he won't be,' interjected John. 'It's much worse … Odin's changing Connie to become some weapon … and it's … all my fault.'

'Johnny, you gotta focus on the now,' said Murray. 'Afterwards, then you can get all depressed over all your screw-ups.'

John slightly grinned, although his grey eyes remained sombre. 'I know you said it doesn't matter,' he said, 'but you need to know that I'm sorry for what I did as a child. I'm sorry that I ruined all your lives; I didn't know what the pills would do. That's no excuse, and I shouldn't have lied …'

'Relax, kid,' Murray said gently. 'Like a good friend of mine said: you've gotta concentrate on the future; don't dwell in the past.' He sighed wearily. 'Like me …' Murray pulled out a flask hidden in his right boot and began to drink again.

'I hope Odin isn't hurting Mack because of me,' said John, concerned. 'I wish I could see if he's all right.'

'Do you, now?' asked Toat's voice. The hologram appeared seated next to him. He smirked and then said, 'Well, then … take a look.' Toat snapped his fingers.

John felt a sharp pain in his head, as if his mind was being chewed by a ravenous flame. His scream was cut short when the sight of the wastes changed completely; he saw the interior of Valhalla. 'Wh-what's going on?' he demanded.

'I sent a command to your nanomachines to temporarily link your vision with Doctor Factorem,' responded Toat's disembodied voice.

John looked around the room he had been given a view of; it was made from the familiar dark blue metal that was common throughout Valhalla. A cluster of cables held a lump against the wall; the lump was Mack. He was strung up like an ant imprisoned in a spider's web. Thin cables constricted his whole body; all he was free to do was weep. However, aside from his obvious emotional distress and predicament, the small boy was unharmed.

'I told you, didn't I?' said Toat. 'He will be safe for longer than your little trip. So, do not waste the time you do have available thinking about him, okay?'

John blinked. The image of the room inside Valhalla became blurry, and then he was looking inside Odin's throne room.

The king sat on his throne of thick entangled cables, and in his hand, he held a simple black remote control, which had only two buttons. Odin pushed one button; Factorem's screams of agony tore through the air, and yet they were muffled as if through static interference. Odin pushed the other button, and the screams stopped. 'I warned you, didn't I, Adam?' Odin said. 'If you ever dare to deceive me, *again*'—he pushed the first button; the hazy screams filled the whole chamber—'I will punish you, *again*! I had expected such insolence a thing of the past; remember *this* happened before!'

John shivered as he swore that Odin's mismatched eyes were staring right at him.

Factorem's deep screams slowly became more distant.

The vision of Valhalla became blurred as John blinked rapidly, and then he blinked once again. He felt somewhat relieved that he was back in the desolation of the wastes, near Toat and Murray, and even the unreadable Saul. 'Next time, warn me about stuff like that,' he ordered Toat, who mockingly saluted and then vanished. 'Bastard,' John muttered.

With wide eyes, Murray stared at John. 'O … kay … well then, I'm all rested up,' he said. 'So, onwards and upwards.'

The pair, plus their additional tagalong, resumed their predestined path over the seemingly endless fractured mirror, which ultimately led towards a collection of structures unlike what John had expected; the skyscrapers seemed to be well-maintained, lacking any of the degradation that plagued Necropolis.

CHAPTER FOURTEEN

cLUNACITY

This new settlement—new at least to John—was also much larger than his usual understanding of a 'settlement', even though that concept had already been challenged earlier with Valhalla.

From the ground, it appeared as if the city was made of a collection of glass towers that spiralled larger as they moved further into the city's middle; it appeared that all were rising to honour a central spire that loomed over all other buildings.

'Seems … nice,' said John.

'Well, it's pretty to look at, I guess,' said Murray. 'But be careful to keep to yourself. Even when on the best behaviour of the full moon, these people can be a slippery lot.'

At the only viewable entrance to the city, a booth was adjacent to the path, inside which sat a man wearing a pure white suit. He stood to attention, yet with a relaxed air about him.

Above the booth was a black bird, listlessly looking in different directions at random.

'Hello, hello, new friends,' said the white-suited man. 'I'm Jerry, your welcomer for today.'

'Yeah, save the spiel, Jerry,' said Murray. 'We're just passing through.'

'Oh, of course, good gentlemen.' Jerry smiled. 'But please allow me to accompany you through our lovely home!' He exited the booth, which was soon filled by another man dressed in the same spotless-white outfit.

'Just bear with it, Johnny,' whispered Murray. 'Loonies love to sermon.'

Unlike Necropolis, the streets were all smooth and without any sense of tectonic disturbance. The shining skyscrapers could be blinding when the rising sun struck them, thus John kept his eyes straight ahead along the street, avoiding irritation over their new 'friend' Jerry, who had begun conversing with the cleric.

'So, are you looking to convert to the One True Path?' asked Jerry of the three arrivals.

The stoic yet amiable Saul, who was still accompanying Murray and John, seemed to flinch but remained composed. 'Thank you for the kind offer; however, I'm here to discuss a matter with the … what do you call them?'

'The Eternal Eclipse?'

'That's the leader, I guess?' said John, despite himself.

'Very astute, young gentleman,' said Jerry. 'The Eternal Eclipse is what we all should aspire to be like! The closest to holiness.'

'Right …' John murmured.

'Oh, very right,' said Jerry. 'Righter than anything in this sad world of ours!' He then hurriedly walked a few paces ahead of them. Along the street were various entrances to the ascending towers—some were vacant, but others had people in similar, if not identical, white suits to Jerry.

Whenever John happened to turn his head towards them, they delivered a warm smile and a friendly wave. He felt nervous at the seeming civility, as often the eyes of a friendly face seemed potentially unhinged.

'Me and your dad first met the Lunatologist stronghold here during a new moon,' said Murray, 'which isn't exactly the warm welcome you get on the "full" moon.'

'Oh, it is to be expected,' said Jerry. 'It's only reasonable that the furthest we are from the Lord's light, the less at peace we feel.'

'I mean, call it what you want, Jer,' said Murray, 'but flaming torches and screaming didn't spell *reasonable* to us.'

'Wait, how does the state of the moon affect your moods that much?' John asked.

Another white-suited person, holding leaflets, approached the group. 'Please, take some of our literature! It will enlighten you!'

'Oh, don't worry, Melrose,' said Jerry. 'I'm enlightening our guests, thank you.'

Melrose slumped but clearly tried to remain smiling.

While daylight filled the street, there were lampposts lining every several metres, which held crescent-shaped lights in slumber. The gutters along the street seemed freshly formed, due to their cleanliness and absence of cracks.

'It's such common knowledge to us, but it is never boring to tell,' said Jerry. 'Humanity is at our best under the light of the moon, and the darker it becomes, the darker each of us feels.'

'I grew up without much sky,' said John, 'so I can't say I understand your meaning.'

'Oh, poor gentleman,' intoned Jerry. 'If you allow me to take you to our visitor's centre, then I'm sure—'

'No, no, we're good, Jer,' Murray interrupted. 'Just the basic tour through the city, thanks.'

'Oh, very well.'

As they reached the centre of the city, they found the foot of the central spire; its large archway was patterned after another crescent moon, thicker than those of the lamplights, yet still less than half-full. While difficult to see for certain, John realised the spire reached so high that a few rainbow clouds were split by it while floating overhead.

'Presumably, this is the location of your leader?' asked Saul.

'Oh, yes,' said Jerry as he sent smiles at a few door-men who were clad in the same white suits as everyone else native to the city. However, John finally realised that the suits each had lapel pins; depending upon the person, the silver moon pin was at a varied state of fullness. 'If not for the Divine Reading, please join us for lunch.'

'I'm not hungry,' said John, and then, after a beat, 'actually, I haven't felt hungry all day … am I sick?'

'More like fixed,' said Toat, without appearing. 'Don't be concerned. Some weaknesses that one might consider *being human* don't quite apply to you anymore, like needing to sleep.'

John's eyes grew wide in understanding.

'You can still join us without eating, ' said Jerry, not privy to the disembodied doctor's update.

'Yeah, well, I'm starving, Johnny,' said Murray. 'The food around here isn't half-bad.'

John nodded.

'It isn't half-good either!'

John's eyes rolled.

'Oh, then a banquet for some of our guests,' said Jerry. 'Please, follow me to a nearby restaurant.'

The peculiar Saul placed his hands on the shoulders of Murray and John. 'It seems we are to part ways here, kindred travellers.' He released them. 'While short-lived, I enjoyed the company for a change.'

'Yeah,' said John. 'You were all right, too.'

Saul smiled and then left towards the large glass double doors that went into the base of the city's central spire.

'Are you guys not bothered by danger?' John asked. 'We're clearly armed, but you don't seem worried.'

'Oh, it's too much worry to worry,' Jerry said with a chuckle. 'On such a full moon state, nobody would likely show any violent tendencies, so your weapons are merely a different kind of adornment.'

'If you say so,' said John.

The nearby restaurant wasn't at full capacity; however, it had enough diners to create a hum of noise and activity from staff, whose own white suits were in a style that included aprons. Murray and John sat at an unoccupied table, as led by Jerry.

'Won't be long,' noted Jerry before he disappeared into the restaurant proper.

'They're not—' muttered John. 'They're not going to try to eat us, are they?'

Murray laughed. 'Ease up a little, Johnny. Loonies are weirdos, but they won't cross any moral lines.' Murray appeared deep in thought for a moment. 'Well, at least during the full moon.'

'Great,' said John.

A plate of prepared vegetables and lentils was placed in front of Murray, who sniffed it with mild indifference before seizing a provided fork and shovelling the food into his bearded mouth.

John sighed, alleviating his boredom by watching the various other diners as well as the odd person walking along the street footpaths—a parade of porcelain-coloured costumes was sufficient to pass the time, at least.

CHAPTER FIFTEEN

A Bright Greeting

After one of the pair had eaten, Jerry cheerily led the remaining duo of John and Murray through the other side of Lunacity; unlike the first half, there seemed to be many neon light signs adorning street faces. While daylight dramatically muted their effect, there was still a cascade of colours present—predominantly blue and red, with multiple shades of both.

'I'm sorry you are choosing to leave so soon, gentlemen,' said Jerry. 'But please feel free to return to our hospitality, especially during any solstice!'

'Yeah, thanks, Jerry,' John said with a shade of suspicion.

Jerry remained amiable as he smiled and waved at the departing duo.

Unlike the glassy field leading into Lunacity, the landscape on the city's other side was a series of rocks and pebbles, none piled particularly high, with the ground being an uneven texture of broken stone.

At last, after a duration of time that John didn't care to record, he noticed another structure that still stood and was free from corrosion and rot. It had the look of a warehouse, but it was more focused on being aesthetically appealing. Its walls held frames of black-tinted glass panels.

The structure was a deep gold colour, although this was at first difficult to determine because countless infinitesimal gems covered it. Jewels of almost every colour decorated the vast building, bordering each tall window. Along clearer walls, shining gems were arranged to form swirling patterns, thereby creating a fresco of a bright cosmos.

Along the edge of the structure's flat roof were clusters of black yet shiny birds; one of the birds glanced at John and then, without even a simple squawk, it took flight.

Murray cleared his throat. 'There it is, Johnny. The place of bargains and the place to find that weapon I think can beat Odin!'

John mumbled to acknowledge the statement.

They continued to walk, albeit at an accelerated pace, over the occasional glass fragments, crunching pebbles and scraping dust from the stones that rested on the city blocks. As they reached nearer their destination, the centre front of the warehouse was vaguely discernible; a large gap that could easily accommodate a heavy vehicle was present.

The golden structure was clearly metal, but not the valuable currency with which it shared the shade of colour. It was seamless, as if it was carved from a block.

John squinted as a ray of sunlight reflected off something that lay atop the left barrier.

John and Murray carefully slid down a small hill made of weathered, light-brown rock.

A sound much like a cannon firing echoed throughout the wasted city; the wind screamed as it was cut by a rapidly moving projectile. A cloud of dust erupted from beside Murray's head on the rock behind them. John started in shock, and then he dived face-down onto the dirt.

Murray remained standing. He looked behind him at the floating dust as it dissipated leaving a roughly circular crevice, about the size of his head, in the rock. It was deep enough to be considered a tunnel.

John looked up from the dirt. 'Get down, you idiot!' he pleaded.

Murray shook his head, and then he bellowed at the warehouse entrance, 'Belle, you silly kid! It's me! Murray!'

John slowly rose to a crouched position; simultaneously, he raised an eyebrow in puzzlement.

'Oh … sorry, Dad!' cried out a female voice from behind the sheetmetal-protected wooden barricade.

'Dad?' John mouthed.

'Come on,' muttered Murray; he offered a hand to assist the knelt pariah; however, John leapt up to his feet without assistance.

They reached an arched columned aperture of the structure's entrance. An engraving along the entire arch seemed to generate pride: *CALEB DE CALIGO'S PLAZA*. Beneath the engraving was the aesthetically stylised phrase: *Bargains are yours to seize.*

The plaza doors were situated at the end of the dark, column-lined entrance hall. Within the decorated hall were two sections of wooden planks; they were piled up over a metre high. The planks were covered in shaped sheets of metal; the pseudo-shield had numerous bullet holes, scratches and dents scarring them. A break between the barriers, right in the centre, could only fit three people if they were walking shoulder-to-shoulder.

The travelling exiles walked through the gap between the double barriers; closer inspection revealed that the barriers extended through much of the entrance corridor. They passed the barriers; between the edge of the back of the barriers and the actual entry were almost exclusively armaments, which were held by racks above wooden benches that lined the wide corridor.

To their left, lying on top of the innermost part of the barrier, was a sniper rifle on a short stand. John recognised it from one of his lessons from the Seniors—it was a particularly large semi-automatic sniper rifle.

Immediately behind the left barrier, on the bench, were seated two girls around John's age. They both had golden eyes with strange diamond-shaped pupils and long hair that cascaded halfway down their backs; however, one's hair colour was cherry-blonde and the other one's hair was black. The sun-haired female had fairly porcelain skin, while the crow-haired female had bronze skin.

The darker girl was calmly reading a book while the lighter girl had one hand behind her head and was sheepishly smiling.

'Really, really sorry for nearly shooting you.' The cherry-blonde girl spoke in the same voice that had called out.

Murray pushed John aside, and then he went forward; he tapped the grinning girl's forehead, and the girl whined in discomfort. 'How many times, little lady?' he demanded. 'How many times have I told you *not* to shoot at me?'

'I said I was sorry … 'bout six times,' the girl said. 'But I thought you could have been Lunatics!'

Murray laid a hand on the girl's head; she winced but then relaxed as Murray merely rustled her hair. He then said kindly, 'I'm glad you've got your wits about you, just like me and John taught you. But remember—the boss, Malik, has reached a temporary truce with the Lunatics. Ah, well …'

John faked a cough.

Murray looked back at the boy, stroking his beard. 'Oh yeah,' he mused, as if he suddenly remembered John's presence. 'Well, Junior,' Murray said while bringing John closer. 'These young ladies are Belle and Claire, the Bright twins.'

'I wasn't really asking for an introduction … wait, did you say: the Bright *twins*?' John said, amused. 'They don't really look at all alike … not in any way I can tell.'

'We get that a lot,' said Claire, monotone, without breaking eye contact with her book.

Murray walked to the opposite bench. 'But look at their eyes,' he said while heaving an esky out from underneath the bench. He retrieved a bottle of beer and then lightly kicked the esky back under the bench.

'You really shouldn't drink so much,' said all three youths, almost in unison.

'What are you? My mother? Lay off,' Murray retorted not-so-calmly.

Down the entrance corridor, a pair of armoured sliding doors glided open; a young woman, possibly a few years older than John, exited the plaza structure. She wore a long, light red coat and had golden eyes with diamond-shaped pupils, and she too had cherry-blonde hair that was tied up in a ponytail. She looked exactly like Claire but shared Belle's hue in hair and complexion. She walked in a graceful yet somewhat childish manner, her arms gliding slowly around her while every third step she took had a small skip attached. 'Dad!' she called out affectionately, and then she rushed to Murray, hugging him. She grabbed the beer out of his hand and began to drink it, to Murray's chagrin.

'Dad?' John mouthed again.

Murray was released from the crushing embrace.

'The Bright girls,' said Murray. 'The twins and the older sister, Teresa.'

John remained silent; he nodded as a greeting to all three. 'But *Dad*, you?' he repeated out loud.

'Oh, right,' Murray said, pausing to pull another bottle from his cloak. 'When I was travelling with your dad, Athena directed us to Malik's place—this here shopping complex. But to stay at this "sanctuary", you must do something in return. We were chosen as suitable for either guard duty or exploration to find things in the wastes that Malik might want. Well, we scavenged about half of the weapons in this hall. Anyway, on one of our earliest searches, about eight or nine years ago, we found Teresa and her kid sisters clinging to her, all alone in the wastes. Well, John an' me, well … we didn't think it was right to leave children alone in this shitty world, so we brought them here, and then we convinced Malik that we could train them to be the best shooters ever. So, he let them stay. The girls told us their names, but they didn't remember their last names. John decided that their last name should be *Bright* because their smiles could brighten any day in this dark world.'

'That's pretty dumb,' muttered John to himself, yet he reflected on the origin of his own name.

'And we've called Murray and John our dad and papa ever since!' Belle cheerfully chimed.

'That's right,' said Murray. 'John and I made the best team. Speaking of which, girls, this is John's son: Johnny Junior.'

John tried to speak up; however, he was interrupted by the delightful glee of both Belle and Teresa, the older girl dropping the now-empty bottle that she had taken. They both hugged John, smothering his face and leaving him unable to speak.

'Your papa was our papa!' Teresa said.

'Yay! You can be our brother!' gushed Belle.

'Girls, let go of him,' Murray said seriously.

The girls fell silent and then sat next to their reading sibling.

Murray gripped John's shoulders. 'I've gotta get something off my chest …. I wasn't totally honest with you, Junior. It's true I don't know where John is now, but …' Murray released John and then sat on the opposite bench. 'A few years back, Malik's personal guard turned against him,' he said. 'We were in his main chamber at the time, trying to … to barter for a larger food allowance for the girls.' He gulped the remainder of his beer and then dropped the bottle. After it clinked on the tartan-tiled floor, he continued, 'Malik's seven elite guards rushed in … they filled Malik with lead.'

John frowned at the visceral imagery, though perhaps this was due to also dredging up recent memories of his own firearm brutality.

'Your dad and me … we had to surrender. But before the guards could disarm us, Malik tore them apart, one by one, with his bare goddamn hands. In their panicked fire, your dad got hit in the gut, left him in pretty bad shape.'

John's face froze as his teeth stuck together in shock and dread.

'After the mutineers were killed, Malik, he healed so … impossibly. I always wondered how, but seeing what that hologram guy did for you, I'm pretty sure that Malik is filled with nanites, too.' Murray sighed with unhidden sadness. 'But … but Malik, the betrayal made him more … unusual. Not that he was the most stable guy to begin with. He offered to heal John, but in exchange, John would become Malik's property. Now, I don't know if Malik healed him or not, but I haven't seen or heard from John since.'

John frowned. 'B-but,' he stammered. 'But where did he take my father?'

Murray scratched his beard, remaining silent.

'I know!' declared Teresa.

John's sights turned to her.

'I mean, I *think* I know.'

'Better than nothing,' said John. 'Please, tell me.'

'When Dad Murray came back and told us that Papa John was gone,' recalled Teresa, 'we were really worried. So, I frequently asked anyone and everyone I could anything to find out if Papa John was okay. Like, only a few months ago, I heard rumours, but only rumours, from a few of the other residents. Since the failed mutiny, Malik had become crazier, and he started to take people as prisoners to settle family debts. Which means it's possible Papa John is held somewhere in Malik's chambers, too.'

Claire glanced at John, and obviously noticing his distress, she attempted to console him. 'Don't worry. I'm sure Malik is the kind of person that takes good care of any *possession* he owns.'

The monotone statement thickened John's dread.

The blue-tinged hollow-man Alistair Toat appeared next to the group.

The girls appeared aloof about his manifestation.

'I'm sorry, but I really must say something,' decreed Toat. 'This fellow you keep calling Malik, is that another name for *him*?' He pointed to a sign above the sliding doors: *CALEB DE CALIGO WELCOMES YOU.*

'Yeah,' murmured Murray. 'He likes to be called Malik as an official title, and it's not good to piss him off, so everyone calls him that. What does it matter?'

Before Toat could respond, John interrupted. 'Wait— you said you only know about technology, not any events or people.'

Toat chuckled. 'I did say that. However, I am also coded with the records of personnel, activities, and experiments of the former Haven facility. And I know a Caleb de Caligo was one among the number who were Uplifted: the once-exceptional scientists and scholars. Now, if Malik is actually my progenitor's old colleague, then I think now is a good time for a reunion. If he remembers me, he may be more agreeable to part with the *special weapon* for which you have traversed the desert. Have you forgotten about Odin and your child friend? Or would you rather focus more on speculative paternal issues?'

John shook his head. 'No,' he murmured. 'You're right, Alistair.' He smacked the sides of his face. 'So, Murray, where is Malik, and why do we even need that guy's permission to take the weapon?'

Murray stood up straight and coughed loudly. 'Because Malik is an alchemist,' he answered.

John frowned deeply. 'A what?'

'An alchemist. They're like some kind of scientist, which makes sense now, given that he was a "scientist" from Haven,' explained Murray. 'But he now uses magic to do all sorts of stuff, like transforming things into different things.'

'That is utterly ridiculous!' scoffed Toat. 'There is no such thing as magic! Nanomachines can consume, reconfigure, and reconstruct matter; however, it is through scientific innovation, not a snap of the fingers.'

'Whether you believe in magic or not,' retorted Murray, 'Malik keeps his most valuable possessions close to him, and the weapon I have in mind can't be picked up like any simple firearm.'

Toat crossed his arms in subtle defiance.

'Teresa, I think you should come with us,' said Murray. 'Your sisters are on guard duty, and I don't wanna protect this kid by myself.'

The older pariah stumbled towards the reinforced doors with John, Teresa, and Toat following suit, albeit walking steadily.

'Good luck!' Belle called out as she returned to her position behind the sniper rifle.

'Yeah. Be careful,' murmured Claire, seemingly disinterested as she turned another page in her book.

'I suppose when we get this weapon,' said John, 'we might also find my father.'

The main plaza doors pinged open, welcoming the exiles, runaway, and quasi-man. The interior of the shopping complex was monumentally big, remaining faithful to the Uplifted penchant for sizeable structures.

High above their heads, ersatz daylight was provided by a large spiral that covered the entire ceiling surface. Along the walls, slogans such as *SHOP MORE, SAVE MORE* were plastered in eye-grabbing large fonts.

A dozen metres from the entrance, a row of checkout stations divided the actual complex from the entry; each station had a lamppost, atop which was a decahedron with a red robotic eye in it, like a gravity-defying bird in its nest.

Past the checkouts, where the actual complex began, it was an odd mixture of miscellaneous objects that only held one definitive connection: they existed.

It was a city made of bed, bath, and … various furniture such as leather lounges, wooden tables, and plastic chairs.

Shelves were clustered together to form separate houses, thereby making it appear like a neighbourhood; one constructed with clumsiness, due to a mismatch of materials and colours.

Some beds were tipped on their sides and forced into bunches, granting them the appearance of a childish fort. However, among the makeshift establishments were actual houses, some being two storeys tall. Most were modest in size, yet they were distinct from the fake forts of furniture.

Spread around and often collected together were small or large gatherings of people, many conversing with their closest neighbours. In each group, at least one person was lacking a limb or appendage; their pale faces showed clear dread over the expense of their existence.

'It doesn't look good, Murray,' observed John. 'Almost as crappy as our village.'

'Well, this technically is just the slums. The suburbs are a bit nicer,' Murray stated. 'This limbo is mainly where the residents of the Plaza live.'

'Slums?'

'You know,' Murray continued, 'the poor neighbourhood; the district lot.'

'I know what slums are,' said John. 'But isn't this place like … a store?'

'Store, yes, and a lot more,' said Murray. 'To thousands of people, it is home; for some, the only safe home that they'd ever known.'

'But these people … so many look so scared,' observed John.

'They ought to be, if they have two senses to rub together,' advised Murray. 'Malik does try to make sure his store provides bargains, but he … stresses the costs.'

'What do you mean?'

'He … well … he tries to make people understand the value of … stuff,' Murray clarified while he rubbed his temples. 'Malik wants people to see how much they're really willing to give up for something they want. He exchanges his goods for anything you hold some personal value in. Even bits of your body. Once a deal has been made, you get what you get. But if you try to steal something, it disappears like magic. I've seen it; some people try to steal from Malik, but the stuff they take just evaporates as soon as they get outside. Then Malik does something that just makes them … dead.'

'Oh, I know this security system quite well,' boasted Toat. 'Caleb's so-called magic is merely trickery.' He adjusted his simulated glasses. 'If I am correct, then in each product, Herr Malik has implanted a swarm of nanites. Unless the nanites are commanded by Malik to deactivate, they are programmed to destroy the product that hosts them when taken outside of this building's perimeters. One who steals an item has their specific genetic signature targeted, and when the product is disintegrated, the nanites then enter that person and destroy their brains.'

'Okay … I suppose that's a good reason why we need Malik's permission,' said John. 'So, Murray, how much will this weapon cost?'

Murray rubbed his eyes and then turned away. 'Let's try to not think about it yet,' he responded. 'But then again, you could, to pass the time. Malik is in Section Nine, and it's deep, deep under us.'

'What?' asked John.

'We're in Section One: the base level,' explained Murray. 'The shopping complex continues under us. All the sections are connected, forming a gigantic spring-shaped thing. Malik's Section Nine is right at the bottom of the coil. Sorry, kid, but me and your dad could never actually get to Malik unless he summoned us.'

John stroked his forehead impatiently, and then he looked at Toat.

'From what I can *barely* surmise from what you just described,' Toat said, 'I believe that Malik has created a secure sub-bunker that is only accessible to others when he chooses. See those visual uplinks? These are the same design as the ones in Haven. Through those, he can see everything in this building; therefore, he can see everything and everyone inside this place.' Toat tapped his chin as he examined the surrounding area. 'You said the sections connect in a *spring*, did you not, Herr Murray?'

John prodded Murray's arm.

Murray stammered, 'You mean me?'

'Yes, I mean *you*,' Toat replied dryly. 'Now, please answer my question: you said *spring* did you not?'

'W-what?' slurred Murray. 'Oh yeah, yeah … a big spring thing.'

Toat sighed. 'Okay … well, I think I can safely assume that it is a spiral structure formation.'

'Which means?' asked John.

'Which means Malik can lock down whatever sections of the coil that he wishes to, therefore making it impossible to keep going down unless he lets us,' Toat responded. 'Presumably, each section has a direct lift to it; however, it seems like they are currently locked down.'

'God damn it … all right, I guess a start in Section Two it is, then,' John said with a groan. 'And hopefully, we can make it down the entire spiral to reach this Malik guy.'

CHAPTER SIXTEEN

TEMPTATION

They followed the large arrow with the words *Adonis Electronics* that pointed down to the entry of Section Two; they arrived at an opening in the floor, which sheltered a wide marble staircase.

'How … quaint,' said Toat, his amusement apparent.

'What's in these lower levels?' John asked Murray and Teresa. 'Anything … dangerous?'

Murray was preoccupied with uncorking a wine bottle with his teeth.

'Not at all,' said Teresa. 'Well, not usually.'

They began their descent into the first of the spiral's eight remaining sections.

As they reached the bottom of the stairs, a friendly-faced, pink-haired young woman dressed in a white-shirted, blue-trousered uniform approached. 'Greetings, valued consumers!' she said, smiling widely. 'Welcome to Section Two: Adonis Electronics. My name's Cherie. How may I be of assistance today?'

John stared at her, bemused. 'We want to see Malik,' he said.

'So, would you like to hear about today's fabulous bargains?' asked Cherie.

'No, we want—'

'An entertainment system that you totally need?' interrupted a second young woman whose hair was crimson red and wore the same uniform as the first. 'I'm Jane, and I can help you with anything that you need.'

Murray began to nervously step backwards. 'I … I think I'll go … gonna check if there's more liquor,' he stammered. 'See ya.' He then clambered back up the staircase.

A third woman appeared. This one had snow-white hair and, instead of a white shirt, a red one; her nametag read *Carol*.

The three ladies grabbed John's arms and pulled him away from the stairs.

'Sir, please allow us to show you today's once-a-year bargain,' said Carol.

'Teresa, what's going on here?' John asked, slightly shaken. His question fell on deaf ears as another white-shirted woman, whose hair was green, conversed with Teresa; her nametag read *Lexa*.

'So, you see, if you buy this digital watch that's on sale now,' spruiked Lexa, 'you can also get this *free* mobile phone … for only a small fee.'

'Oh, wow, really?' said Teresa with a polite sincerity.

Many objects in Section Two were difficult to distinguish, as the lighting was lowered to mimic dusk, although hundreds of glowing and flickering screens could be clearly seen—some shining out from thin, wide grey boxes, some merely floating in the air—while various computer screens that lined the subtly curved walls were mostly blocked by silhouettes of faceless people.

A large portion—nearly a quarter—of the section was cordoned off behind a black wall and was divided into separate rooms; this section could be assumed by the presence of numbered doors along the wall.

John was dragged by the three oddly strong individuals towards the opening of a corridor made of lights and sounds. Before he could begin to gather his bearings, John was forced to sit in a soft, comfortable lounge chair.

Carol smiled widely. 'Now, sir, please allow us to show you our latest television models.'

John's head was grabbed from behind by Carol; her index finger then went into his nose, causing him to sneeze. His gaze was forced forward, and his head was then trapped by a web of straps clasped around his forehead. He tried to stand again, but his arms and legs were restricted by straps attached to the chair.

The chair John was trapped in began to move.

Cherie and Jane pushed the chair down the corridor of mixed sights and sounds; the flashing and humming caused him to become slightly disoriented. Sounds all completely unrelated buzzed and shouted in the exile's head. 'Look, I don't give a damn about your sales pitch!' John exclaimed. 'Just let me out of this thing and take me to Mal—'

A blinding light consumed his sight. The light dimmed and was replaced by a mixture of images of grass-covered hills and gentle ocean waves on white sand beaches, as well as lazily moving clouds.

'We have such sights to show you.' A melodic voice from a three-dimensional silhouette addressed John. 'How may we tempt you to purchase?'

The image on the massive television became a view of a rainforest; the noise of a hundred creatures chirping, clicking, buzzing, and screeching assaulted John's ears.

'Dammit!' cried John. 'Shut it off!'

The screen fell to black. The only sound that remained was John's quickening breaths. As he sighed in relief, the screen resurrected itself, filling his entire field of vision. While his ears were filled with horrid, broken shrieks, the screen displayed a fast montage of flames, tidal waves, and various people dying by gunshots, stabbing, and increasingly gruesome ways.

'The bargain also includes over one hundred film titles on VR to improve your pitifully boring life,' pitched the silhouette, its soothing voice changing to a harsh one with a tinny echo as the bass faded. 'Which can elevate your sensory experience for greater plateaus of delight and—'

'Shut up!' shouted John. 'Shut up! Shut the hell up! I don't want anything from you, except for Malik's location! ... Alistair! Where are you? Get me out of this!'

John furiously thrashed about, utilising all his limited movement. He stopped as he felt an increasing heat around the straps that bound him. The straps on his arms became thinner, until they ripped apart as if they made from ancient paper. John was released from his restrictions, and then he stood up, amazed.

'We're having a data rejection,' the voice of Carol said.

'Oh craps! The program is shutting down!' cried the voice of Jane.

The atmosphere around John began to waver, and then it shattered into a thousand pieces, each piece holding an image of the area to which it was attached. The pieces fell, slowly spinning, revealing that the back of the pieces were a flickering light blue.

The world around him shattered the same, all the pieces vanishing into a blinding white light.

Then all John could see was red. He quickly realised that he was staring at the inside of his eyelids. He opened his eyes. John was huddled on the ground, just in front of the chair into which he had been forced. He stood up and saw that Teresa was still intently listening to Lexa. 'What the ...' John grumbled.

With a puzzled expression, the blue-tinged Toat examined him.

Section Two was the same as it had been, except it was filled with a dull artificial light. The silhouettes of people mesmerised by their own computer screens were slightly viewable. They were a dissimilar collection, with ranging superficialities; one thing that they had in common was that their eyes were so bloodshot that they were almost entirely red, and there were rashes on their faces from being burnt by their tears.

Some of the screen-enslaved mindlessly chuckled at their screens that were filled with action and adventure while some breathed heavily as they stared lustfully at much more scandalous forms of entertainment. Each person had parts of their bodies missing, some more than others; one greasy male lacked arms and legs, and he merely mashed his computer's keyboard with his nose and chin.

John glared at the three women who had forced him into a psychedelic reality; however, they were too occupied to share attention with him.

Carol was scolding the other two. 'What have I told you about making the damn pitch program too intense?'

The other two stared at the floor as if they were children being lectured by a parent.

'B-but, we had no choice,' stammered Cherie. 'Malik has increased the quota of items we have to sell, and—'

'No excuses; especially no attempts to throw blame unto our boss for your mistakes,' interrupted Carol. 'Remember the last time you tried to excessively increase the pitch level? The man was in for eighteen hours, refusing to buy *anything*, and he almost died. We can't be that extreme to the consumers; we only need subtle and sexy!'

'Con-consumers?' stuttered John. He sneezed; a silver pill the size of a pea flew out of his nose onto the floor. John picked up the pill. 'What the hell is this?' he asked no-one in particular.

Toat hovered closer, examining the item with a look of prejudice. 'It seems to be a compact version of an interactive computer probe,' he observed.

Carol ceased scorning the first two, and Lexa too fell silent, stopping her watch pitch, which caused Teresa to sigh disappointedly. Lexa hurriedly stepped to join her co-workers.

Carol stood tall and proud, with her hands on her hips in a pose that screamed out irritation. 'I'll have you know,' she lectured, 'That isn't a *probe*, it is one of our special and better-than-reality sacred gems provided by Malik himself.'

'Sacred?' tutted Toat.

'That's right, Mister … Hologram!' retorted Carol. 'A sacred gem from Malik enables us to effectively sell his great products. But those are only the store models; we actually sell the sacred gems, too, which can be programmed to be used as an individual's own better-than-reality reality.'

John tried to march to the women; however, he was still disoriented. He stepped on the side of his own foot and fell ungraciously onto his side.

'Honestly, sacred gems!' Toat scoffed. 'No, no, no, you deluded dainty dandelion. I mean, listen to yourself: do *blessed* and *programmed* really fit together? That small *probe* in my young friend's hand is just a machine. A machine made to influence one's mind to suit your little sales pitch. A probe made to force the desperate and disillusioned further into madness … From what I saw just now: you rammed a cerebral spike up this boy's nose! You must really be terrible merchants to have to resort to such deviousness.'

Carol turned beet red, clenching her fists. 'Quiet, you! We were hand-picked by Malik himself!' she cried. 'And what the hell do you know about anything? Malik is our boss, a majestic god to us! *He* made us strong with his alchemy so that we achieve profits, but only so he can have resources to help others.' She pointed. 'You see those nobodies at the computers? They were miserable before Malik graced them. All he takes from them is what they don't use anyway. These freaks never ran, jogged, or even walked, so they happily give up such things that they don't need; Malik's love for us is far more than what our consumers take and lose!'

John laughed, finally managing to stand without swaying. 'Malik sounds like a grifter,' he mocked. 'To resort to digital smoke and mirrors to even sell.'

Carol became a rumbling ball of fury, like a child refusing discipline. Her mouth was now ajar, as she was clearly ready to roar; however, her colleagues stopped her.

The grinning pair made of pink Cherie and red Jane held onto their raging co-worker, ensuring a tight seal over the Carol's mouth.

'Ah-hum … I think our manager has said too much already,' said Lexa, wearing a sheepish grin. 'Thank you for coming to Adonis Electronics; we hope to see you again soon.'

'Hope we can hang out when you finish work?' asked Teresa.

'Sure thing, girl,' responded Jane while keeping a firm hold on her superior.

'Karaoke!' said Lexa. 'Can't wait!'

'Can we just see Malik?' asked John.

Lexa didn't respond as she and the others moved further away; she simply waved to John while she assisted her co-workers with their angered manager.

To take his mind away from the odd, unhelpful situation, John examined the pill probe that he held between his index finger and thumb. 'Hey, Alistair, what is this probe thing?' he asked. 'How come the nanites didn't stop it?'

Toat hummed as he examined the orb probe again. 'Well, they did … eventually,' he responded. 'However, they didn't interfere initially because they're not programmed to stop a separate mechanism's function unless commanded to, or if the program is lethal to the host.' He prodded his index finger straight into the probe, and then after a second, he retracted it. 'Just as I thought,' he said. 'That probe there is inactive, in a sort of stasis, without a connection to a human's brain stem. When it is active, it downloads data from a host server to activate a specific program.'

'Which means?' asked John.

'It means that this *"kleiner"*, or small, bug is as good as dead until it digs into someone's mind,' replied Toat. 'And whichever section it is closest to, it will connect to that section's frequency, which will force all that bargain and sales shtick into one's brain.'

John nodded in acknowledgement as he placed the probe into his right coat pocket. 'Well, I guess we should try and ask for Malik in the next section,' he said.

'Hang on for just one second,' Teresa interjected. 'I gotta go get Dad back.' She then half-ran and half-skipped back up the marble stairs.

A moment later she returned, dragging Murray behind her. He was muttering and trying to break free, like an incredibly upset infant.

'Hey, Murray, nice to see you again,' said John with a false smile. 'I have a small query … Why the hell didn't you tell me about the little brain probe?'

'Well … ummm … I did try to warn you,' replied Murray as Teresa released him. 'It was implied!'

'When?'

'I thought you got the gist of it when I ran back up the stairs,' Murray said, 'Besides, I didn't want to risk going on another digital drug trip. The last one really, *really* hurt.'

'How did you and my dad manage all these years then?' John demanded.

'That's why I said it was really hard to see Malik: he only calls off his employees when he feels like it; otherwise, you could get forced into a sales pitch,' he responded. 'But when Malik summons you, the staff will stop their sales pitch and ensure you are left alone to get to your meeting with him.'

'That would have been good to know earlier, but oh well,' said John. 'Come on, if we have to, we'll go through this place section by section; eventually someone will tell us if Malik's willing to meet with us. And as for their screwed salesmanship—we'll just have to be on our guards.'

Murray nodded dejectedly, and then they began their path to the next section through Adonis Electronics.

They walked past the seemingly lifeless people who were engulfed in a reality beyond reality.

'Murray, I'm curious about these people,' John admitted. 'Do they live down here or something?'

'That's pretty close to the truth—if you can call it living,' replied Murray. 'The people who were up on the base level, Section One, I'm sure you saw their fear. That's because they worry continuously over the cost of their families' wellbeing and what will happen if they ever die. So, they purchase only necessities that are brought up to be sold on the base level. But those who actually live in the sub-levels, like here in Adonis Electronics, they have abandoned everything except their obsessions. They sold everything to Malik to maintain their *hobbies*. When they run out of wealth or commodities, they begin to sacrifice parts of their bodies until they have nothing except their basic desires. They're practically zombies.'

'That is messed up,' said John.

'Yep. Addiction's a terrible thing, Johnny,' Murray replied before drinking out of a bottle he pulled from his cloak.

John looked away, opting to not remark on the latest consumption. 'Hey, Alistair,' he said.

'*Ja.*'

'How were those sales reps so strong?' John asked. 'I mean, I thought I was enhanced by nanites, yet they dragged me along like it was nothing.'

'Well, you can probably guess it was because of Caleb de Caligo, or their *precious* Malik,' responded Toat. 'I heard one of them say something like "magic", which likely means Malik has further developed his biotechnology. He did invent the compound known as Huon.'

'Malik is the creator of Huon?'

'*Ja.* Well, as a part of a team,' Toat explained. 'But he did develop a lot of it on his own, and it seems to me that he has created an improved version. Normally, I can detect Huon's presence in an individual; however, I couldn't detect anything in those girls.'

'Damn … could my nanites make me stronger than the Huon carriers?' John asked.

'They already are,' Toat responded. 'The nanites consistently try to make their host overcome any threat; therefore, if someone starts to overpower you, they'll find a way to help you out. That said, please spare me from further nanomachine questions; it would take too long, and you wouldn't understand anyway.'

John nodded, wide-eyed, in acknowledgement.

They reached a dividing wall that marked the separation point between Sections Two and Three; on the left side, the sleek black wall's subtle curve was a few steps away from the doorway between Two and Three.

'Hey, what's with all those black doors?' asked John.

'Where? The VIP rooms … oh, you don't want to know,' replied Murray. 'I looked in there once, and it was *not* a pleasant sight … I still shudder at the memory … So, don't go in there … ever … Seriously, if I hadn't been drinking already, I would've been driven to drink … Anyhoo, let's keep going.'

CHAPTER SEVENTEEN

THEY LOVED CAKE

Bacchus Burden, the sign said as John and his three allies entered through the door. Sections of Bacchus's Burden mimicked the appearance of grocery stores that John had read about in books, as well as substantial sections of the plaza's main floor; however, divergences arose with the congealed piles of sludge along the aisles.

Bloated individuals sat or lay in food or filth, half of whom had grown so obese that their humanity became doubtful. Piles of food were gathered around each of the hundred blobs, who were given sufficient space as to not spill their food into their neighbour's pile.

Some of the morbidly obese lacked at least a single arm and leg; they used whatever appendage was left to shovel pulp into their gullets. The sight was saddening, while the stench that filled the area choked almost every other odour out of the air.

'This … is depressing,' said John. 'Murray … what happened to these … people?'

'Oh, those who live in Section Three, Bacchus Burden, live only for one purpose: to feast,' he shared. 'Those who were once victims of their hunger ended up sacrificing everything; some were just too desperate to avoid starving again. Gradually, they forfeit their eyes, then their ears, sometimes an arm or leg, sometimes their teeth, but they always eventually give up parts of their brains.'

John felt very disturbed and yet equally sympathetic at the sight of the gorging creatures. He finally felt a sense of gratitude to the Seniors of Seven, despite how strictly they kept order and how their protection used a veil of deception. He had no recollection of facing any hunger above mild, which even then was temporary.

'They get a kind of lobotomy that makes them incapable of anything except eating, but their minds never know when they're full, so they just keep … eating. Something in the gruel deforms them into these sorry states.'

'Well, this place is horrible.' Toat grimaced. 'Let's hurry through to get out of this grisly sight; the next section has to be better.'

The group carefully began to tread around the filth, wincing as their footsteps squelched in muck, but they stopped when they heard a squeaking noise.

A person wearing a red hazardous material suit was pushing a wheelbarrow full of slop. 'Oh, great,' they said, their voice muffled by the suit. 'Looks like consumer ninety-seven is gone.' He released the wheelbarrow, and then he stomped towards a recently-deceased fat man. 'Oh, hi there!' he said to the group. He gripped the fat man's arms and began to easily drag the corpse.

'Where are you taking him?' enquired John.

'Oh … you people may want to leave,' replied the hazmat-suited man. 'The other workers of Bacchus's Burden are having time off, so it's just me today. I don't think I'll be able to help you as I'm a tad busy, you see.' He pushed the fat man's corpse right next to a person who had taken an appearance that was a mixture between a boulder and a thick worm. With its plump and stubby arms, it immediately tore at the fat man's corpse, hurriedly dismembering the body and devouring it piece by piece.

The creature deconstructed and devoured the remains no differently from the paste it consumed until the fat man had no remains at all.

'What the hell!' cried John.

'Oh, yeah; sorry, folks,' said the hazmat-suited man. 'Normally, we dispose of the dead fatties after closing time, but I've got a busy schedule to keep. Time's a factor, 'cos if they get too rotten, the others won't eat 'em.' He returned to the wheelbarrow of slop.

'Wait!' called out John. 'Do you know if Malik wants to meet with us? I mean, he didn't stop us at Section Two.'

'Hang on, let me check,' the man replied, placing a hand against his head. 'Nope. Sorry, I can't rightly tell …. Well, goodbye!'

'Oh, that just sucks,' muttered John.

John and his allies continued to step through Section Three, avoiding the reach of the porcine people and stepping over the miscellaneous goop and scraps that littered the floor.

However, Teresa occasionally risked her safety by prodding a lump of fat to see it jiggle.

'Murray, how the hell do the people in any other Section even get food?' asked John. 'Everything just looks like slop anyway.'

'Fortunately, the regular grocery store is on Section One, and there is catering for some other Sections, so you don't have to go through this nightmare to get food,' Murray responded. 'This level is for the most desperate, poor fools who feared starvation more than this consequence.'

'It is times like these that I'm glad that I don't have a body,' mused Toat.

CHAPTER EIGHTEEN

THE AVARICE OF MAN

They entered Section Four—Mammon's Mercy—almost becoming blind due to its brightness. The entire area was filled with flashing or glowing lights that together took up the entire spectrum of colours imaginable. Massive words such as *WIN* and *LUCKY* were carved into the walls, made from gold; the lights seemed like jewels that were encrusted into the gold.

Mammon's Mercy was filled with the sounds of cheers, cries, and ringing. The whole lengths of each wall were adorned with crank-operated poker machines.

The central area of the section had tables spaced around it, all of which were occupied by at least five gamblers and one dealer. Some of the tables had green tops, as if to show the gamblers some kind of nature that they had refused by entering the games.

Along the inner wall, large screens were displaying various sporting games; in front of the screens were numerous men and women whose hands were filled with pink and blue tickets. Some were cheering for their wagered-upon team while others were yelling furiously.

Occasionally, a man dressed in dark trousers and a pin-striped shirt would wipe the screens with a large cloth as saliva from the obsessed betters kept flying out of their mouths onto the glass.

'Uuuuhhh … can we be quick here?' stammered Murray. 'P-please? Last time … I, uh, was here … I kind of lost half of my bullets … and my shoes.'

'It's all right, Murray, relax,' soothed John. 'We'll just keep marching through.'

The group walked to the nearest table, where a card game was underway; Murray pressed his hands against his head and closed his eyes, blocking out the sights and sounds of Section Four. Players of this game were already clinging to either a bundle of golden coins or a bag filled with paper money. The dealer had grey balding hair, and he wore dark trousers and a white shirt that had red pinstripes down its sleeves, completed by a shiny purple vest.

'Excuse me, sir?' John asked.

'Sorry, gentlemen … and lady, no new players for now,' responded the dealer.

'No, we're not here to play,' said John. 'We want to know if Malik's willing to organise a meeting with us.'

'Just a moment,' replied the dealer, who held a hand to his ear. 'Nope, I'm sorry, Malik is not sending any messages about special guests to Mammon's Mercy at this time.'

'Oh … okay, thanks anyway,' John said.

The group went through the glitter and gold of Section Four; Teresa held onto Murray while he was whimpering.

The constant and persistent cheers and jeers were so loud that any other noise was rendered redundant. The noise never ceased.

The four companions reached the dividing wall between Sections Four and Five; the noise at this point only sounded like a grumbling stomach that no amount of wealth could fill.

'Murray, why did you freak out back there?' John asked.

'Oh, well, I have a bit of a gambling problem,' Murray replied, seemingly slightly embarrassed. 'When I first found this place, I gambled away everything I had on me: weapons, bullets … clothes. But thankfully, your dad helped me out, and because of his help, I only bet one bullet every year … Except for the year that Malik took your dad; that's when I bet half my ammo … and my socks … and four toes.'

'It's okay, Murray,' consoled John.

'Yeah, see, you're feeling better already,' reinforced Teresa.

A man dressed like a butler passed by. He was carrying a tray that held a dozen glasses of wine. Teresa grabbed two of the chalices, giving them to Murray, who drank them immediately. Murray's breathing slowed to a relaxed pace.

'By the way, why do those other people keep gambling?' John quizzed. 'It looks like a lot of them already have a lot, so why would they risk losing it?'

'Oh, them? They got the gambling bug worse than me,' Murray responded. 'They can't ever stop. For them, it's not about winning; it's about playing the game. Some want to make sure they have more than anyone else in the room. And some of them lose so much they're forced to make a deal with Malik: they forfeit the part of their brain that maintains logic and common sense.'

'Is that actually a thing he could remove?' John asked.

'Yes, Junior. Don't doubt Malik's abilities,' Murray replied. 'He is the great *alchemist*.'

CHAPTER NINETEEN

ADDICTED TO RAGEAHOL

The dividing wall between Sections Four and Five, like its prior fellows, had a doorway located at its midway point. Above the door, a sign read *Menoetius Arenas*. The loud cries of encouragement and disparagement ran throughout the atmosphere.

The noise created a more overwhelming array of sounds than the casino in Section Four. There were several fields and courts, each divided by a continuous grandstand that spread around like the veins of a leaf.

While athletes forced themselves towards and beyond self-destruction through their excessively strenuous running, sprinting, and sometimes spinning, people in the stands were consumed by rage and pride.

The audiences roared and spat and swore at the far more physically adept who played their particular games. On a column of basketball courts that ran through the middle of Section Five, the players' shoes squeaked with each step they took.

John recognised one of the contests of strength and stamina from a screen inside the gambling arena of Section Four.

'I'm not technically alive, but seeing them makes *me* feel exhausted,' said Toat, running a hand through his hair.

'The players and spectators are customers,' remarked Murray. 'They love—and I mean absolutely adore—their sports, so much that they almost boil over from their passions. The last things that they own are their passions. But never mind them; be careful around the refs and the snack-vending guys in the stands. They may have those little, what did you call 'em … probes.'

'So, these people running about … they're doing it for fun?' asked John.

Murray nodded in response.

'Okay, I can see that it's exercise and honing agility and strength. But what about the people in the stands watching? Are they relatives or friends of the players?' John asked.

'Some of them are,' Murray responded. 'But a lot of them are just watching for a good time.'

'Why?'

Murray opened his mouth to respond; however, an egg-shaped rugby ball plummeted through the air, straight through hologram Toat, striking the ground and then bouncing up to smack John's chin.

John swore out of surprise rather than pain.

'Little help?' asked a union player.

Teresa picked up the ball and tossed it back towards the rugby field.

A basketball bounced away from a court; a bald referee ran to retrieve it.

'Hey there, has Malik alerted you to any meetings he might be having?' asked John, somewhat fatigued.

'Wait one moment,' replied the ref. He placed his hand against his ear. 'I have received an alert of sorts.'

Both teams on the court ceased their weaving movements, instead, standing at attention in two lines; both lines faced John, subtly impelling him to the centre of the court.

'What's the alert?' John asked, sceptically viewing both now-unified teams, which were being joined by the court's spectators, descending the stands to join the players in their lines.

The ref smiled. 'Just survive.' He then blew a high-pitched sound from his whistle, launching the gathered athletes and audience at John.

John swerved and ducked away from chaotic limbs seeking to either grab or punch him; as the crowd engulfed him, he slid down beneath their legs, emerging from out of the scrum.

Players tripped over audience members and vice versa in an attempt to intercept John's smooth manoeuvring. He had to dive as an audience member flung their whole body at him.

John dashed into a gap in the swerving grandstand, weaving around its wooden supports while increasing numbers of the pursuers found themselves trapped in the wooden web. Exiting through a different gap between the seats, John's legs were grabbed by colourful-shirted individuals. He fell face-down, striking every seat down the seven levels until smacking his forehead on the floor.

John moaned, but he didn't cease his movement. He pushed his hands against the floor, launching himself up to stand again. He then resumed his sprint until he had to swerve, his boot-heel squeaking on the polished court.

Two bulky players almost caught him between them; however, John managed to roll away, leaving the pair to collide with each other.

Above the court, a large net split apart, unleashing a rain of balls; when struck, John was neither hurt nor slowed, though he almost tripped over the rubber spheres once they landed.

Several members of the chasing crowd collected a ball each and then quickly flung them at John.

'Stop it—that's annoying,' muttered John as balls flew over his head or ineffectually bounced off his back.

Another shrill tone from the ref's whistle caused the crowd to stop their assault. Those who collided with the floor or one another softly rubbed their sore limbs.

'Okay, you can go now,' said the ref.

John scowled at the ref, the crowd of athletes, and the audience, and yet he and his group continued downwards nonetheless.

'That was different from usual,' said Murray. 'But Malik does enjoy his games.'

'Then he must be expecting us?' said John.

'I doubt anything could sneak up on him,' said Murray. 'And if he really wanted us to turn back, he wouldn't just have made you play a dangerous game of tag.'

CHAPTER TWENTY

OBSESSIONS

The companions entered while Toat silently chuckled at the sign: *Voracious Vending*. Inside Section Six were rows of shelves; the shelves were filled with knick-knacks and colourful objects that were all adhering to some form of idolatry: whether it being ancient characters of fiction or long-dead persons of infamy.

Most of the customers had hidden themselves; however, some couldn't hide the sounds of their giggling giddiness.

'Yecch … what a dreadful sight,' said Toat.

'I suppose, but it's not that bad, Alistair,' John mentioned. 'At least it all looks sort of clean and almost inviting; a hell of a lot better than the other sections.'

'The section is not what disgusts me,' decreed Toat. 'A lot of these people are idiots; they are small-minded and stupid. They idolise self-loving egomaniacs and over-pampered prima donnas! I can see and hear them all, clinging to pieces of junk made in the image of their worshipped individuals.'

'Malik uses his alchemy to create everything here,' Murray remarked.

'I know that!' said Toat. 'But he would've had to have based this … junk on something.'

'That means it has some historical merit,' said John.

They walked through the aisles between the shelves, occasionally stepping over people who lay slumped on the ground, giggling mindlessly, or rolling side to side and embracing an item or more.

'What's wrong with these people?' asked John.

'Basically, they sold their souls,' responded Murray.

'How?'

'They've given up everything, just like the others. They gradually forfeit all their thoughts and memories ... except for the ones that are about the *heroes* that they worship so much. Each to their own, I say ... except maybe with some stuff.'

John and his allies carefully traversed through the aisles, their eyes almost hurting from the glittering shine of the products that lined certain aisles. They relied upon Toat to alert them if some skulking employee was about to push a probe up into their heads.

Teresa accidentally stepped on a plastic doll that lay idly on the ground. 'Oops,' she mumbled.

A loud cry of absolute anguish caught their attention. 'Wha— What have you done!' cried a greasy-haired, balding, mid-teen boy.

'Oh ... I'm so sorry,' apologised Teresa. 'I'll get you another one, I promise. Please don't worry!'

'*No*! Nothing you can do can undo this ... this travesty!' squealed the boy. 'My ... my precious, you killed her! You ... you're a murderer!'

'Look, buddy, she said sorry and she'd buy you another one,' said Murray, 'So get over it!'

'No. No. No,' mumbled the boy. 'I ... I have nothing ... I *am* nothing ... Malik won't give me another.' The balding boy bawled loudly, and then he began to smash his head repeatedly against the floor. A cracking noise sounded the end of the smashing, and then a small waterfall of crimson flowed from the damaged skull. The boy lay motionless, face-down in a pool of his blood and tears.

Teresa, mouth agape, clung to Murray.

'That's what happens,' said a tall, thin man, 'when you stan women.'

'What?'

'Being a cuck always ends in death.' The man leant towards John. 'Remember this lesson, boy.'

'I don't even understand what you're saying,' John admitted. He and the rest of his compatriots began swiftly walking away. However, the tall, thin man trailed behind them, habitually scratching his uneven facial hair.

'Go away,' said John.

'I'm not following you,' said the man, eyes gaunt from insomnia. 'I'm only going this way, too.'

'Sure,' muttered John. 'Where are you going?'

'I don't see how it is any of your business,' said the man. 'What I do is in the service of the great man Malik.'

John stopped, leaving Murray and Teresa to pull up shortly ahead of him. 'Can you take us to Malik directly?'

'Obviously not,' said the man; his full denim outfit then creaked as he slouched. 'Such filthy creatures are to be kept away from our Malik.'

'Well, excuse us for being filthy.' John began walking again.

'No, not you, gentlemen,' said the man, lurking alongside the aisles. 'That female creature. Such cringe.'

'Okay, you're just blabbering nonsense again,' said John. 'Go away.'

The tall, thin man continued to trail the small group; they changed directions in an adjacent aisle, yet he still followed. They tried to hide behind one of the various standees, yet the man reappeared as soon as they left cover, his swishing denim attire alerting them to his lurking.

'Listen, creep,' said Murray, 'if you don't back off …' His hand hovered over the gun in his holster. 'I can make you back off.'

'Do not be absurd, sir,' said the lurker. 'I'm trying to be ready to help.'

'Help for what?'

'For when the female *rees*,' said the lurker, shuddering in disgust. 'Females are always so temperamental; you can never tell when they will become hysterical.'

'Well, I can break your nose,' said Murray, 'and remain calm while doing it.'

'Such cringe,' said the lurker. 'Are you a white knight or something?'

'I'll give you nighty-night,' said Murray; however, his advance was halted by Teresa's grip on his arm.

'Please don't, Dad,' she said. 'Just ignore him.'

'*See*! *See*! Hysterics,' growled the lurker. 'That's what you get for being a white knight! Some female to assault you!'

'I'm sorry for being hysterical,' said Teresa with a hint of disdain. 'Please, just leave us alone.'

'Why won't you date me?' asked the lurker.

'What?' muttered John. 'You just went on about hating women, now you want a date?'

'Stay out of it, simp,' said the lurker. 'If not for you white knights, a specimen of Chad like me could have easily gotten with that girl already.'

'Really?' John said with an eye-roll. 'That fast?'

'Obviously,' said the lurker, 'I am a good Lunatologist man.'

'You don't look like one,' said Murray.

'What? Is there a rule about what Lunatologists can look like?' the lurker replied with a sneer.

'I'm a little rusty,' said Murray, 'but I think one of their rules is that you must wear white clothes.'

'I'm allowed to be an exception!' said the lurker. 'Such good Lunatologist men, such as I, are given allowances, and we have women flock to us, even if the quality of female is so sub—'

Murray punched the lurker.

'White knight!' cried the lurker. 'White knight! Cuck alert!'

Murray punched him again, but hard enough that the lurker clearly lost consciousness, slumping against a long cushion that had a pattern of a person on the pillowcase. 'That wasn't hysterical of me, right?' said Murray.

'Seemed reasonable to me,' said John.

The trio continued past the unconscious lurker.

'You know not to listen to creeps like that, right?' Murray said to Teresa.

'Oh, I know,' she said. 'They're annoying, but I can deal with them by myself.'

'Well, you shouldn't have to,' said Murray. 'And when I'm around, you won't need to, okay?'

'Yeah.' Teresa nodded.

John pondered for a moment. 'Are all "good Lunatologist men" really like that weirdo?'

'I don't know,' said Murray. 'I guess the ones I didn't need to kill seemed better than that creep.'

CHAPTER TWENTY-ONE

GOD LOVES VIOLENCE

When they reached the doorway that led to Section Seven, Teresa had returned to her normal cheery disposition. The sign above it read: *Mars Armaments*.

'Oh no,' muttered Murray.

'What's wrong, Murray?' John asked.

'Awesome! This is where Lionel is!' said Teresa happily.

'Who's Lionel?'

'Lionel … he's like a prodigy with weaponry; he can repair or even improve almost any kind of gun, and he is one of the best snipers around. If it's weapons, he knows all about them.'

'Oh … okay … then. Why aren't you pleased about meeting him?' John asked Murray.

'He almost killed John and me when we first arrived,' Murray advised. 'So, he always acts overly nice to me, to reconcile … or something.'

'If it's that minor of an issue,' said John, 'why didn't we just come here first to see him?'

'Well, you were all fired up earlier,' retorted Murray. 'Besides, with the lifts deactivated, we can't get to him unless we go through each section one at a time.'

'I guess so,' said John. 'But if we can't find him, do we keep going to Section Nine?'

'No,' replied Murray. 'It's impossible to get into Section Eight, let alone Malik's chambers, without the presence of one of his elite minions.'

'Well, let's hope we can find Lionel.'

Throughout Section Seven were countless firearms, swords, knives, bows, arrows and explosives, all neatly displayed within glass cases and multi-level storage racks; often the weapons were right next to a potential customer, almost taunting them by being just out of their reach.

'Geez, if we could get all this, maybe we could kill Odin without Malik's special weapon,' said John.

'Ha! If only it were that easy,' Toat replied. 'You know very well how powerful Odin is, so you must understand that conventional weaponry cannot kill him.'

'I know,' John retorted. 'It was just a thought.'

Occasionally, their pace was slowed by a distraction: someone screaming in agony. Some individuals were strung upside down and were being dunked up and down repeatedly into a basin of scalding liquid. Some people were tied into what appeared to be tanning beds; however, their screams and the smoke cascading from them displayed that they were there for neither rest nor recreation.

One man lay on a bed of nails, trying desperately to tense his muscles to prevent the sharp points from digging further into his flesh.

Another individual had to keep his chain-bound limbs taut as, if he slackened, his stomach would slip down into a vat of molten iron.

'What did they do?' asked John. 'Kill someone?'

'Yep,' Murray replied. 'Eventually, that is. To pay for an instrument of harm or death, you must endure a certain amount of agony yourself. That way, Malik believes that by suffering as much as or more than your intended targets, then you've earnt the right to maim or kill.'

They spotted a thin man around Teresa's age, and she hugged him in welcome.

The lean man released Teresa; his face was somewhat similar to a citrus fruit: round and a little bit rough. He was dressed in conflicting camouflage clothing: his shirt and trousers were yellow and brown, to be hidden in a desert; however, they were covered by false foliage that would suit jungle warfare better. He then went to hug Murray.

'Hey! Don't you dare hug me!' ordered Murray.

'Dad, relax, you know he's one of our friends,' said Teresa.

'Yeah, relax, Murray; you know me better,' reassured Lionel. 'You know I would do anything to protect Terry and her sisters. And anything for my best buddy Murray!'

'I know, but please don't do any of that affection stuff while I'm here,' Murray replied with a grumble.

John and Toat stared silently.

John then coughed to break the silence. 'So, Lionel, I was told just now that you know things,' he said. 'My point being: do you also know a guaranteed way to get to Malik?'

'Oh, that's easy, Murray could've told you,' replied Lionel. 'Murray, don't you remember that silly jingle that used to play like a hundred times every day? The gist of it was: if you want to meet the leader, all you must do is dial 1800 362.'

'Well, that's a *great* help, Lionel,' muttered Murray. 'But we don't have a phone.'

Toat chuckled. 'Yes, you do, ignoramus!' He hovered next to Murray and tapped Murray's left wrist. 'The Jackal, like many devices, is also a telephone.'

Murray pulled up his sleeve and pressed a button on the silver device. A monotone computerised voice intoned, 'Hello, thank you for—'

Toat typed on the holographic keyboard that hovered above the Jackal device.

'Mobile phone function: activated. Please dial the number that you want to call,' said the Jackal. A blue-tinged number keypad replaced the keyboard.

Murray looked at Lionel, and then Lionel repeated, *'One eight hundred, three-six-two, that's whatcha gotta do.'*

The Jackal began to chirp a dial tone, followed by a repetitive ringing. It stopped when the call was answered: 'Hello, and a pleasant day to you, valued consumer,' said a merry pre-recorded voice. 'Your location has been traced, so please wait; someone shall meet you di-rect-ly.'

The Jackal had tedious music funnelled through it, which stopped when the device closed the connection. The keypad vanished and the device returned to sleep.

'Now what?' asked John.

Murray stroked his beard. 'Now, we wai—'

'Hey there, valued consumers!' interjected a loud, friendly voice.

They all turned around to see a sinister-looking man smirking behind them. He wore an outfit made entirely of black leather, which had some white patches that showed that it had once been completely white but had simply been covered in black shoe polish. The leather had gold studs planted along various seams and his shoulders and spine. His hair was a mohawk; however, it was long and limp, as well as dark and greasy. Piercings were stabbed into his face, seemingly all over, and some had small skull-shaped jewels attached to them. He wore large combat boots with mismatched shoelaces and rusted iron spikes protruding from the toes. 'We really appreciate your call,' came the friendly voice from the frightful man. 'My name is Phil, and if you would please follow me, Malik is awaiting you presently.'

The companions, now including Lionel, began to follow the contradiction-incarnate Phil. John frowned at the oddly merry man, but he still followed with the others.

They walked past more people "paying" for their weapons; many of whom were burning themselves to compensate.

'Hey, Murray, what's with this Phil guy?' John muttered.

Murray hummed and then answered blankly, 'Ever since that incident when Malik's personal guard tried to kill him, he started to pick the most random people to be in his personal staff.'

John's fists remained tense in suspicion.

'I wouldn't overthink it, Johnny.'

CHAPTER TWENTY-TWO

Forlorn Frauds

Following Phil, the companions arrived at the dividing wall between Sections Seven and Eight. Another doorway had a different sign above it, which read *False Friends*. The door had no handle and was merely a plank of wood. Phil placed his palm upon the centre of the door; it slid open, allowing access through it.

A vast hall was revealed through the opened door, or would have been, if not for the greenery. A slice of jungle filled the entire area. Lush leaves dangled from twisted branches, and tangled bushes encased every odd tree base.

'Welcome to Section Eight: the petty False Friends. This place is where Malik's insurgents enjoy their just deserts,' said Phil, seemingly maintaining his struggling grin due to his numerous piercings. 'Follow me, please, gentlemen and lady.' He walked through the doorway, his jewellery clinking softly.

The group followed Phil, albeit slightly hesitantly.

'Umm … Murray, why is there a jungle underground?' asked John.

The jungle hummed and chirped and croaked as unseen shy and sly creatures watched them.

'I don't know the how,' responded Murray, 'but it's a rainforest thriving under artificial sunlight.'

'Wow, the mysterious jungle!' said Teresa merrily as she and Lionel started to chase each other through the trees.

'Don't worry about them,' said a clearly irate Murray to John. 'That's the odd little way the kids always act.'

The jungle floor crunched and rustled as footsteps pushed onward.

'Are you sure they should be running around in a place like this?' asked John.

Murray chuckled. 'Lionel don't look like much, but believe me, he's an expert survivalist and natural born killer … who happens to be like a child.'

'Uh … huh,' muttered John, the rustling of the leaves and branches as Teresa and Lionel ran through them distracting him. A low branch scraped John's forehead, causing him to swear in surprise.

'Oh yeah, sorry,' said Phil. 'Watch your heads, folks: low branches. Okay.'

The cut on John's forehead sealed, and then it vanished; the only proof it was ever there was a small amount of blood that had escaped before the cut healed, which he wiped away with his sleeve.

'Well, well, you must be special guests,' said Phil while holding a hand upon one of his pierced ears. 'It seems Malik wishes to meet you with no further outside interruptions.'

'What do you mean?' asked John.

'Well, I've just been informed that the boss desires to meet with you,' responded Phil. 'You should feel lucky; most people have to be on a six-week waiting list.'

John felt heat emanate from his coat's right pocket. He buried his hand to discover the source of the rising temperature, then retrieved his hand and opened his palm to see the heat source. The small silver pill lay in his hand; however, it was glowing light orange. 'Alistair, what's wrong with this thing?'

With his index finger, Toat tapped the probe. 'It seems that that poor little probe is overheating,' he responded.

'But why?'

'Well, I think it's because we're nearing the source of all the transmissions within the Plaza,' replied Toat. 'Much like rays of light, the transmissions are singular, with each Section providing a node, or prism, to befit the light comparison; the node directs specific programs for the specific Section. Perhaps this deep into the Plaza, none of the individual programs can be channelled; I suspect only the levels higher than this one have nodes to direct an assigned pitch from the entangled programs into the probe. I guess when it's this deep, instead of one, all the programs are sent to the probe.'

'So, that means it is downloading the "sales pitch" for every department?' asked John.

'That's the general idea of it, *ja*,' Toat replied while adjusting his glasses.

John returned the now-orange probe to his right pocket, its heat stifled by the coat lining.

'Wow, ain't you a clever little bee,' said Phil, jeering at Toat.

Toat grumbled at the passive yet sarcastic remark.

The group's steps were never silent. Loose twigs cracked, grass rustled, and mud squelched each time they trod.

'Help me … please … help,' pleaded a frail and starved voice from an unseen origin.

A few drops of blood rained onto the jungle floor.

John looked up; he was shocked to see several people hanging from the top of various trees as if they were merely branches, almost severed from the tree itself.

Only five people were distinguishable from the flora; however, they were just the ones who weren't completely camouflaged. The five above the group were hung upside down like bats, with their feet roped together and tied to the tip of the trees.

'Phil, what the hell are they doing up there?' John demanded.

'Hanging around,' replied Phil, simultaneously happily and sardonically.

'No, I can see that. I mean *why* are they up there?'

'Do not concern yourself with such trivial things,' said Phil. 'They are simply given some time to think as to why they believe they're more knowledgeable than Malik …. Now, come along.'

They all followed Phil; John tried to ignore the weeping and moaning of the tree-strung people.

Toat, however, chuckled quietly.

'What about those people? What are they doing?' asked John. He pointed towards a line of tables that had leaves growing out of them and seemed to be severely warped tree trunks. Upon each of them was a different person who was tied tightly down by metal clamps formed from the table's wooden surfaces. Each was being regularly whipped with barbed chains by odd prison guards dressed entirely in full-body black suits with zippers tightly closed to keep the suits together.

'Lying.'

'Oh, haha, Phil,' replied John. 'Why are they *lying* under restraints like that?'

'They asked for it,' said Phil. 'They wanted to lie, so here they are …. Now, come along.'

John's suspicions of Phil, and especially the enigmatic fallen Uplifted—Caleb Caligo, or Malik—grew thicker with the forest's own growth. Eventually, the agonising cries of the people were no different than whispers among the other wildlife, but the smell of blood remained present.

'Here we are,' announced Phil at a stone shrine.

The stone carving was the same size as him; however, it was sculpted to depict a figurine of a muscular and faceless man. The stone figurine held a serpent triumphantly above his head while under its right foot was the disembodied head of an elderly bearded man.

Phil pressed his palm against the shrine's base.

With a hiss, the solid statue split into several equal pieces that shifted away from each other, pushing a portion of dirt, grass, and leaves away as they did so.

The shrine slid away, revealing a circular iris hatch. The hatch opened, shifting another portion of dirt, grass, and leaves further away as it widened. The hole became wide enough for a dozen people in a group huddle to fit through. A circular platform then arose from where the statue had been.

Phil stood on the platform, with a smile that appeared to once again struggle due to some piercings, and then he gestured for the others to join him.

The circular platform had a large enough surface for a group of ten people to stand and extend their arms outright, yet John's group stayed close together.

Phil clapped twice, and the platform began to descend slowly, but it gradually gained speed.

The platform snugly slid down the hollow cylinder from which it came; above it, the statue slowly re-formed, re-covering the entrance. The sound of dirt scraping was barely audible.

For several minutes, the group stood in silence; the only noise was an occasional cough, as well as the lift's constant muzak ringing in their ears.

CHAPTER TWENTY-THREE

THE HEART OF CALIGO

With a *ping*, the lift platform stopped moving. In front of the group there was a wooden door, which clearly clashed with the dull metallic hue of the lift shaft. It slid open.

Phil exited first onto a tiled mosaic with a colourful floral pattern that covered the floor of a large and otherwise white room. The room that the group had entered was sterile and cold in appearance; the only exception to the whiteness was the tiled floor that Phil stood on.

Phil moved to face the wall behind him; he placed his palm against it. A tone rang, and a section of the wall became semi-transparent, misty, and then vanished. Phil skipped through the opening; the group followed, walking.

John cursed as he was struck by the sheer, almost blinding, coldness of the adjacent room. His breath was visible; the heat of his exhalation became viewable as it formed short-lived vapour clouds. He embraced himself.

Lionel and Teresa hugged each other while Toat and also Murray seemed to be unaffected by the sharp dive in temperature.

The iced-over room was considerably larger than the contradictorily surfaced room with which it shared a wall. It was nearly half the size of the jungle that lay above it.

All through the freezer were oddly shaped sculptures that were fused with every surface in the room; the floor itself was uneven and covered by lumps.

'Wh-what th-the h-h-hell?' stuttered John through the icy air.

His query was not of the low temperature, however, but rather the truth of the ostensible statues that appeared before him as his eyes adjusted to the ice veil.

Hundreds of people were frozen in states of terror and agony. Some were paused in their positions of clawing over their immediate neighbour in a hapless attempt to escape. Every single person was chained to the surface, which captured them further in a prison of ice.

On the wall opposite the room's entrance were embedded a pair of onyx doors. Around the doors, parts of the frozen prisoners had been broken off and planted, forming a sickening arch.

Outstretched arms with open hands were cruelly attached to the arch; some were statically gesturing to the doors, some offering a handshake, and some were forced into a frozen greeting wave.

At the bottom of the cannibalised arch, legs protruded so they seemed to form an iced chorus line of them dancing independent of bodies. Eyeballs were encrusted into the arch, thereby becoming pseudo-gems that couldn't ever blink again.

Phil obviously noticed John's total contempt for the room. 'Oh, don't worry about these silly people,' he said light-heartedly. 'They are enjoying their just punishment for their treacherous ways. Anyway, right through those doors is Malik.' He gestured to the group. 'I have been instructed to wait here for your return, so until then, please enjoy the grand privilege of meeting with the great alchemist and creator and boss of Caligo's Plaza, Malik.' He then sat on a pile of sleeved arms and cloth-covered rears that were clustered to make a chair coming out of the wall.

John scowled at Phil while carefully stepping over the frozen bodies on the floor; some were stuck in their failed attempts to reach out for assistance.

Lionel and Teresa appeared to have mostly adjusted to the chill; they were prodding the fingers and cheeks of the frozen people.

John, however, was harshly affected by the freezing climate, as he had never experienced such biting cold because he was accustomed to an arid, sheltered atmosphere.

Toat rolled his eyes at the shivering boy. He lay a hand on John's shoulder. 'I'll send a message to the nanites to regulate your body temperature, shall I?'

John nodded frigidly.

Toat's hollow hand then glowed, and John instantly felt at ease in the chilly hall.

'Ah … thank you.' But then he frowned again. 'Murray, is this frozen hell new to you?'

Murray shook his head. 'No, Junior, I'm afraid this place existed when John and I first got here all those years ago,' he responded. 'Though, with less bodies at the time.'

'Why didn't you run the other way?' John asked.

'Desolation can seem worse than danger, Johnny,' said Murray. 'The devil you know.'

The black doors then opened inwards, inviting them into the chamber it held.

The group walked into the proverbial heart of Caligo Plaza's structure.

Malik's chamber wasn't as freezing as his 'trophy room', although it was still cold enough that the travellers could easily distinguish their breath from the room's air.

The interior floorplan of the chamber was the shape of a bisected circle; the black doors were at the centre of the curve.

The floor of the chamber had miscellanea such as towels, tools, and even toys tossed carelessly around its surface.

Along the chamber wall protruded a long workbench, which was split into two, as it had a gap for the black doors and yet another gap at the opposite wall.

The workbench was littered with test tubes, bent plastic pipes, glass containers holding bubbling or stagnant liquids, and Bunsen burners, as well as whole sets of items that normally belonged in a scientific laboratory.

In the break in the workbench, at the opposite wall, was a machine composed of a thick cluster of pipes and tubes, with digital and analogue clocks stuck out like contusions. This large device had neither a distinguishable beginning nor end. Holes and openings were along the machine in arbitrary patterns. The machine stole the free space of the gap in the wall, as well as reaching up to the ceiling.

The curved ceiling held thousands of squares, each holding videos from every part of the Plaza; every person either seemed unaware that they were being watched or glared with simultaneous spite and fear at the camera lens that silently observed their every movement.

The entirety of the clustered machine was not viewable as it was blocked by a golden throne and a tall, subtly muscular man. He wore an outfit that appeared to be made entirely out of belts stitched together. Black and dark-brown belts with shiny silver buckles covered his arms, with loose straps flapping slightly every time he moved. His torso was covered by a mesh of silk-sewn belts mimicking and exceeding the colour and pattern of a rainbow.

Blue- and red-striped belts were linked alternately and wrapped around each of the man's legs like the bandages of a dead pharaoh. His pale bare feet were oddly unaffected by the specks and thin sheets of ice that covered the floor.

He flicked switches and twisted knobs that were attached to a control console in front of the messy machine.

Steam and a flashing variation of red and green light shot out of the holes along the machine and then, almost as fast as they had been generated, they disappeared. From under the machine of twisted, nearly mangled pipes, a tray extended itself, and sitting on the tray was a pile of ostensible fruit.

The tall man effortlessly cradled the fruit. He then lifted it towards the ceiling. Above the bizarre mechanical creation, a wide tube extended down, and then a vacuum sucked up the fruit, swallowing it up. It retracted once the fruit had been taken.

The man turned to the group. His head was hairless; however, it seemed that he had eyebrows painted on as thin lines, and each ended in small spirals. His eyes were only uneven violet pupils. His fingernails and toenails were all polished black; however, each one also had different language characters imprinted with gold: every single one of them said—

'Malik.' Murray greeted the athletic-looking man as he approached the group.

Malik returned the greeting somewhat shyly. 'Oh … yes, hi, Murray.'

'Nice clothes there, Malik,' said Murray. 'Those buckles must've taken a while … still, I'd say it's a step up.'

'Oh, well … thank you, Murray,' said Malik timidly. 'Speaking of, um, clothing … you know how I feel about that silly hood of yours.' He was now only a few paces away from the group.

'Huh? Oh, right. But I thought you'd made an exception this time,' asked Murray, almost fearfully. 'Since you allowed these kids down here, too. Besides, my daughter here hasn't seen me without it … so I thought—'

'I thought I already told you,' interrupted Malik, seeming slightly bolder. 'Take off that hood in *my presence*!'

Murray sighed sadly. 'I'm so sorry you're here to see this, Terry,' he said to Teresa. He then gripped the top of his balaclava and slowly began to remove it. He gritted his teeth and sucked in air as his pain clearly intensified. As soon as Murray had removed his dark-blue balaclava, the reason he needed it at all became clear.

His scalp was completely absent, only a paper-thin layer of flesh remained. His nose had been removed, displaying his nasal cavities, and no longer obstructed was the broken sniffing sound it made as he breathed. Murray's face still had skin; however, most of it was scarred by thick now-sealed slashes. His emerald eyes held deep anguish and agony. As Murray pulled a flask from his robe and drank its content hurriedly, he pocketed the balaclava.

Teresa's eyes widened with terror and filled with tears of sadness. She grasped onto Lionel, who tried to hug her gently to lessen her horror and sorrow.

'My god,' John simply swore.

'Yeah, I know, but I did tell you, Johnny,' Murray said, pausing to drink again. 'Malik just *loves* to make us understand the costs.'

Malik smirked as he walked up in a shuffling manner to Murray; using a polished fingernail, he scratched the bloody skull once, causing Murray to swear loudly. 'Calm yourself, Mar. You did learn the value of life,' Malik said before grasping Murray's facial hair and pulling it.

A tearing sound emanated as glue on Murray's face struggled to cling.

Malik tossed the removed beard onto the glassy floor, revealing Murray had been wearing a false beard to hide an unnaturally formed cleft lip. 'And I showed your insignificant friend how I fulfil everyone's desires, leading you along section-by-section, playing with you at times.'

'You mean you wanted to meet us the whole time?' seethed Murray while rubbing his uncovered reddened chin.

'Of course I did,' responded Malik. 'You didn't think that my minions forgot to probe your minds in every section after Two, did you? After your friend managed to stop the first sales pitch program, I told everyone to stand down, barring a few little romps—but I couldn't resist! Anyway, I was interested to see that you *wanted* to meet me, since you always hate these little meetings, face-to-face.'

Malik glanced at Teresa and her growing tears. 'I see you never told your cute little girls, not even the eldest,' he scoffed. 'You never told them what it cost for you to keep them here … and feed them … and for me to tolerate Scarface and *you* bringing along parasites.'

'But I've … I've told you a hundred times, they are invaluable,' explained Murray. 'We were just fami—'

'Shut up! You know my word is truth, and if you counter that, you're a dirty liar,' exclaimed Malik. 'Anyway, since you were such a looker, I made sure that everyone would *look* at you!' He gasped a quick scorning giggle. 'Remember, it was your choice.' Malik was still giddy. 'To pay for the additional consumers, that is, leeches on *my* establishment and *my* resources, you would either give them to me when they blossomed. Or you would forfeit the quality of yourself that I saw as your best, and since taking your obedience would mean making you a vegetable, I took your looks.'

John frowned, trying to make sense of the deranged concept of appearances having monetary value.

'And Scarface couldn't assist in the bargain because he already belonged to me, so you had to pay all that extra debt on your lonesome, so you lost your head, or at least part of it. Didn't you, Mar?'

John clenched his fists angrily. 'You bastard,' he fumed. 'Caligo, you bastard, I'll—'

'Stop, Herr Smith,' Toat intervened. 'Something, besides the obvious, is wrong here.'

Malik slid back towards the throne in front of the cardiovascular-like machine.

'Are you really Caleb de Caligo?' asked Toat.

'Oh, of course I am, *Alistair von Toat*,' Malik replied to the hologram.

'How? What happened to you?' asked Toat.

'I should ask you the same thing,' countered Malik. 'You seem … so ghostly, Alistair. What happened to me, you ask? Why, do my mannerisms frighten you?'

'No, you were always unusual, to say the least,' said Toat. 'But how are you so young … and athletic … and tall? You were always the short, unimposing, fat-faced twit, yet comfortably such. How could you change yourself so drastically? And Murray told us that your head had been shot apart; however, it healed somehow …. Yet I don't detect any medical implants; you aren't scarred nor have any seams …. It's like you *naturally* evolved. Caleb never altered himself; he would even refuse the rejuvenation chambers in Haven. Could the outside world change such strong beliefs?'

Malik pivoted on his bare feet. 'Caleb de Caligo *was* my name,' he said. 'And I have the memories of a lifetime to prove it.'

'So, you're a clone,' observed Toat.

'A rather tacky label, don't you think?' said Malik, with a brief pout. 'The original Caleb was held back by fear. He could have achieved greatness, but his stubborn commitment to remaining "pure" meant he needed a test subject.'

'I see, but Factorem wouldn't allow human experimentation, not even on a clone,' said Toat, now wearing a subtle frown in contemplation. 'That explains Caleb's departure from Haven. He spent a year in isolation before abruptly leaving without a word.'

'Yes, the basic Caleb—let's call him … my *father*—was carrying me in an incubation pod,' said Malik. 'He took over this abandoned place—providing shelter and supplies for free, if you can believe it—and raised me among the filthy people.'

'He couldn't have given you his memories until, at the minimum, puberty,' surmised Toat. 'I understand—it is the same technology my progenitor used to create me. Yet instead of an empty cloud, you were a sapient child, flooded by someone else's life, when your own had hardly begun, yet begun it had.'

'Oh, don't pity me, Alistair,' sneered Malik. 'I was born a genius, granted physical potential the old me could never acquire. Upon receiving original Caleb's memories, I merely gained experience; I wouldn't need to waste years in research he'd already covered. I could stand above all.'

'Caleb was always unusual,' said Toat. 'However, as strange as he was, I'm shocked his experiments were done to a child… even if it were an artificial one.'

'Well, you know he had a predilection for fear,' said Malik, the uneven violet pupils of his eyes darting about. 'Fear of mortality affects all, even "pure" Caleb de Caligo; the pure man who buried cerebral implants into my skull. I don't hold a grudge for his experiments; they were a useful guide as I continued his work, eventually integrating them into myself.'

'It's disappointing to learn about Caleb's forsaken morality,' admitted Toat. 'Such biotech should never be explored on a subject, not until the data has been perfectly proven in theory.'

'Despite my own innovations, Caleb did wonderful work on me. Perhaps he was more artist than scientist?' Malik became timid again. 'Anyway, you were always so cruel to the underdog, Alistair. Almost every Uplifted at Haven was so infatuated with the tiny robot bugs that most other research, including "my" own, was deemed redundant. But biotechnology is always much nicer and cleaner than that synthetic junk. My head was blown apart, but not enough to prevent my glorious recovery,' Malik said boldly, his shyness re-dissipating. 'I saw your tick-ridden pal there; could he survive such an injury? Doubtful, considering he could get overpowered by some *little girls*. How pathetic.'

John grimaced, finding a growing agitation towards the self-proclaimed alchemist; he reached the realisation that he might despise hubris even more than cruelty.

'To be considerate to the bug boy, I had provided each of my minions with a single concentrated dose of Sama; an improvement on the brilliant, though obsolete, Huon, and that one dose is enough to strengthen them for the rest of their lives without an eventual rate of decay, like Huon. My children can beat anything that *you* can make.'

'But this new data conflicts with anything I know as possible ...' Toat mumbled.

John's heart quickened with more visceral rage as he looked from the grisly maimed Murray to the one who caused it; Malik's self-aggrandising added annoyance to John's anger.

'I keep the very best of my creations for myself, obviously,' Malik continued with a smirk. 'I made an advanced Sama dose for myself, which I aptly call Sempiternal; it perpetually sustains my body. Through exhaustive experimentation of my forebear and my own innovations, I managed to defy nature's rules by evolving into the magnificent sight before you.'

'I see. So, that's why I couldn't detect the introduced liquids,' mused Toat. 'The dosage and concentration are so perfect it becomes indistinguishable from one's natural biology .... The years have indeed enabled your genius to grow beyond what the old Caleb could accomplish.'

'Why, thank you,' Malik expressed, bizarrely bashfully.

Murray fell to his knees; the stab of the combination of the chill and open air seemed to be attacking his bare skull and overwhelming him.

Teresa and Lionel each grasped one of Murray's arms, preventing him from falling further. Teresa's tears still rained and then fell to become ice droplets before hitting the floor.

'However, "Malik", like most of Caleb's own work, your Sempiternal carries flaws,' Toat said.

'Does it now?' scoffed Malik.

'You cannot ever leave this frozen chamber, can you?' retorted Toat. 'I remember a similar project by the original Caleb that failed miserably: the Kratos compound. It was rendered ineffective in temperatures lower than ninety-five degrees Celsius. So, it seems your Sempiternal experiment has countered this problem, yet too effectively. This chamber is about negative ten degrees Celsius; I suppose that is the optimal climate for your Sempiternal ... therefore, you are trapped in your own *kleinen* experiment.'

Malik laughed heartily, which scratched the air audibly, like a rusty chain against tin. 'Oh, well done. You got me. Yes, I can't leave, but I wouldn't say, I'm "trapped"; why would I want to leave?' he argued. 'I have over a thousand faithful servants to act out my will, and I can control enough of the plaza's functions with my cerebral implants. Everything else, I control right here.'

Out of the floor in front of him, a small dais arose. Atop the risen console was a keyboard with hundreds of keys adorned with various insignia.

Malik typed faster than one's eye could catch; seemingly arbitrarily. His fingers cracked and danced along the keyboard as if he was tugging a puppet string with each digit.

On the screens, all employees of Caligo's Plaza stood up rigid, and then just as suddenly, they returned to their duties of restocking, selling, and bartering.

'Yes, yes, brilliant,' said Toat, clearly unimpressed. 'But this self-aggrandising exhibition deflects from your clear hypocrisy. That technology is an imitation, and what's more, the whole building, your workers, and all your products contain nanomachines. If you hate nanites so much, why do you use them so abundantly?'

'I never said I *hated* nanites per se, Alistair,' replied Malik. 'Much like my genetic template, I only despise Factorem's *obsession* with them.'

'Ah, yes, but on the topic of obsessions, why do your minions think you're an alchemist, and to some, you're even a god?' asked Toat. 'You know quite well that the Uplifted aren't deities; did your *father*'s principles fail to pass to you?'

Malik leant on the throne with his elbow while he rested his head on his hand. '*I* never *said* that I was a god,' he responded. 'Old Caleb made himself a charity for them, but I'd established myself as an alchemist and an altruist … the people are the ones who then decided that I was *a god*. My powers and knowledge are akin to one, so I thought, *Why not let them think what they want?* I allow them to call me a god, if they wish, but no-one's forcing them, Alistair. Besides, if the shoe fits—' He glanced at his bare feet. 'Proverbially speaking, of course.'

'Naturally, clone Caleb,' said Toat. 'Yet, for a purported *god*, you are quite the coward. You cannot leave here, but neither do you allow people into your inner sanctum, unless they are at a disadvantage in the sights of—I assume—one of your brainwashed valets or using their families as hostages.'

'That is not cowardice,' retorted Malik. 'I give so much freedom to the consumers with my bargains; isn't it, there-fore, good business to regain some of the balance? The consumers are filthy parasites, but when I ensure they are obedient, they no longer gnaw away my resources—they nibble; a smarter tactic to enforce docility, rather than let-ting any parasite go feral, or worse, infect my solitude.'

'Your surveillance web is absolute,' said Toat. 'How could any so-called *bargain* allow anything resembling bal-ance to appear? Caleb was also weak, but he'd be surprised that you felt it necessary to maintain a dictatorship.'

'Now you're being melodramatic,' mused Malik.

'*Verdammter Tyrann.*'

'Why don't you just speak English?' Malik spat. 'Pick a language and stick with it; preferable, you just quit that ugly native tongue.'

'Better an *ugly* language than an ugly personality, you rudimentary Rumpelstiltskin.'

'Sorry to break up this … teary reunion,' interrupted John.

Malik turned towards the young exile.

'But I have a question,' John announced, with fog from his breath veiling the rage in his eyes. 'Where do you keep your secret weapons?'

Malik sheepishly shuffled towards the group. Without losing his re-assumed peaceful demeanour, he forced his palms forward to strike Lionel and Teresa, causing them to fall back onto their own palms. He then let Murray lean on him while he pulled him to the throne.

John remained static; utterly puzzled by Malik's manic movements.

CHAPTER TWENTY-FOUR

THE COST

Malik leant Murray against the keyboard console column while he tapped a sequence.

An unseen pedestal underneath the throne rotated it.

John was taken aback by the throne's recently revealed side. Three death mask-like faces lined the throne's lower region while another three were along the top, and at the midst of the throne's surface, a seventh—a living, weeping man's face—was crying tears of icy blood.

'Malik … th-this is monstrous … even for you.' Murray gasped. 'Especially for you.'

Malik blushed like a small child who was concealing a recent mischief.

'I wondered, for years,' continued Murray, 'what you did with their remains. There wasn't even a rumour about what you did with them … it's your personal guard that tried to kill you, but how are they still alive? If you can call this life. But I saw you kill them.'

'Well, I did, but they weren't dead for too long. I gathered up their itty-bitty pieces and brought them back,' boasted Malik. 'I considered reconstructing each individual but with strict obedience programmed into their thick skulls

… But then I thought it'd be more appropriate to forge this fabulous collage of heads—much tidier without those superfluous bodies. All they experience now is the sting of their betrayal … emphasised by the strategically placed probes in the pain centres of their minds. Unfortunately, now the only one who hasn't gone brain-dead from the pain is my favourite bodyguard.' Malik stroked the centre face, which scowled in pain and hatred. 'You should have quit before you were "a head".'

Murray groaned, trying to stand upright. 'Listen, Malik,' he said, 'I promise, I'll listen to your damn stories next time, but right now, my friend needs a dose of the Inferno solution.'

Malik coughed out a single laugh. 'Does he?'

'Caleb, what is the Inferno solution?' asked Toat.

Malik kicked Murray, who fell back onto his right side; he used his right arm to prevent his bloody skullcap skin from scraping the frozen floor.

'I don't explain things more than thrice,' replied Malik. 'That's why I need my minions … now, Mar, be a good boy, you can tell them.'

Murray looked up at Malik, seemingly uncertain whether he had permission to share revelations. Malik nodded in approval.

Teresa and Lionel dived towards Murray to help him sit up straight. John walked to Murray's side, with Toat in tow.

'The Inferno solution is a drug that counteracts Huon,' said Murray. 'Whenever you breathe inside Caligo's Plaza, you inhale airborne Huon particles that are being ventilated throughout the building. It isn't enough to enhance strength or intelligence, but it's enough for his purposes. The Inferno solution is the response to anyone openly speaking against Malik or is a threat to his authority …' Murray took a deep breath. 'Or if they leave without … without settling an outstanding debt … the Inferno solution is shot out of the walls of the plaza, injecting the dissident. The solution destroys Huon in their body, often inducing paralysis. But … but the pain receptors stay active and are attacked, making the person feel like … like they're burning alive. They are then taken … to be imprisoned—'

'No, no, no, enough details,' interjected Malik. 'And I don't *own* a prison, they are art galleries. You remembered rather well, Mar. Bravo. Feeling hellfire? Now, that is a fate deserved of a traitor.'

Toat hummed in thought. 'Oh, that is ingenious, Caleb,' he said. 'At last, you have truly impressed me!'

Malik bowed graciously as if he had received an ovation and tapped a key on the console's panel. A column arose from the iced floor, cracking through a thin sheet of ice; it rose to the summoner's elbows.

Sitting on the column was a glass case. The case's bottom was covered with red silk and it cradled a row of seven syringes, each filled with fiery orange liquid; the colour constantly yet slightly shifted.

'One dose of Inferno solution … I wonder … normally it would cost significantly more than you could pay,' expressed Malik while stroking his chin. 'You know what, Mar, you have been a great asset over the years: killing crazies, gathering some neat salvage. Hence, I'll be generous: for your special bargain today, you can either surrender your daughters to me—'

'That won't happen, ever!' Murray growled.

'Okay, so I guess that you choose the second option,' declared Malik. 'Like your friend, Scarface John, you will be my slave, until death or trade.'

'Since you brought that up … where is John Salt?' demanded the son.

'I'm sorry, what'd you say?' asked Malik mockingly with an open hand on his ear as he approached John.

'Where. Is. John Salt?'

'Oh. Him. Mar's pal … yes, Scarface was my janitor for a year—'

'Your what?!' asked Murray.

'*Jan-i-tor*. Yeah, I fixed him up after he nearly died,' said Malik, the over-enunciation of the first word dripping with mockery. 'To repay me, I made him keep my gallery clean; whenever you dropped in, I kept him locked in one of my lab cabinets. I didn't want you to get any crazy ideas of rescuing him.'

John's anger at Odin was burdened by guilt, yet his contempt for Malik was unbridled. He felt hatred for the self-styled alchemist more than he had thought possible. The spite felt suffocating.

'But I arranged a deal with the Lunatics, about a year ago now … a treaty actually, and one of the conditions for the peace was that I give a few odds and ends to the Loonies; hence, I gave up my sword collection *and* Scarface. The treaty has lasted a whole year thus far, regardless of your little imps knocking off a few every now and again; I surmise those Loonies really like swords, or Scarface is great at scrubbing toilets.' Malik laughed loudly, his cackle assaulting every side of the chamber.

John clenched his fist and punched Malik's cheek.

The laughter stopped as Malik spun a half-rotation from the force of the strike. He fell onto his face, and then weakly, he turned to look up at John. Malik rubbed his reddening cheek. 'That really hurt, you little bastard,' he moaned. The alchemist rose, scowling his twirl-ended brows. 'You know, just for that, I'm taking Mar *and* his greedy girls,' he announced, like a spoilt child. 'And you, young ruffian, can leave … empty-handed! You'll appreciate my resources when you're left with nothing to choke on!'

John gripped Malik's throat with his left hand.

Malik, however, struggled in vain, and even though Malik was taller than John, he seemed dwarfed by John's strength; the loss of domination caused sheer horror, which was clear in Malik's pin-prick eyes. He gripped John's wrist, but no amount of effort from his jerking arms could dislodge the grip around his throat.

'Oh … okay, you can take the Inferno solution, but not the girls,' bartered Malik.

John reached into his coat's right pocket, his hand returning with the glowing white pill probe; its heat burrowed into the cold air, creating small white clouds around it.

Toat chuckled next to Malik. 'Sorry, Caleb; looks like the boy isn't your standard bargaining type,' he taunted. 'And you know, I almost forgot to compliment you on your sales pitch device. Truly clever.'

'Feels horrible to be helpless like your *consumers*, doesn't it, you demented freak?' John demanded as he continued to hold Malik's neck tight. 'How does it feel to be helpless, like everyone trapped in your twisted deals?'

'I didn't force anyone,' Malik cried out. 'They all knew what they were getting into. I only provide an outlet for those parasites! It's not my fault they overindulge! I've tried it *their* way; gave them plenty of autonomy, but they are rats! They tear and rip at one another to get the juiciest offer; they need a firm hand to rule them, otherwise they'd fall back into an insane frenzy.' He tried to struggle out of John's grasp; however, kicks to John's shins were ineffective, thus Malik was held tight. 'Now, p-please, please, please, let me keep my products! The consumers need me … they'll die without me! They need the bargains to give purpose to their insignificant lives. Come on, please! Let me go … If you let me go, I'll get Scarface, I mean, I'll get your dad back for you!'

John froze.

'He's lying, John.' Murray gasped. 'Once he makes a deal, he never, under any circumstances, changes it.'

'No. *No*! No! It's mine—all mine! Do you hear me?' Malik squealed and kicked. 'I made it, I earnt it, you can't take anything from me!'

John held the petite probe in the palm of his hand and then he forcefully shoved it up Malik's left nostril; it automatically crawled deeper into Malik's cranium. John threw Malik onto the icy floor.

Malik sat silent and then broke into painful screams. He gripped his scalp and rolled and twisted about, his belts' buckles clinking against the frozen floor. His eyes then became totally bloodshot, the red capillaries seeming to pierce his violet pupils, and his screams of amalgamated fear and uncertainty rang out.

Then silence fell.

Malik impotently lay on his back, his head tilted to the side, leaning his cheek on the cold floor. Thin plumes of smoke poured up out of his nose like a chimney.

John continued to glare, trembling from the anger that had erupted through the scuffle.

Tears of blood trickled from Malik's eyes as he mumbled, 'The bargains … The bargains.'

On the ceiling's screens of the frozen chamber, Malik's minions collapsed, only to instantly rise again, shaking their heads as if woken from a dream. Hundreds of the immersed "consumers" who were barely entangled within their cravings appeared to snap out of their dazes and slowly they began to walk away from their obsessions. However, many people continued to indulge their compulsions, simply with less fervour. A sense of peace seemed to settle among them despite them continuing their habits.

Yet the indulgence of idleness didn't last ….

Screens displaying footage from Adonis Electronics showed images of the technologically-engrossed individuals, many of whom lacked a few or all limbs, falling into the glass screens of light with which they were obsessed. The screens cracked while the users dozed peacefully.

In Bacchus Burden, the beyond-morbidly obese worm-people howled, as they couldn't continue feasting, their bulging bodies beginning to convulse. The fat slugs leaked fluorescent yellow bile, and then each one slumped down onto their faces.

The 'glitz and glamour' energy of Mammon's Mercy became different for the majority of the gamblers; they seemed less dazzled by the bright flashing lights, but they appeared to rather view them as unnecessary and garish. Nevertheless, they still greedily grabbed their tokens in their arms like a bundle of wheat and then hurried to the vast selection of cashier windows.

The employees posing as referees in the sport of Menoetius Arenas released a shrill cry through their whistles; the players and fanatics alike collapsed in clear relief. The heat of the arena finally must have breached their nerves, and the colosseum's tense humid atmosphere gradually dissipated.

In Voracious Vending, the giggling gits ceased their whispering glee and emerged from their respective lairs. They tossed their former idols' iconography onto the floor, as if its value now seemed to have lost the previous perceived value.

The men enduring the severe torture of their senses in Mars Armaments, as well as the individuals imprisoned in False Friends, simply stopped their cries; shackles unlocked, and vines lowered captives. The former prisoners look puzzled by their sudden freedom but also relieved. The torturers shook their heads as if waking from a dream; they began to help their former victims to stand or they placed a comforting hand on their shoulders.

On the back of the throne, the last sapient face seemed to make a peaceful smile, and then his eyes dulled as he passed away.

'Looks like the connection of Caleb's warped clone is completely cut,' said Toat. 'I'm almost impressed by how much of the madness was controlled by his mind. While it won't be an entirely smooth transition, unleashed from his control, the consumers are emancipated from their hells, whether by their own realisation or by death. I, too, suspect the employees from the less sadistic sections will continue their work, however, with greater individuality, and presumably no more cruelty.'

In the screen displaying a view of Section Two, the three subordinates of white-haired Carol were now reprimanding her—the crimson-haired Jane jabbing at her prior superior. Carol sulked as the girls criticised her fanaticism as well as her dismissive attitude towards the customers.

Among the sight of the over-bloated corpses in Section Three, a lone figure could be distinguished. The hazmat-suited man grudgingly mopped the vast mass of filth and grime. Although his face was covered, it was evident from his aggressive jerks that he was angrily cursing his occupation.

'I'm sorry that so many seem to be still trapped,' said John. 'I thought being released from Malik would give them freedom.'

'That they have now, Herr Smith,' said Toat. 'Caleb was partially correct in that he didn't give people their vices—he exploited them. However, thanks to your impulsiveness, there are many who will now have the chance to escape their sins.'

John gave a slight grin, feeling his rage at Malik collapsing as the man himself had. He acknowledged the information that the Plaza had been completely changed because of his sudden outburst. He glanced at Murray, who was lying on his back with his head held up by Teresa and Lionel.

Teresa gently stroked Murray's ruined face.

John rushed to Murray. 'Put your balaclava back on! Protect your face, your damn scalp!' he ordered.

'No, Junior, I don't think so,' mumbled Murray. 'The only reason I needed to stay alive was to stop Malik imprisoning the girls with him. But now, he can't hurt them. Besides, they don't … don't need me now … they've got each other, and that's good enough.'

Teresa started to cry. 'No, that's not true, Dad.' She wept. 'Papa John and you were the first ones who showed us kindness. Papa John has gone somewhere, but you can't go too! Not yet; not now.'

Murray grinned, his scarred face contorted and pale.

'You are not giving up yet, idiot, not when we still have a lot to do,' said John. 'We still have to rescue Mack and stop that would-be god, Odin.'

A colony of nanites bolted out of John's palms and completely covered Murray's head, forming a platinum cocoon.

The titanium mask around Murray's head throbbed and pulsated.

The silver mask evaporated then clustered itself into a cloud again; it returned to John.

John opened his hand; the cloud sank into it like water into earth.

Murray wore a look of total shock, which spread to Lionel and Teresa; Murray's face and scalp had been regenerated. Murray felt his face and head in clear disbelief, touching skin on top of his head for the first time since Malik had gradually robbed it from him. 'How?' he stammered, his emerald eyes darting side to side.

Toat chuckled. 'Well done. Bravo, boy!' the hologram complimented. 'But I too am curious. How did you know how to do that?'

'I … I just wanted to help,' replied John, almost equally surprised. 'I think it's like you said: the nanites do anything that their host commands. I wanted Murray to be healed. The nanites must have felt it, too, so then I just knew what to do. It's like they're giving me instructions on how to control them, because I just knew how.'

'Nanites with empathy?' said Toat. 'Rather, let's credit your intuition.'

Teresa jumped up and hugged John. 'Thank you, Johnny!' she cried. 'Now, all together we can rescue Papa John. You heard Malik—Papa's with the Loonies. So, let's get him!'

John smiled and gently pushed Teresa back. 'Thank you, Teresa; I want nothing more than to find my dad, but there is something I have to do first,' he said. 'For once, I can stop something terrible from happening.' He used his screwdriver to pry open the glass case that contained the seven Inferno solutions. He grabbed one syringe of the orange liquid, holding it in his right hand. 'So, this is the weapon you brought us here for?' asked John.

'That's the stuff,' Murray confirmed. 'Since I saw Lucy again all those years ago, I tried to find something that could stop Odin. When John and I were taken into Malik's circle of trust, I found out about the solution and how it reacts with Huon. But after John disappeared, the cost was too high, and even if I managed to get it, I couldn't risk my life by going after Odin. If something happened to me in Valhalla, making me absent for more than a month, Malik would take the Bright girls. But, thanks to you, we're all free.'

John looked at Malik; the smoke from the fallen alchemist's nostrils had lessened, blood from his nose and eyes formed a cold pool around his head, and he still whimpered, 'The bargains. The bargains.'

'What's going to happen to this place now he's like that?' John pondered.

'He always had an overinflated sense of his importance,' responded Toat. 'So, despite what he said, the plaza doesn't really need Caleb for it to function … after the reconstruction was completed, it never did. In the event the core controller is disrupted or, in this case, utterly shattered, then the main computer system will continue to act independently.' Toat pointed at the pipe-ridden machine. 'Even his "alchemy" apparatus will continue to absorb waste matter and turn it into produce, and the chamber will implement an automatic assembly.'

'Wait … Malik's products are made of crap?' John asked.

'Well, not *always*—any material will do,' replied Toat. 'Everything has the same base elements as the components of another. This machine recycles a lot of matter, which indeed would include excretion.'

'Yecch!' John groaned, then he glanced at Malik. 'So, what do we do about him?'

They all stared at Malik's fallen form.

'Just leave him,' Toat said indifferently. 'Despite and because of his self-aggrandised evolution, he'll be in that state for a few weeks, thus he is a problem outside of immediacy.'

The group shrugged and then nodded, although Murray walked over to Malik and kicked him in the gut. He then rejoined Teresa and Lionel. 'Do you want me to hold onto the solution for you, Johnny?' he asked.

'No, it's okay,' replied John. The Inferno solution syringe lay in John's palm, and he sent a command through his thoughts. Small tendrils grew from John's palm, engulfing the syringe lengthwise and then swallowing it into his flesh. The syringe and tendrils disappeared into John's palm.

'That's … gross,' observed Murray.

'I suppose it is, a little bit,' affirmed John. 'But it'll be safe and unbreakable in there.' He pulled back his sleeve to look at his forearm momentarily; it had a slight hue of silver as the nanites thickened to guard the solution. He then joined the others as they exited Malik's chamber through the black doors.

CHAPTER TWENTY-FIVE

THE BIRDS!

Outside of Malik's inner sanctum, the iced 'trophy' room had warmed slightly, and the temperature continued to gradually rise. Phil sat slumped on the melting chair of body parts. The group approached him.

Lionel patted Phil's leather-clad shoulder. 'Hey, buddy! Are you okay, Phil?' he checked.

Phil opened his eyes and lazily sat up. 'What?' His voice was strained. 'Who's Phil? I'm Bernd, if anyone cares … which nobody ever does.'

Lionel helped the piercing-covered man to his feet.

'You're burnt?' John asked.

'No, idiot, Bernd is my name,' Bernd said in a manner that sounded as if he had not slept in years. 'And why is it so freaking cold here? Last thing I remember was tripping on acid watchin' a music video … man, what time is it?' He examined his painted black leather outfit, staring at the white patches. 'What the hell am I wearing?'

Bodies began to slowly tumble from the wall, torsos slipped, and limbs limped; their frozen cells slithered away.

The group returned to the white room; the wooden doors that guarded the lift tube had vanished, and in their place was a continuation of the white wall.

'How do we get up to the surface now?' asked John.

Toat smirked and clicked his fingers; to their left side, a pair of shiny lift doors appeared from the wall. 'When Malik was disconnected from the network, I was easily able to access the system's mainframe to discover *all* of the *kleine* tricks of the plaza,' he boasted. 'And there *is* a way to exit this section, even when it's in total lockdown.'

Toat clicked his fingers again.

The lift doors pinged open.

The unlikely group entered it, with plenty of space to spare.

As Toat clicked his fingers once again, the doors closed, and the lift began to ascend.

'It really works by snapping your fingers?' asked John.

'No, it's called showmanship, *Kind*,' responded Toat indignantly.

When the lift reached its peak, it stopped with a light hiss. The doors pinged open.

The group was situated near the line of checkout stations of the Plaza's Section One, near the shabby shacks constructed from shelves and furniture.

Murray rolled his head side to side; it seemed he was readjusting himself to the sensation of skin stretching over his scalp.

'Lionel, is there a sick bay or hospital somewhere in here?' John enquired.

Lionel nodded.

'Then can you take Phil … err … Bernd there so he can recover?'

Lionel nodded again.

'I'll help,' said Teresa, allowing Bernd to lean on her shoulder as well as Lionel's. Teresa and Lionel then began to skip away, much to the blatant irritation of Bernd.

'Dad!' a voice cried in alarm. Belle ran into Teresa. 'Oh, Terry, where's Dad?' she pleaded.

Teresa pointed towards John, Murray, and Toat; she and Lionel continued to assist Bernd.

'Oh, Dad! I've been looking for ages!' cried Belle, embracing Murray.

'It's okay, Belle, I'm here,' consoled Murray. 'I've gotta see what's wrong.' He then appealed to John. 'Can you help out again?' he asked him.

'If it can be quick,' said John. 'I need to get going before time runs out. I must stop Odin, no matter what it takes.'

Do you have the strength? scoffed a cruel voice echoing inside John's skull.

John felt as if his head was burning from inside. He fell to his knees, gripping his head, growling in agony. He looked around in abject terror.

'What's the matter, Johnny?' asked Murray.

Did you really think you could escape my grasp? mocked the voice. *Ever since you thought you escaped, I've been tracking you. I admit, you vanished from my scope for a while, but now I know exactly where you are.'*

'O-Odin, h-how are you doing this?' stammered John, gasping from the stabbing and gnawing sensation in his skull.

I am a god, you demon, said Odin's voice. *Nothing is beyond my grasp.*

'What's the matter, kid?' asked Murray.

John's eyes became light blue with vertical pupils akin to a reptilian eye. He smirked, with a malicious aura emanating from the grin. He looked up at Murray. 'Well, aren't you a sight for sore eyes?' said John, with Odin's spiteful voice echoing him.

Murray and Belle fearfully stepped back away from John.

'Who the hell are you?' demanded Murray.

'Now, now, is that any way to greet your dear older brother?' mocked Odin via John.

'Theodore?' beseeched Murray. 'What have you done to Johnny?'

'You behold Odin; and your precious demon will be fine,' Odin said. 'One of my agents delivered the information that you are in that buried satellite. So, I sent a wonderful present, waiting for you to emerge.'

'Take me to the entrance!' ordered John in his own voice.

Belle and Murray held John's shoulders to keep him standing.

And while John grasped his burning cerebral cortex, Odin's cruel cackle taunted the trio.

'The entrance is where the problem is!' said Belle.

The trio reached the entrance, passing through the sliding doors and into the entry corridor. Claire was positioned behind the large sniper rifle while, behind her, upon a metallic lounge, were seated two panting men in tattered, bloodied, and dirtied white business suits.

The two men each wore a pendant around their neck, adorned with a small silver crescent moon. One of the men was bleeding profusely from the side of his head as one of his ears had been torn off. The other man hugged his own abdomen, trying to keep his intestines from tumbling out.

'I will release my hold over your mind, demon,' spat Odin's voice. 'I am a god, after all; it wouldn't be righteous if you didn't have a chance to fight for your wretched little life.

'You will fight as well, Murray, unless you'd prefer to run away again. Enjoy my gift; from my heart to all of you.' Odin's cruel laughter rang in John's ears, but it gradually faded into silence.

John stood without assistance, as the blinding migraine had faded with Odin's laugh. His eyes reverted to their original grey colour. He glared at Murray. 'Why didn't you say you're that monster's brother?' demanded John.

'That's not important now,' uttered Murray. 'You didn't need to know.'

'Didn't I?' John almost seethed. 'Damn it! Well, he was in my head, so I saw some of the things in his …. Most of it was blocked, but I did see what he was sending, and it was—'

On the rocks and dust that littered the path into Caligo's Plaza was a black swarm. The dull brown of the earth wasn't visible as a flock of what seemed to be close to one hundred ravens perched themselves all over it. The cloud of black sat cawing and twitching.

'It wasn't birds,' John thought aloud.

'Of course! *Verdammt*! Why didn't I realise it before? Nothing survived the Cataclysm,' said Toat, gripping his own head. 'At least, no wildlife has returned to *this* region; these black birds are synthetic organic entities. They are serving as Odin's vassals—his eyes and ears! That's how he found you so quickly. Now, I'll create a firewall to prevent another occurrence of possession, Herr Smith.'

'Okay then, umm … Belle, what happened to these guys?' Murray asked, turning towards the two men in pain.

'I have no idea,' replied Belle, dumbstruck. 'They weren't all bloody like this when I left to find you.'

'These Lunatics were stupid,' came Claire's monotone reply.

'Lunatologists!' said the one-eared man, exhausted. 'We were sent here on our monthly recruitment trip. By the time we were leaving, all those freaky birds were there. When we tried to leave, the damn things went berserk and attacked us. But when we retreated here, they … went back to being really still, but really creepy.'

'*Halt die klappe*! I'm trying to think,' declared Toat. 'Odin wouldn't just send sorges to peck you to death; because of my carelessness, he knows of your nanites and their regenerative capabilities … therefore, the birds must be hiding something …. We may as well confront the problem. John, go out to them.'

John sighed with great lack of enthusiasm, and then he slowly began to pace towards the ravens.

When the black birds noticed John, they ceased their twitching and cawing; their beady black eyes shone red. The ravens started to flap their wings, and then they took flight.

The frightening flock of ostensible birds flew around each other in a spiral formation, thereby taking the appearance of a black-feathered tornado. Then, one by one and at an increasingly rapid rate, they burst like water balloons. However, instead of water, a dark-green fluid, which seemed to contain silver glitter, plummeted and splashed onto the ground.

As the twister continued to rain jade, the fallen fluid crawled together, forming an expanding lump of green with silver sparkles. Eventually, every raven had erupted, while some black feathers continued to float downwards; the green globule grew larger with each additional crawling liquid joining it. The silver-dust-polluted emerald substance made a horrid bubbling sound that became louder as it enlarged. The mesomorphic matter began to throb and rearrange itself.

'Gross,' scoffed Belle.

John cautiously stepped back into the entry corridor, unsheathing his Bowie knife.

Claire fired ten consecutive shots at the gelatinous mass. Five bullets went straight through; small dust clouds exploded as the projectiles struck the ground behind it. The other five bullets were stuck halfway into the green globule; the bullets were dissolved by clustered pockets of silver. In one fluid motion, Claire pulled out the empty magazine, tossing it over her shoulder, and then she reloaded the rifle with a full clip.

Two columns developed from the globule's top, assuming the shape of a pair of giant spider legs with gorilla paws at the ends. Twenty more columns of green substance slithered from its lower body like eyeless, mouthless serpents, taking the shape of tentacles; some of their tips were crab-like pincers and some grew multiple twigs along their edges, forming centipede legs.

Thick, thorn-like protrusions emerged from the globule's front. Between the giant spider-leg shapes, the form of an enormous turtle's head grew, which also had four ram horns and massive vampire bat teeth.

The jade glitter-filled substance stopped its rapid shifting and solidified. The green hue faded as its shell was born around its body. Its torso became white and its spikes and edges black, therefore appearing like a tundra landscape.

The spider legs became a dark grey, almost indistinguishable from black; strands of grey hair extended from them. On the reptilian head, a large, vertically blinking eye opened. The maroon pupil darted back and forth, searching for its believed tormentor.

Claire fired again; the bullet sped and then struck the eye, unleashing a torrent of green blood that thickly sprayed over its front and on the ground. The creature bellowed with the cries of its multiple crudely amalgamated animals, and then the creature went limp, its head lolling to the side.

John stared at the creature. 'No way it was that ea—'

The creature, Odin's unleashed chimera, then roared, its limbs thrashing madly.

Claire fired the nine remaining rounds in the clip; each shot striking the chimera's head, causing it to look like green goo being pummelled by an invisible sledgehammer. As Claire prepared to reload again, one of the clawed tentacles extended and clamped onto the rifle. The rifle was ripped right out of her hands; she stumbled and then ran to her twin and adopted father. The pincer holding the firearm snapped shut, breaking the rifle in half.

Its giant, gorilla-handed spider legs grasped onto its own mashed mound of a head and then tore it off. The open neck became a maw into which the mangled head was sloppily shoved. The toothless maw shut.

Atop the headless neck, lumps developed and throbbed. Three thick snakes broke through from the lumps; each snake had a hissing mouth and scalpel-sharp gnashing teeth. Two of the snakes had the heads of grey wolves; they growled ferociously at the group.

On the chimera's mountainous torso, another vertical blinking eye opened; it accommodated the chimera's whole gut, with its frontal thorns seeming to be thick eyelashes.

The creature roared at the people perched behind the entrance barrier blockade.

Within its cacophonous howls, John heard a grumble that sounded almost like his name. 'Umm … Alistair, how do we … do we kill it?' asked John hesitantly.

'Well, it's a hydra-type chimera, so I'd say … with quite a lot of difficulty,' responded Toat.

'Well, no shit,' growled John. 'You know what I meant by *how*?'

'Most chimeras, especially complex creations like the hydra, have a central core or artificial brain,' said Toat, the hydra wriggling and clawing closer. 'That brain is what drives it and keeps it from falling apart … again … particularly needed for a composite combination of critters that are genetically incompatible. Deactivate the brain and the whole thing returns to its harmless liquid state.'

The hydra clutched onto the entrance columns to drag itself slightly faster; the wolf heads reached forward, biting at the air in front of it. The chimera's body caused the battle-beaten barrier to merely crumble under it.

'We've got a helluva lot of firepower to use,' exclaimed Murray.

'I think now would be a good time to use it,' said John shakily as he struggled against his nerves to stand up to the hulking horror clawing closer. 'You, Lunatics, help too!'

'Lunatologists! It's a legitimate religion,' said the one-eared man. 'Anyway, Gary's too hurt to move, let alone fight.'

'That doesn't mean you can't,' Toat pointed out.

The one-eared man hummed, frustrated, but he grudgingly stumbled over to Murray, who was next to a rack of firearms.

Claire and Belle were each given a rifle and a light-machine gun; the one-eared man was given two automatic-fire pistols.

Murray merely unholstered his Callahan pistol. 'Shoot its eye again!' he yelled.

However, just as he uttered the command, the hydra's eye slammed shut while its tentacles dived towards the defenders.

John cut at the tendrils, only managing to bat them away.

Claire, Belle, and the one-eared man fired persistently at the hydra; the bullets either bounced off or simply had their tips pinned into the creature's torso.

The hydra's left gorilla paw grabbed the wounded Gary and then hugged him against its body. In doing so, its bodily protrusions spiked straight through Gary's weakened flesh.

'No, Gary!' cried the one-eared man. 'May Luna save your soul.'

One of the wolf heads engulfed Gary, swallowing his corpse whole.

Murray fired the Callahan until each chamber had been emptied. The resulting explosive blasts around the hydra's heads knocked everyone, except for John and Toat, from their feet.

Those who had fallen slowly stood again; all cautiously aiming at the smoke cloud that hung around the chimera like a blanket.

The smoke vanished, revealing the chimera once again being headless; however, in the opening of its neck, more lumps throbbed and expanded themselves. Six eyeless snakes bloodily sprouted from the lumps faster than an eye could blink. They were followed by three maroon tendrils, which each ended in a thick yellow talon, one of which was similar to a cactus.

'Where can we get more explosives?' demanded John.

'Mars Armaments: Section Seven,' stated Claire. 'I'll go and get some.' She sounded moderately more energised.

As Claire started to run into the plaza, two snakes chewed the root of their neighbouring cobra. The cobra fell onto the ground; its tail grew and took the shape of a scorpion's. The detached cobra darted after Claire.

The one-eared man, Belle, and Murray, who grabbed a machine gun, had resumed fire on the hydra with their respective weapons and couldn't stop to cut off the cobra.

The cobra's tongue, actually a squid-like appendage, shot out and wrapped around Claire's ankle as she was running, causing her to fall. The cobra's tongue retracted while it slithered speedily forward, lime-coloured saliva profusely leaking from its mouth.

John jumped onto the large cobra and, using his blade, pinned the serpent's head through to its jaw to the ground. It writhed, irritated, as its feast was a foot away. The riflemen couldn't cease their barrage to assist, as they had to counter the hydra's frantic attempts to crawl closer. 'Alistair, can you destroy that thing's core?' John yelled over the gunfire and pinging of falling shells.

Toat shrugged. 'Probably not,' he replied. 'But I can momentarily stall it.' His eyes then emitted a bright-blue glow; the hydra and its cobra fell limp.

Claire freed her leg from the cobra's squid-tongue.

The shooting stopped as well; they carefully lowered their aim.

'Go … get the blasted bombs, *Fräulein,*' Toat ordered Claire.

Claire resumed her sprint to the Mars Armaments.

John pulled his knife from the cobra's head. 'What are you doing?' he asked Toat.

'Something similar to what Odin did to you,' responded Toat, clearly straining. 'He disabled your body by transmitting a frequency into your head. However, like me with the chimera here, Odin cannot kill you through wavelengths alone. Also, like me, he couldn't maintain the signal for long.' Toat's eyes returned to their dull-grey colour.

The hydra twitched and then became limber, gradually resuming its crawl towards the group, with its tendrils dragging its mountainous mass towards the defenders.

CHAPTER TWENTY-SIX

LIVING NIGHTMARE

Two of the hydra's snake heads simply plopped off its tundra-like body, joining their cobra brethren. Five of its tentacles detached and grew wolf heads. All eight of the abominations slithered into the plaza, meeting screams of terror from its residents.

'I don't think the hydra can fit through the doors itself,' uttered John. 'You guys, get in the Plaza to kill those damn snake things.'

Murray, Belle, and the one-eared man ran into the plaza.

The hydra's eye reopened; its bloodlust was so intense that it seemed to cry tears of hatred. A dozen half-formed centipedes and a hundred ants crept out from beneath its tentacles.

'Alistair, can you distract the hydra for a bit?' asked John while vainly slashing at the lashing and often creeping tendrils and stomping on the creeping small bugs.

'Okay, but I cannot maintain my holographic form farther than a hundred metres from my CPU, which is around your neck,' said Toat. 'So, don't wander too far.'

John sprinted towards the plaza's sliding doors to assist his comrades; Toat hovered in mid-air in front of the chimera's rage-filled eye. A cluster of tentacles tried to form a wall to block John, but he dived through a gap between them and kept running.

One of the tentacles pelted towards John, wrapping around his right leg. His run turned into a hop. The scaly tentacle compressed, crushing John's leg at the knee. He growled in pain while stabbing at the sturdy tentacle.

John's blade finally broke through the tentacle's shell, releasing a steady stream of dark green blood and a bitter scent. It released John then squirmed back to its body.

John's freed leg continued to crack and snap, and he felt as though it was being stabbed from within. However, when the pain subsided, his leg had healed. He ran into the plaza.

Six bodies lay maimed on the floor, each missing a limb and appendage due to the monsters' attacks if not earlier amputation to pay Malik. The bodies emitted a strong stench of iron that assaulted John's nostrils.

He followed the clap of gunfire and screams of terror. The trio of Murray, Belle, and the one-eared man were firing at the hissing horrors. The wolf-headed creatures had gone deeper into the plaza than John could go before surpassing Toat's broadcasting limit.

The snakes ignored and were even disinterested in the bullets bouncing off them, as they were relishing in ripping out the entrails of consumers.

The cobra used its taloned tail to impale a man, and then it chewed its prey's neck; the man's larynx was crushed by the cobra's jaw, thereby rendering him unable to scream.

The brown snake coiled itself like a spring and then, using its beak-like snout, it dived through the torsos of a cowering couple. Golden tokens claimed from the casino in

Section Four joined the shower of their blood; the snake's brown skin was painted red as it left them.

The naturally red snake sadistically swallowed a screaming obese person who had just escaped from their gluttonous habits in Section Two; they became a lump in the snake's body before shrinking as they were dissolved by strong stomach acids.

John gritted his teeth. He knelt, laying his free hand on the floor. Through his palm, his nanites consumed a fist-sized chunk of the mysterious metallic matting; this loss of the structure was hurriedly self-repaired.

John's symbiotes fed the broken-down material through his system, through his other hand, and finally into his Bowie knife. The blade softly illuminated a white light, lengthening it moderately while its density increased a hundredfold, becoming a tempered sword.

John charged at the closest serpent. With a strong strike, he decapitated the red snake; its red skin became slathered by its own green blood. The red snake's body flopped about like a fish out of water while its jaws continued to mindlessly bite the air around it.

The brown snake slithered closer towards a cornered family of three; as it leapt, John kicked its head. It crashed into a pile of wooden chairs serving as a shack.

The snake emerged from the timber, facing the exile, bloodlust emanating from its drooling mouth. The brown snake coiled itself, ready to spring. It jumped, mouth gaping, fervent to feast upon flesh. John ducked and fed the snake the length of his blade, slicing the top of its head off.

The brown snake was left with its lower jaw, and it could merely consume its own gushing green guts.

The cobra stood, glaring menacingly at John. However, before it could make another sound, the cobra disappeared in an explosion, its flesh slopping to the ground and its blood falling like raindrops.

As the smoke cleared, Lionel was dancing triumphantly on the green bloody pool that was the cobra. A now-hollow grenade shell pinged onto the sleek store floor; Lionel loaded another grenade into the launcher module that was attached to his carbine.

Behind Lionel stood Teresa clapping and grinning, along with Claire, who remained expressionless—both girls held an RPG launcher under each arm.

The red and brown snakes' bodies persisted in writhing, despite their seemingly mortal wounds.

'Yay! Well done, Lionel!' cheered Teresa.

'It was sure easier than those wolfy bastards,' returned Lionel. 'Aw, yeah!'

John smiled slightly, but briefly, as his grim visage returned. 'Murray, Belle, Lunatologist: you guys help the injured,' he ordered while sheathing his blade. 'Lionel, Teresa, Claire: you help me blast that damn thing out there away.'

Lionel placed his gun's strap over his shoulder and then grabbed an RPG from each of the girls. He tossed one of the rocket launchers to John.

All armed, they ran back towards the entry hallway.

As they exited the plaza, the group spotted Toat yawning while floating in the air; the hydra was furiously trying to bite, claw, or even just touch the hollow man.

Lionel and Teresa knelt; their rocket-propelled grenade launchers sat on their shoulders. They fired, and the projectiles spun around the air like dragonflies as they made their way to their target.

Upon impact, the explosion that the shots caused was unexpected to John as they burst into thick white clouds. The whiteness casually danced higher, eventually revealing the chimera caught in a prison of ice.

'What … what?' John muttered, confounded.

'I retrieved the closest explosives I could find,' said Claire. 'Two sub-zero warheads, and two high-explosive rounds.' She fired her rocket; the high-explosive round swivelled through the air almost gracefully. As it impacted the frozen abomination, a fiery explosion roared and ripped through the ice. The hydra looked like it had been feasted upon by a larger creature.

John growled in frustration when the chimera's tentacles twitched and its splattered green goo gradually slithered back towards it. He detached the high-explosive warhead from his launcher, dropped the launcher, and then ran towards the hydra. Using its own spike-covered torso, he climbed up the mass of the monster to reach the gaping crevice in the creature caused by the blast.

John shoved the explosive into the green swamp-like flesh atop the hydra, and then he stomped on it, forcing it in further and deeper. He jumped from the hydra, and while doing so, he sent a fine silvery mist from his hand into the chimera. The unleashed legion tunnelled underneath the warhead, carrying it into the belly of the beast itself.

The nanoscopic squad self-destructed to detonate the explosive.

Flames tore through the creature, devouring its flesh and cooking it while rending it to pieces. Green blood and goo splattered all over the entry corridor; small globules, however, still crawled towards the main body.

A small silver sphere fell out of the falling slop. It bounced onto the ground with a *ping* and then rolled.

John picked it up between his index finger and thumb. It seemed to have engravings all over its surface, mirroring an overhead view of a maze. 'Is this its core?' he asked.

'Indeed, it is, Herr Smith,' answered Toat, returning to ground level.

John held the hydra's core in the palm of his hand. He closed his fist around it, squeezing tightly. The sphere cracked, unleashing small dancing electrical sparks. John compressed it tighter still, and the core crumbled; he dropped it, causing it to disintegrate into silver sand.

The hydra's body fell limp; it began to melt like ice in the sun. Its body lost its colour and form, becoming dark green like its blood. The hydra's body bubbled down into a pool of green fluid, and the snakes in the plaza and the creeping creatures, similarly, melted into green puddles.

The group, bar Claire, who seemed utterly indifferent to the whole situation, sighed in relief.

The sheer amount of empty bullet casings that littered the entrance corridor's floor was ankle-deep. Many of the shells still had thin plumes of smoke slithering into the air.

John softly kicked through the shells, causing them to ping and clink. 'How long before Odin realises his monster is dead?' he asked.

'I don't think he would care, even if he does,' replied Toat. 'That pitiful mixture of a hydra was probably intended more as a terror attack than an assassin.'

'Who's Odin?' asked Teresa.

'Not a very pleasant or reasonable person,' responded Toat while adjusting his oval-rimmed glasses.

Murray, Belle, and the one-eared man exited the plaza.

'How are the injured?' John enquired.

'Well, the ones who aren't already dead should be fine,' said Murray, wiping sweat from his renewed brow.

Belle giggled, pointing at the pool of green blood. 'It melted!' She laughed childishly.

'Anyway, how are you feeling, Lunatologist?' asked John.

The one-eared man groaned. 'Look, I'm fed up with that crap.' He moaned. 'My name's Franklin, not Loony, not Lunatic … wait, you did say Lunatologist, didn't you? Well, excuse me—I'll think I'll pass out from blood loss, okay?'

'Chill, Franklin. For a Lunatologist, you don't seem too bad,' said John.

'Um, thanks?'

'Lionel and Teresa, can you take your new friend to the infirmary?' John asked.

Lionel and Teresa locked arms around Franklin. 'Okay-dokay!' they responded simultaneously. 'Come along, Franky.' They pushed the semi-belligerent Franklin into the plaza; empty bullets jingled as they were shifted by the duo's merry march.

'Back to the great rescue, Herr Smith?' Toat probed.

John nodded affirmatively.

'Well, if you want to be faster, you can use your nanites to lessen your weight and increase muscle strength, ergo making you far swifter,' Toat suggested.

'I'm coming with you,' announced Murray.

'No … you really shouldn't,' John countered. 'You've just recovered from a long near-death experience; you can't risk what I've given y—'

'No, Johnny, I really should!' interjected Murray. 'Odin's an evil bastard, but he's still my brother; I'm sorry I didn't tell you sooner … if you have to kill him, so be it, but I'll be there for him at the end.'

'Dammit … all right, fine,' said John. 'But I need to hurry to make it back to Valhalla faster … I apologise in advance.'

'Apologise for wh—'

John placed a hand on Murray's forehead before he could finish his question; nanites reacted with Murray's brainstem, knocking him unconscious. John draped Murray's body over his shoulder, lifting him up, and then he began his departure.

'Wait!' implored Claire.

John turned to face her.

'Thank you for saving his life. Please make sure he stays safe … and when you guys get back, we can all look for Papa John together.'

John smiled slightly and nodded; he broke into a sprint, his speed not hindered by Murray's unconscious form.

CHAPTER TWENTY-SEVEN

RUNNING BEFORE TIME RUNS OUT

John ran with the weight of Murray over his shoulder and Toat flying effortlessly by his side; he ran, remembering the rocky road and smooth dune route to Valhalla.

Approaching Lunacity at night, it offered a more powerful presence, as its myriad lights illuminated the surrounding area and climbed up the sky itself. Lights were organised into patterns mirroring the stars themselves—although the real ones were smothered by light pollution.

While a white-suited greeter tried to run alongside John, his pace was too swift, leaving the man panting, hands on his knees. Just as swiftly, the runner reached the other end of Lunacity, leaving its vibrance behind him.

Dust flew up as John ran; it floated momentarily, then it either vanished with the wind or resettled upon the earth. John slowed his pace when he heard Murray groan to signify his reawakening.

'Well, well … seems like Herr Murray is more resilient than you thought,' said Toat, smirking while crossing his arms.

'Put … me … down, Johnny,' Murray implored.

John knelt, planting Murray's feet on the ground, allowing the older exile to stand on his own.

'What'd you knock me out for?' asked Murray while rubbing his forehead.

'Sorry, but I needed to move fast, and it's not like you'd just let me carry you,' replied John.

'Okay … fair enough, but now, aside from a slight headache, I'm feeling like my old self,' Murray said. 'So, we don't have to stop to rest at all.'

A raven glided down and then perched itself on rubble close to them. It stared with its beady red eyes at the travellers while cawing innocently. Murray unholstered his handgun and shot it; the black bird was consumed in a plume of flame and smoke. All that remained of the raven was crumbling ash and scorched feathers.

'A bit excessive, wasn't it?' asked Toat.

Murray shrugged as he holstered his gun in the pouch on his gold belt. The exiles and hologram retraced their path towards the vast crevice that contained the Valhalla facility.

'Murray, why didn't you say that Theodore King was your brother?' John asked.

'What difference would it have made?' Murray sighed. 'Would you have trusted me more or less? Would it make you reconsider killing him? No. I didn't tell you, but only because you didn't need to know; you needed to focus on rescuing my nephew rather than feeling uncomfortable around me because of my brother's actions.'

'I don't plan on killing anyone,' said John, 'if it can be helped.'

'I don't know if my brother could even see reason anymore,' Murray said with seemingly heavy mourning. 'Imprisoning his own son and nephew to suit some twisted plan …'

'Hey, Alistair, can you tell if Mack's all right?' John asked.

'I cannot say,' said Toat. 'Odin has placed a firewall around Valhalla's servers, so I cannot hack into the system without actually being inside the facility.'

'Okay … well, then, can you tell me what the hell that hydra thing was?' asked John, still shaken from the mere thought of the beast's presence.

'To, I assume, pass the time? Well, you know, it was another chimera,' responded Toat. 'The hydra contained nanites, which were programmed with a template of the monster and would always try to keep its shape, even after being completely ripped apart or contained in nearly a hundred separate vessels.'

'I know you said that chimeras have a constant order to kill,' said John, 'but why did the hydra start to break pieces off itself to attack anyone randomly?'

'The hydra was insane,' replied Toat. 'The core of the chimera commands its subordinate nanites to upkeep its body, but when it is whole, its urge to kill causes it to splinter; the overwhelming bloodlust is almost always due to a human element.'

'What does that mean?' asked John.

'Chimeras have no higher awareness from so many different animals,' said Toat. 'Therefore, a human mind, or a copy of one, needs to be implanted into the core to provide order over all of the intermingling instincts.'

'So, Odin was responsible for all that bloodshed at the Plaza,' said John. 'He made a copy of his mind for that thing.'

'Odin wouldn't copy his own brainwaves,' Toat advised. 'He wouldn't dare risk the creation of another self; no, he would have used a much weaker mind than his own.'

'Did you determine whose mind was in that thing?'

'Ja.'

'Who was it?'

Toat sighed. 'I'm afraid that creature's mind was a duplicate of that *unglückliches Kind*, Mack.'

Murray gritted his teeth.

'Now, now, not to worry, Herr … *King,* apparently …' said Toat, 'the *real* Mack won't remember anything that the hydra experienced; its mind was a copy of Mack's, not the original. He probably did not even notice Odin borrowing his memories.'

'That doesn't change the fact that a part of Mack was tortured with those other creatures,' said John. 'Was he so badly hurt that he went insane?'

'No,' replied Toat. 'He *almost* went mad; the child did not desire to kill. He was lashing out in panic. His fear would have driven any usual person completely out of their minds. The bloodshed was caused by the maddened creatures within the hydra; the animalistic natures mistook Mack's cries for help as a rallying cry for battle.'

'I suspect Odin's hand was more of an influence,' said John. 'He did seem obsessed with making me suffer.'

'Well, you know my hypothesis,' said Toat. 'You could try asking the traitor himself; the closer we get to Valhalla, the sooner you will have to face him.'

The ground ceased cracking and crunching as the exiles and quasi-human scientist reached the soft yet coarse sands of the vast, desolate desert wasteland.

CHAPTER TWENTY-EIGHT

HOMECOMING KING

After half a day of nonstop travel, they had arrived at the edge of the minefield that encompassed Valhalla. Murray pulled up his sleeve, ready to utilise his Jackal device.

John raised a hand to stop him. Instead of allowing Murray to use the Jackal, John knelt, ramming his fists into the minefield. A pulse wave emanating from his hands caused the sand to appear akin to calming ocean currents. The sands shifted, jumped, and then became static once again.

'What did you do?' asked Murray.

'I disabled the entire stupid minefield,' replied John. 'Or at least half … I think.'

Murray checked his Jackal; a small picture of an envelope with the word *NOTICE* underneath appeared on its screen. Murray pressed it and a message appeared, hovering above the device: *Valhalla blast zone signal lost*. It vanished when Murray pulled his sleeve down. He hesitantly stepped one foot onto the minefield's boundary as if he were checking the stability of a rotten wooden floor.

John casually walked onto the field.

Murray jumped onto the minefield; he sighed. 'Well, now that it's nothing more than any other sand plain in a desert, let's keep going,' he suggested while catching up with the pace of the younger pariah.

John and Murray then began to run, returning up the invisible trail that they had originally taken. They were travelling along the trail much faster, due to the growing sense of urgency within them both.

As the exiles were close to the entrance of the android boys' cavern and the arrogant arch at the foot of the hills, they rapidly slowed their pace.

'Murray, I need you to go back to Seven for me,' said John.

'What? Why?' Murray asked, undoubtedly confounded.

'The Seniors know about Odin, and I think they have for some time now,' John said. 'They know more about negative technology and counter-inventions, so they must know something about their weaknesses.'

'The Seniors? Those lying old bastards!'

'I know that they're self-righteous and manipulative bastards,' John admitted. 'And yet we may need them to help us stop your brother. Odin is too powerful for us to leave out any options for help.'

'Yeah … I guess it's worth a try,' Murray replied with a grunt. 'But how the hell can I get their attention out of that giant castle of theirs?'

'You'll think of something,' John replied simply.

Murray sighed, appearing reluctant, but then he turned towards the hills around Valhalla and began walking.

'Uh … Murray, Seven is that way.' John pointed towards the opposite horizon.

'Excuse me, Johnny, I haven't been to that pit for over ten damn years.' He growled, stomping past John. He then walked over the dead minefield, which still held particles of glistening silver sand, towards the ruins and—beyond that—the fortress-like structure of Seven.

A creaking noise broke John's attention away from Murray's slightly intoxicated march.

A trapdoor opened from the sand; a small grey-haired android wearing a dirty white shirt and blue overalls emerged. 'Hey! It's my man, John,' said Richie. His head then twisted to yell into the cavern, 'Hey, guys, look who's back!'

Howie and Leo climbed out of their cavernous hiding place.

Howie spotted John, and then he darted around to jump onto his back.

John didn't fall this time.

'Was it you who disabled the minefield?' asked Leo. 'Did your quest for a secret weapon pan out?'

'It did,' said John. 'And I'm glad you guys are here, because I need you to initiate a new mission.'

'Really?' asked Howie excitedly.

'You do?' asked Toat with amusement.

'Well, a mutual friend needs your assistance,' John answered. 'But he may look a bit different to you. He's on his way—'

'To Seven to convince your village leaders to help you stop Odin,' concluded Howie.

His brothers, John, and Toat stared at him.

'What? Can't I know stuff too?' said Howie.

The others still stared silently.

'Oh, okay. I have really great audio receivers. I heard them talking about it.'

'Oh, right … that actually makes sense.' Leo peered towards the horizon. 'I guess that's Murray out there … unless my optic sensors deceive me, Murray has … not got his hood-thingy on.'

'Oh, that is quite the change for Murray,' said Richie sincerely. 'Thanks for the heads up, my man.'

The trio of androids began to casually stroll towards the direction that Murray was heading.

'Wait!' called John.

They turned to face him.

'Make sure the Seniors don't kill him ... and you shouldn't kill them, either.'

The androids resumed their pace; however, Howie turned to John again. 'Trust us, we wouldn't do such a thing!' the orange overall android said with a half-grin.

John raised an eyebrow, but he smiled as he watched them head towards Seven.

'Well, what now, O Brave and Wise Leader?' asked Toat.

'You already know,' replied John. He then added, 'You oh-so-witty mad scientist.'

CHAPTER TWENTY-NINE

THE ÆGO OF ODIN

John marched towards one of the swerving metallic paths that was carved into the base of Valhalla. He ran so fast up the path that in comparison, his earlier ascent seemed to have taken months. He reached the arch at the end of the path, beyond which was one of six elevated pathways that led to the top entrance of Valhalla. 'When will Odin know we're here?' he asked Toat.

Before Toat could answer, the dodecahedral structure in the pupil of the canyon's eye dissolved. It melted into a silver liquid that was absorbed into the platform that had held it like water into a sponge.

'Around now, I think,' said Toat. He vanished back into his control core cube.

The former entry platform now held a dark grey, hour-glass-shaped object.

John's quick pace enabled him to reach it within minutes.

The opaque hourglass was almost the same size as the exile; black domes were embedded into its upper and lower faces. They lit up red, appearing like Factorem's cybernetic eyes: red sclera, with white-rimmed red pupils.

'Is that you, Doctor Factorem?' John asked the hourglass shape.

The top eye receded into the hourglass. Out of its dwelling, whipping cables shot out, and then they swiftly bundled together. At the end of the cable limb, a spike grew so quickly that it seemed to have been fired out.

The limb rapidly extended; it impaled John through his gut, just below his sternum. The boy coughed blood onto the mesh of dark cables.

The hourglass shape itself loosened and broke into several other cables, all swivelling and then wrapping around the limb.

The limb grew thicker and longer so that it lifted John above it; his blood, flowing from underneath his chest, was pattering onto the platform. His nanites struggled, but they couldn't regenerate John nor interfere with their superior brethren that were in the limb.

John tried to scream, but he could only gasp as the air was stolen from his penetrated lungs.

The spike, which protruded out of John's back, split, and then it became like a grappling hook. The limb lifted John higher. It then, with accelerating speed, spun him around. Spinning faster and faster, it soon became a blur.

The boy's blood splattered a red ring around the limb.

The grappling hook folded back into a spike, releasing—or rather throwing—John.

The boy was flung through the air, flying and then falling towards Seven. However, his flight through the whistling and stinging air didn't force him that far. Instead, he plummeted down into the ruins of Necropolis.

With disorienting momentum, John crashed through the higher floors of one of the city's four gothic towers—weathered windows shattered, desks became splinters, cubicle sides cracked, plaster ceilings and walls fragmented, and monstrous statues tumbled—until John fell out of the opposite side of the building, with a trail of dust and cascading scraps of paper following him.

The force from the falling exile was so mighty that the ancient skyscraper crumbled, causing it to fold into its neighbour, and then both buildings collapsed into each other, dispersing dust, grey stone, and dirty glass throughout the city.

John's plummet continued unimpeded until he crashed through the tiled roof of one of the few still-standing and long-abandoned houses. His forced momentum caused the old home to collapse into itself, with a large dust cloud erupting in its place. The wood splintered and fractured, the tiles crumbled, and then the house was nothing more than another pile of rubble.

John sat up; his nanites had clotted his wound and strengthened his skeletal structure as soon as he had been tossed, and they were hurriedly repairing their host. A chorus line of red strings shot out of the boy's chest cavity like fishing lines.

John's symbiotes consumed wood and rock to rearrange the atoms to replace the flesh and blood stolen from John. The red strings reeled in, and then the cavity closed; the skin that had been damaged now appeared like calming storm clouds or water when struck by a stone.

John sighed when he felt his wound had been healed. 'You know, you guys could've warned me about that damn spike thing,' he said to the nanites. He then stood up and bolted towards Valhalla.

But then he stopped short of the inactive minefield as an odd sight captured his gaze.

From behind the hills of Valhalla, a thick tendril of a single cable extended; at its tip was a flat platform. Standing atop the platform were two figures.

The behemoth tendril bent down, and then it reached the opposite side of the sand field. Its passengers stepped from the platform. The thick cable swiftly retracted back into the canyon, whipping up gusts of wind in doing so, driving the dust from the fallen buildings back into the earth.

Of the two figures, one was profoundly more muscular and moderately taller; the sunlight gleamed from Odin's shining shark smile, and he brushed a loose strand of his silver hair to join its slicked-back brethren.

Next to Odin, the slightly shorter figure was clad entirely in black robes in a similar manner to the Seniors; however, the figure's head was completely wrapped in royal blue bandages, with some gaps atop its head revealing light-grey hair. The bandages also had an opening for the figure's left eye, which was filled completely with a red light. It wore red boots like Odin. Around its hips was a silver belt made of a chain.

Odin and the dark figure both began to walk across the sand field towards John, who stood rigid.

The pair stopped mere metres from John.

Odin had less grey skin covering his metal skeletal structure than he had during their prior encounter; his silver ribs were easily visible, as the grey skin struggled to stretch over his sternum and around his back and hips. His arms still had most of their flesh left, as before, while his shoulder blades had no covering at all. His few remaining innermost organs were contained within a hybrid of flesh and metal muscles on his waist. What skin did remain also struggled to hold down throbbing green pipe-like veins. 'Greetings, once again, demon,' jeered Odin. 'Are you prepared for your final judgement? Prepared for your long-awaited punishment?'

'Spare me your long-winded threats,' said John, squinting. 'I acknowledge my fault and responsibility for making you into what you are now, and I'm sorry. I'll say this once: release Mack and stay away from Seven, or I will be forced to make you.'

Odin stared at John silently, his red right eye glaring at his fellow pariah. He then crushed the silence by laughing loudly, an increasingly cruel cackle. 'What? I appreciate your bluntness,' asserted Odin, 'but no matter what a demon does, my divine mission of salvation will come to pass.'

'Salvation?' repeated John.

'Yes, the Sevenites have nothing to do with the schemes of the Seniors,' said Odin. 'They are prisoners just as I was; I will show them mercy. The Seniors believe that time and design will allow utopia, but I know the truth … it only takes power and a strong will. Therefore, the people shall be liberated into my hands. I will give all of them a stronger dose of Huon and, through my will, they shall be reborn as my unstoppable soldiers, ready for a revived world.'

John feared the reality of Odin's plot. He already understood the threat to Seven, but the dark ambition expanded the danger to the odd, though friendly, Lunacity and all of the people in the Plaza, including his self-appointed yet endearing adopted sisters, the Brights—John dreaded the suffering that would be done to just two settlements he knew, and he couldn't comprehend the many unseen who would also be mercilessly subjugated.

'Only the Seniors will perish,' said Odin. 'And with all their planning, all their control, time will reward them with the grave … is that not the best way to punish them, demon?'

'What do you think?' said John. 'I won't allow you to turn the Sevenites into your puppet army. While brief, I recall how vile it is to be connected to your mind; so much hatred is poison. The villagers don't deserve to feel as rotten as you do. And the Seniors may be bastards, but that doesn't give you the right to kill them.' John's hand hovered over the hilt of his sheathed blade. 'Now I have nanites like you, I can stop you, but it doesn't have to be this way. Please, stop yourself, now.'

Odin laughed again. 'I'm sorry, but did you *really* believe for a second that you could even hurt me?' he mocked. 'You've already proven that you can't best me; otherwise, you wouldn't have so kindly asked for my surrender. No. You are merely a freak, and we are divinity.'

'And *we* being you and who else?' demanded John.

'In due time, demon, in due time,' Odin responded. 'First, I would like to congratulate your impressive and swift slaughter of my creation.'

'Alistair told me that you made a copy of Mack's memories and imprinted them in that monster's mind,' John said.

'Yes … took you some time to notice,' asked Odin.

'I know that Mack would be angry at me for dragging him into Valhalla, even wanting to kill me for it,' John admitted. 'But why did you make that monster start arbitrarily massacring people in the Plaza? They were innocent, so why would you target them?'

'Innocence is as relative as cruelty,' Odin calmly replied. 'Yet I programmed no such instinct to kill. I just used an already constructed chimera, admittedly a rough creation, then implanted a copy of the little boy's memories into its core, although the chimera didn't realise that it wasn't the *real* Mack, so to answer your question: the innocent boy just snapped … misery loves company.'

'Speaking of miserable company,' John said quickly, to contain his building rage, 'who's your friend?'

'I think you mean *your* friend,' Odin retorted, placing a hand on the mummy-headed figure next to him. Odin's red eye shone as he gestured to the figure next to him. 'Come now, show your old buddy that you're okay.'

The figure rapidly unravelled the blue bandages from its head, carelessly tossing them onto the ground. The figure's hair was a light grey, almost white like Odin's, but it was thicker and wildly unkempt. His skin was pale but still retained some flesh colouring, unlike Odin's.

'C … C … Connie?' John asked, terrified at the evident answer.

The figure opened its eyes; both were organic and yet they were filled with unnatural red light.

'Close enough … but so much more,' advised Odin.

'You monster! How could you do that to your own son?!' John yelled.

'Exactly—*my* son; it's only natural for him to join his father in godhood,' said Odin. 'He once was the son of that shadow of a man, my mortal identity, but now he is my son once again, worthy to be the son of the mightiest of all gods.'

'You bastard!' roared John, unsheathing his Bowie blade. He pulled his arm back and then lunged towards Odin.

Odin caught the blade with his left hand; he crushed it as if it were merely frail glass.

Odin then made a fist with his right hand and punched John's chest with so much force that John was knocked over a metre back, with all his ribs fractured.

John coughed blood, groaning in agony. However, the pain subsided quickly as his bodily regeneration speedily re-aligned the bones and sealed the ruptured blood vessels. John then stood up.

'I must really thank Doctor Toat for deifying you,' Odin taunted. 'Thanks to his work on you, your demise could last for days, even months … and there will be such agony that you will be begging for death—'

'I'm here, too, you poor imitation of a greater myth,' Toat said, his hologram appearing next to John. 'I'm here, so stop your tiresome rambling.'

'Yes … there you are,' said Odin. 'Thank you for making this child into a god. His suffering can last so much longer than his sickly, soft, pre-Promethean body could withstand …. Now, introductions are over; you shall cower before my divine wrath. Behold those ruins.' Odin lifted his right arm to point at the vast decrepit remains of Necropolis; small clouds of dust still lingered throughout the city blocks. He pointed. 'Watch as I bring order to destruction.' Odin opened his lifted hand, his wide palm facing the ruins. On Odin's metallic palm, a small sphere of the purest black light generated.

The black orb expanded, with bolts of white electricity twisting and twitching around it. The sphere of light expanded further, and it now appeared like a translucent view of a planet, with a black mantle and white core; from it emanated an eerie blue aura.

Toat exuded absolute terror.

The sphere of light was larger than Odin, yet it still clung onto his palm and didn't touch the ground, with no evident effort on his part. The bolts of white electricity became more frequent and erratic, lashing the air like a flurry of whips.

Odin's muscles flexed, and he gritted his teeth.

The light orb ceased expanding, and then it started to compress itself. The white core was again dominated by darkness. The sphere compressed into a size no larger than an apple; the white lightning crackled audibly while rapidly whipping at every direction.

Odin grinned. 'You ought to kneel, demon,' he said.

John stared at him, confused.

Odin forced the orb of pure black light forwards; it flew above John's head.

The dark sphere shot through the air, swerving to avoid any desolate figure or structure with an agility that suggested sentience, until reaching the very midst of Necropolis.

Odin closed his fist; the orb stopped dead in the city's epicentre, and then it dropped onto the ground. As soon as the smallest curve of the dark light touched the cracked road, the sphere erupted.

An explosion of white light almost instantly enlarged to devour the entirety of the ruins. Every rock, splinter, speck of dust, every structure, every statue corpse—everything that the light enveloped evaporated into molecules. The molecules broke up into atoms. The atoms then ceased to exist.

John stared, in shock, at the dome-shaped explosion. The bright white explosion was horrifying to behold, not just due to its sheer destructive power, but also due to its total silence.

The silent white cataclysm lingered for moments, and then it faded like an inverted sunset. In its wake, it left nothing—no light nor shadows; it was a void of emptiness.

A hole as wide as the blast in the ozone exposed the darkness of space and its bright stars; day became a false night. This vacancy didn't last, however, as the world tried to correct its loss.

The void sucked in light first in a whirlwind of the colour spectrum, and then matter followed suit.

John lost his footing as he was dragged by an ocean of sand flowing into the hollow.

A thunderous chorus of howls erupted as the void was filled by a maelstrom of matter. Earth and light flooded the region of nothing, spiralling simply like water down a drain.

A sonic boom assaulted all directions to signify the loss of existence had been reimbursed. Instead of the ruins of Necropolis, now there was a relatively flat plain of sand and dust; the rusty sky above it held spiral rainbow clouds, which returned to their regular flight pattern quickly.

CHAPTER THIRTY

BLOOD BROTHERS

A small patch of sand rustled and then burst as John pulled himself up out of his enforced entombment. He stood up, spitting out sand and patting dirt out of his hair and from his face.

In a daze, the boy struggled to gather his bearings. Although still far apart, the fortress-like structure of Seven and the hills that contained Valhalla seemed to have crawled slightly closer than they had been before.

Some of the iron shielding on Seven's walls appeared to have bent towards where Necropolis was no longer; small fragments of the metal had been torn off like paper and had been dragged a hundred or more metres from their station, revealing the oft-eroding cement walls that they had guarded.

The hills around Valhalla had crumbled slightly. The partial flensing of the mountain's stone skin revealed sections of metal mountains that were hidden under them.

Odin and Colonel hadn't fallen; they began to calmly walk towards John.

'You fool, Odin!' Toat chastised as he reappeared. 'You cannot use antimatter as a weapon!'

'I disagree,' retorted Odin. He pulled the skin on his right arm back like a shirt sleeve, revealing his forearm as hollowed and filled with three transparent orbs between his radius and ulna bones. In each of the orbs were two smoothed pyramids, which were positioned in their containers so that they appeared to be mirror images. The pyramid tips met at a tiny white sphere that emitted an eerie blue aura. 'Magnificent ... isn't it?' he mused; he pulled the skin back down his arm to re-cover the orbs, and the split epidermis sealed when it touched the flesh of his hand. 'Look around ... my antimatter bomb works beautifully.'

'No! You conceited cretin!' yelled Toat. 'By using antimatter in its basest form, you risk ripping not only the planet, but tearing reality itself apart!'

'Oh, please,' Odin said dismissively, 'do you really think that I would use it so recklessly? I've been analysing the variables and possible outcomes of the generator for years. I merely miniaturised the channelling of antimatter that *you*, so-called Uplifted, couldn't use to its full potential.'

Toat scowled.

'What does he mean?' John asked.

'I don't know,' responded Toat. 'Parts of my knowledge about antimatter have been ... corrupted. All I know is that it has the potential to be either the perfect generator of endless energy or the weapon of nightmares.'

'Yes ... When I possessed that wretched child through you, dear doctor, I removed your knowledge of antimatter,' snarled Odin. 'But I left most of your data as it was, so you wouldn't notice: all you can remember about antimatter is that it makes such a weapon that it would inspire awe and dread.' He grinned proudly, which displayed his sharp teeth. 'But enough of that for now ... You, John Smith, will face the vengeance of your old friend Connie or—as he has been reborn—my son, Váli.' Odin sent nanites through his feet into the ground.

A throne of crystal-like glass grew from the ground as if it were a tree.

Odin seated himself tall on the throne. 'Váli is powered by an antimatter core,' he boasted, 'continuously pumping energy throughout his system. He will never tire, never stop, and is forever undying. Now, my son, face the monster that killed your brother and for far too long has plagued us; destroy him.'

Váli stood attentive and utterly expressionless. He charged at John, fist held back, and then he launched forward, striking John's left cheek.

John was hit with such force that he was launched, twisting through the air. His flight, however, was stopped by Váli's left knee rising to crush his stomach. Váli's right elbow struck John's head, sending John face-first to the ground.

John looked up at his assailant; Váli's red glowing eyes displayed no emotion, and yet they seemed to especially lack mercy. Using his right heel, Váli stomped repeatedly onto John's back. John screamed agonisingly as every collision broke his spine, which was rapidly repaired only to be cracked again.

Váli ceased his stomping and lifted John by enclosing his arm around John's neck. Váli's right fist hit John's face, then his head, then his face—each strike unleashing more might than the last.

Despite John's nanite-fuelled regenerative abilities, the punches were so fierce that almost every surface around John's head was leaking blood, which pattered onto the sand beneath them.

'What are you doing, Smith?' Toat demanded. 'Why don't you fight back?'

Váli released John; he then punched John's chest, sending him backwards while still on his feet, which scraped along the ground.

'I … I can't,' replied John, just before receiving Váli's kick to his right shoulder.

'What? Why?' exclaimed Toat.

'Be-because … I can't hurt Connie again,' responded John, resisting his body's urge to vomit blood.

'Guilt won't help anyone!' Toat reasoned.

'It-it's my fault … everything!' John continued his sorrow. 'I ruined so many lives … I-I killed Tommy …. I made King the ruler of Valhalla …. After everything I'm responsible for, I can't hurt my friend again.'

Váli headbutted John, clutched his arms, and then began to repeatedly ram his knees into John's gut. Váli let go of John briefly, enabling himself to grasp his old friend's throat with his left hand.

Odin cackled cruelly and clapped tauntingly, obviously relishing the 'fight' before his mismatched eyes.

Váli's right hand audibly cracked as he pulled it back into a fist.

'I'm … I'm so sorry, C-Connie … you were the best friend, but I only gave you pain,' stammered John through his suffering. 'If you can hear me, please … please, know I'm sorry.'

Váli's fist shot forward. However, it failed to meet its intended target; John's left hand caught the strike and, like a Venus flytrap ensnaring its prey, compressed around Váli's right fist.

Váli released John's throat, and despite not having any distinguishing traits, his red eyes focused on John's seemingly sentient left hand that encompassed his right.

John looked at his left hand; his face contorted from the beating as well as confusion. Váli shook his right arm, trying to shake off John's hold of him. Váli started to pummel John's left arm with his own, but his action didn't disrupt John's grip. 'Wh-what's … going … going on?' asked John, feeling ill as his vision became blurring.

'Idiot! I warned you, didn't I?' Toat reprimanded. 'Your nanites will do anything and everything to keep their host safe. Even if that means that they must take control over your body!'

John's right hand jammed into the ground while his left endured the assault and maintained its hold on Váli.

Odin sat up straight. His eyes, or at least his blue left eye, indicated that he was intrigued by the unfolding event.

Through John's right hand, particles of sand, and some metal specks, were devoured by his nanites; they absorbed the material, enabling them to duplicate themselves, exponentially increasing their numbers. John screamed as he felt as if volcanic eruptions were contained beneath his skin. His left hand released Váli, who leapt backwards to observe and try to analyse his changing opponent.

John's left hand joined the right in the ground, allowing the nanites to absorb more matter to create more of their kind.

Both of John's hands then soared out of the dust, compelling him to stand in the process. Every single one of his pores began to leak blood. John screamed as crimson fluid seeped through his skin, the burning pain tormenting his senses.

The exterior coat of blood darkened slightly, it then hardened, becoming stronger; gradually, it became like another layer of skin over his flesh.

John stood, the top of his body bent over, his arms and head limply swaying. Then he stood upright and sombre; his skin was covered by dark red shroud, and his eyes were emitting red light.

Odin leant forward on his glass throne, his interest now clearly elevated.

John charged towards Váli, who charged likewise.

Their movements were almost echoes of each other. Both stretched an arm back, prepared to punch each other. When they were a breath away from clashing foreheads, they launched their respective strikes.

They commenced in a volley of inhumanly strong strikes. An unseen spherical boom grew each time their fists collided with their adversary's; the shockwaves made their presence known by the rings of earth fleeing from the pair.

The sheer power of the strikes caused the ground to shake; even the air around them seemed to tremble.

However, this tremendous show of might ended as their clenched fists hit the opposing foe's cheek. John and Váli were forced apart by the strength of the connecting strikes.

John and Váli ran at each other again.

This time when they met, John stopped dead in his tracks.

Yet Váli persisted in his attack; he furiously, albeit pointlessly, pummelled John's gut.

John's shining eyes faded to their regular grey and white; his head turned towards the left to face Toat, although with great strain, as his neck seemed to be commanding him to keep facing forwards. 'Ali-Alistair … make it … s-stop,' he begged. 'I-I'm trying to … trying to hold the nanites down, but … but I can't stop them much longer. I c-can feel them … they're trying to help me, but their help … is making me try to kill Connie … please make it stop.'

Toat swore loudly, and then his holographic body vanished.

The control core cube around John's neck latched onto his chest, retracting the chain that had held it. The silver cube liquefied into a minute, gravity-defying puddle. The mercury-like substance seeped through John's solid blood shield, as if it were rainwater into the sea.

Váli ceased striking John as his arms and head bent back; he stepped away from his opponent, whereas John fell onto his hands and knees, screaming as agony chewed his flesh like a carnivore gorging on meat.

John's exo-epidermis began to crack—white light being freed from the fractured shroud. He screamed so loudly that it wasn't too far from being a horrifying roar.

Váli stared intently at the agonising boy, his red eyes fluctuating.

'Stop standing around and obliterate that fiend!' ordered Odin.

Váli ignored his father's command and continued to watch John's tormented struggle.

John's solid blood armour completely disintegrated into powder that passively fell from him as black dust. His cries were then silenced as something crawled up his throat. Four times in succession, John belched black bile onto the sand. The regurgitated substance glistened under the sunlight. John coughed; a small silver object, which appeared like a writhing wad of gum, jumped out of his mouth. It squirmed and then morphed into a small silver cube.

Toat's human-sized projection shone from it; he stood next to John.

John picked up the silver core and shoved it into his vest's inner pocket.

Toat offered a hollow hand to lift John up, but John realised the hologram's limitations—Toat's offer was merely an attempt to be friendly, so John stood up by himself.

'What's that black sludge?' asked John, wiping his mouth on his sleeve.

'Nanites that I deactivated,' replied Toat. 'Not all of yours were destroyed, fortunately. However, I did have to expel quite a lot of them to ensure removal of the source of radical manipulation. It's near impossible for anyone to have their body filled with nanites and maintain control of all of them properly. Anyway, be more careful now, as you are significantly weakened.' Toat then vanished.

'I am tired of this,' announced Odin. 'Váli, my son, kill our bane!'

'N-no!' Váli countered, a hollow echo under his voice; the red light in his eyes was now fading, and his natural grey irises peeked through the bloody aura.

'What did you say?' asked Odin, his right eye shining strangely dark.

'W-we h-have to stop this … father. It won't bring back Tommy,' stammered Váli, falling onto his knees while his self of Connie clearly began to emerge from the subconscious. 'What you're doing … is wrong … Mother would be terrified of you; she wouldn't recognise what you've become … it makes you even worse than … than the Seniors … and you told me you were better.'

Odin slammed his right fist on an arm of his throne; the glass cracked, leaving slithering crevices down the throne's side. 'I *am*, and *you are* greater than them in every possible way!' he shouted. 'I also told you that to destroy evil, one must use force; it's because of Smith that your mother and brother are dead! He nearly killed you! So, now obey the one true god's order: slaughter that monster!'

Váli gripped both sides of his own head as if he were keeping it from splitting in half. 'G-get out of my head!' he yelled. 'I'm not … not … not a murderer.' He slumped onto his side in a fetal position.

Odin growled angrily; as he rose, the cracks in his glass throne spread, causing it to lose pieces of itself onto the earth.

Halfway up the side of the Sevenite structure, a clicking noise came from a large protrusion, which appeared to be cylindrical like the tail-end of a large aeroplane. A circular iris-like doorway screeched open; sparks leapt from the sliding door.

A silver ramp extended from just underneath the doorway, reaching down until its end was slightly buried in the sand a couple of dozen metres away from the three warring entities.

CHAPTER THIRTY-ONE

BATTLE OF THE GODS

At the midpoint of the ascending wall, out of the round doorway and onto the silver ramp, walked nine figures. At the front of the two lines of four was the red-vein-patterned and golden-cloaked Senior Masutā.

Behind him were the black-covered Zero and crimson-clothed Soar.

Behind them were two other Seniors, one clad in white, Lux, and one in green, Radar.

Behind them were Richie and Leo.

Finally, at the rear, were Murray, who yawned wearily, and Howie, who walked in a mock march.

Murray and the sorges were placed together at the edge of the ramp, while the Seniors positioned themselves shortly away from Odin.

'What the hell kept you?' asked John wearily.

'Sorry, but they didn't take me shooting explosive rounds at the fort too well,' replied Murray. 'They brought me and the boys inside to give us a trial or something, even after the boys proved that they were Haven sentries.'

Howie smiled at John, detaching his left hand to wave it with his right.

'It took that thunderstorm noise to convince them that Odin's attack was near,' Murray continued, 'but the shockwave that happened, it messed up their gate thing, so they had t—'

'Silence!' interrupted the deep voice of Masutā. 'I've run out of patience for the unalive children and you, drunkard.'

Murray crossed his arms defensively as Masutā marched towards Odin.

'Theodore King, you unwieldy child … what is the meaning of this chaos?' demanded Masutā. 'This is inexcusable usage of dangerous technology, which you cannot possibly comprehend. You're risking the stability of the planet and the survival of humanity itself.'

'I am in no mood for your vile pretension!' Odin growled, an orb of black light materialising in his right palm. '*Senior Masutā!*' He pelted the orb.

It struck the Senior leader's chest. The orb burst into a white light that devoured through Masutā's golden attire.

As the white blast faded, there was a void of nothing in the place of the Senior Masutā. The gap in existence was quickly filled, hauling the other Seniors and slamming them together; they then fell onto their backs.

Odin stepped to his fallen son and stomped on the boy. 'I still have some work to do on you, Váli, my son,' he seethed.

Murray ran up to Odin and grasped Odin's steel-like shoulders. 'Stop this, Ted,' he pleaded. 'Forget about the past. You don't have to take revenge on anyone. Just stop now, before you lose yourself completely.'

Odin scowled at his younger sibling. 'Are you really trying to give *me* advice, my worthless little brother?' he spat. 'You … you disgusting whelp … You expect a god to bow to your pathetic whims?'

Murray released his hold and stepped back in obvious shock before Odin punched his brother's stomach, causing him to fall back on the ground, gasping for air.

'Even as children, you were a scrawny runt!' yelled Odin. 'A whiny child starving for affection, completely dependent on attention from Lucy and me. And then you had the gall to side against me. Your ability to garner pity is astounding! Years after you abandoned your own blood for Salt, our beloved sister abandoned my new pantheon for you! She felt guilty about alienating you traitors and wanted to reconcile.' Odin bent forward as his hand gripped around Murray's throat, and then he stood to lift his brother in the air. 'I haven't seen her for years, and, until he fell into my domain, her son was living with those damn androids. I expect that she died in the wastes … all because of you!'

'She's still alive.' Murray coughed, struggling for more air than the grip around his throat would permit. 'I saw her eight years ago … she told me you had gone insane … and she was going to warn the Seniors … she was afraid for her son, and she was right, too, since you are now holding our nephew captive.'

'My son was murdered by a demon,' Odin said. 'If she lived, why would she abandon her own child? Besides, what do you know about anything? You know nothing, you piece of trash.' He pulled back his fist, preparing to strike his brother, who struggled for breath.

'Stop now!' commanded a baritone voice.

Odin looked at the Seniors; the white-clad Senior Lux stood in front of the other three. Odin then demanded, 'You exiled him, the same as me, why does his fate matter?' He dropped Murray, who gasped with his air pipes no longer compressed.

'Because he's your family,' said Richie. 'And ours.'

The sorge trio had moved to cover Murray. Richie was positioned directly between his brothers and the King brothers. Despite Richie's small stature, he stood tall against Odin.

The older King glared at them, and then he kicked Richie in the ribs, sending the small sorge past Leo and then tumbling and rolling on the ground, stopping short of the Seniors. Odin seized hold of Howie and Leo under his arms. He dragged them away from Murray. He compressed his arms like a guillotine, instantly crushing the android boys' necks; black blood sprayed out of ruptured synthetic veins and arteries. Odin twisted himself slightly until he broke away the heads of the sorges.

The bodies slumped onto the ground, black blood pouring from the neck stumps.

Odin dropped the heads, and then he crushed them, one by one, underfoot; small bolts of electricity and blots of black blood escaped when the craniums were smashed. With his red right eye blazing ferociously, he stomped towards his prone brother.

'Dammit! Stop it, Teddy!' pleaded the baritone-voiced white Senior.

Odin froze and mechanically turned to face the Seniors. 'What did you say? You dare call the greatest god in existence *that* insipid moniker?' Odin snarled while slowly pacing towards the Seniors. 'I only allowed three people to call me that, and since they are all dead, who the hell do you think *you are*?'

The white Senior pulled back their hood, letting loose long blonde hair. The Senior's mouth was covered by a dark mask, and as the shadows dissipated, they revealed eyes that were green and held immeasurable yet restrained misery. 'I am who I am,' stated the voice. The white Senior pulled their mask down below their neck. 'Murray is right, I am alive,' said the white-clad Senior, now with a calm, female and almost angelic voice. 'Teddy … you have become so much worse than the last time I saw you. You have lost yourself to your rage; pointless anger at an ignorant child.'

'Lucy,' said Odin. 'So, you have betrayed me, too … joining the damn Seniors?'

'You—you're his sister?' uttered John as he broke from his stupor. 'At my sentencing … you helped me escape the death penalty. Why would you do that? It's my fault your family was torn apart; why save me?'

'Don't flatter yourself, kid,' responded Lucy calmly yet grimly. 'I wasn't defending *you*, but defending what is right.' A tic in her eye suggested she wasn't as composed as she seemed. 'I do hate you, but I know it wasn't your fault nor your intention to ruin so many lives. Besides, one should never mix their emotions with their duty; thus, after joining the Senior Order, I decided not to retrieve my son. I was once Lucy Lambwell, but now I am merely Lux, a saviour in the service to the people of Sevenite.'

'You callous witch!' yelled Odin. 'All those years, I worried about you; all those years, I sent my ravens to scour the desert for you; all those years, I mourned you, but now … now I find you exactly like *them*: another sanctimonious Senior.' A black orb emanating a haze of blue appeared in Odin's right hand. He thrust his palm forward, sending the antimatter orb towards his sister.

Soar grabbed her shoulders and spun her around so that his own back faced the sphere of void.

The black ball of energy buried into Soar's back; however, it didn't burst. Instead, it burnt as a small sphere of white fire, with flickering strings of red electricity hissing around it. Soar's roar of pain sounded more terrible, due to his gravelly voice.

With shock in her eyes, Lux turned to face him. 'Soar, what have you done?!'

'Soar, you utter fool,' scolded Zero. 'You waste your life, your wisdom, for this child?'

Soar laughed with tiring exertion. 'Forgive me, Zero.' He gasped. 'It was a reflex … At the moment, my flesh is containing the explosion … temporarily … so please, Zero, protect our peo—' His plea was cut short as his body was devoured by silent white light.

Zero pulled Lux back from the consuming light. The void made was filled, and yet the remaining Seniors didn't fall into the vacuum again.

Lux fell to her knees.

'Guard her, Radar,' Zero ordered the green-cloaked Senior.

The Senior nodded in acknowledgment while kneeling next to Lucy.

Zero tilted his head from side to side, causing his neck to crack. 'Now, King, you really are quite the nuisance,' he said. 'You've got a grudge, I can understand that; hell, I even sympathise, but what I cannot tolerate is you murdering my people for that bitterness.' He ran with unnatural agility and darted around Odin, his black cloak sounding like the beating wings of Odin's vanquished ravens. Zero captured Odin in a headlock. And then he faced John, his red eyes gleaming. 'Smith, tear his arm off!' the raspy-voiced Senior commanded.

John stared stunned at him.

Odin struggled wrathfully, attempting to break free.

'Boy, didn't you hear me?' shouted Zero. 'Tear his right arm off! Hurry!'

John, although still stunned, nodded, and then ran towards the Senior and imprisoned self-purported god. He took hold of Odin's right forearm and began to pull.

Odin kicked John and crystal-like stalagmites grew around Odin's grounded boot, slowly piercing Zero and John; however, this didn't stop the tug-of-war with Odin's upper limb. Odin's arm creaked from the strain as Zero's grip tightened and John pulled away, partly to avoid the piercing shards of glass that continued to grow.

John tumbled back with Odin's right arm in his hands.

Odin screamed in agony; in place of his arm, a shoulder stump spewed out dark violet blood. The blood poured down his right side, staining his loose leggings and the dirt that he stood upon, as well as the glass spikes.

John stood and threw Odin's arm away while muttering, 'Yecch!'

Zero darted to stand next to John. 'Well done, boy,' he said.

Odin's screams of pain altered into laughter of madness. 'Do you think I'm defeated?' From Odin's limbless shoulder, thin cables shot out, whipping through the air. More and more dark grey cables sprang out of the stump. They calmed their frenzy by clustering together; they were beginning to assume the shape of the missing arm. Over Odin's new metal mesh-muscle arm, platinum skin slicked down, covering the dark grey cable mesh. Odin grinned while clenching and unclenching his regenerated fist.

'Wh-what the hell?' stammered John.

'I anticipated your limb could grow back,' said Zero as he bent down to pick up Odin's disembodied arm. 'I just wanted to remove your *ultimate* negative weapon.' He threw the arm to Radar, who caught it while still kneeling next to Lux.

Odin's smile changed to a sneer. 'It matters not,' he said. 'Even without the antimatter bombs, I can kill you all.' His red right eye became a blur, as Odin hurtled towards Zero. He grasped the Senior's throat with his left palm as spikes dug into the Senior's neck and volts of electricity were unleashed.

Zero growled as he fell onto his face, totally numb.

John turned on his heel and began to sprint towards the rigid castle ramp.

Odin's metal fist launched towards Lux; however, the green forest of Radar's back shifted to block its path. Odin growled in frustration, settling for kicking the Senior's back and sending him and Lux to the dirt. The mad god growled again, and then he began his own run to follow John. 'Where has your bravado gone, demon?' Odin roared. 'Running like your coward of a father!'

John flinched but kept running until he had reached the shutter doorway, when he felt the ramp tremble. Despite the ramp's rigidity, Odin's thunderous steps sent tremors upon each footfall.

John slammed the top button alongside the entrance, which caused the iris-like door to snap shut behind him. However, Odin's fist burst through it, and as John fled, the metal door began to be torn as if it were wet paper.

Breaching the ripped-apart door, Odin advanced as John vanished down a steel-mesh staircase. He then stormed the castle, lifting the long table in clear frustration, its red cloth falling from it before he tossed it against a white wall; the wall was scraped while the table shattered into pieces and splinters.

Odin followed John into the first of the shooting ranges. John's elbow shattered a glass case, from which he received a handgun and its magazine; he loaded the weapon and quickly aimed at Odin. John fired ten consecutive shots.

Dimples briefly appeared on Odin's face and neck as the crushed bullets ineffectually bounced away.

John's eleventh shot pierced Odin's left eye—blue becoming dark violet as his blood erupted from the pierced lens.

'Stop it,' seethed Odin as he tore the pistol away from John's grip, crushing it in his hand while dark violet poured down half of his face. The self-appointed god seemed unaffected by the loss of his remaining organic eye, as he continued to glare through his cybernetic red one. Odin grasped hold of John; spikes shot out of Odin's chest to impale the boy in place. Parts of Odin's own silver ribcage became dislocated from his sternum to claw into John's flesh further.

John was trapped in Odin's clutches.

Odin ran down the firing range, straight into the concrete wall, using John to guard himself from the brunt of the impact. The spikes then retracted and ribs rejoined their fellows, relinquishing their stabbing clutch of John.

Two javelins of crystal grew from beside Odin. He snapped them from their proverbial roots then used the pikes to pin John. The crystalline spears pierced through John's torso, pinning him to the wall.

John cried out, his arm striking down to break one of the transparent impalements. A third and fourth crystal javelin pierced through John's shoulders, stealing what little range of movement he had left.

Odin repeatedly punched John, which broke the spears. He punched further until the sheer power of the hits cracked the cement wall against John's back.

The strikes pushed the boy deeper into the wall, causing a tunnel to be formed until he was forced through the concrete barrier.

John's nanites absorbed the invaded remnants of the crystal spears, but they left him with the sting of their stabs.

Odin crashed through the tunnel, making it wider with his surging muscular form in the process. Crushed concrete followed him as dust, and his cybernetic eye shone with not just light, but also with fiery rage and hatred.

CHAPTER THIRTY-TWO

REVENGE

Within the bowels of the Sevenite castle, Odin swung John's body, slamming him onto the floor; Odin then rammed his right elbow into the young man's gut.

John gasped as air was driven out of his lungs, and he was pushed through the rock floor into a large cavern; a cavern that was hidden further underneath the castle. He fell through the air only to land with a smack on the cavern floor.

The cavern seemed to be as large as the Sevenite castle itself. It wasn't formed naturally, as the ceiling and walls were smooth and painted with a mural of a black spiral composition, and the floor was decorated with mosaic-patterned bricks.

John rolled onto his stomach and then strained to stand while dust showered down from the cavern ceiling's new hole.

Within his sight was a relatively round pool that took up the majority of the cavern floor's surface area. The pool's depth was impossible to determine because its base was hidden under the liquid that nearly filled it entirely. It was an indigo ink, violet colour, illumination of a purple grotto.

John realised that his suspicions were correct about the location of the Sevenite supply of Huon.

As he started to crawl towards the pool, a loud thump echoed behind him. He turned, and the first thing that caught his glance was the red light of Odin's right eye.

Odin's left eye had healed from the prior gunshot, and he chuckled as he slowly walked towards the crawling boy. 'Can you feel your end approaching, wretch?' he said while stepping closer, blades of glass grass springing around each step. 'Will you grant me the gift of your pleading? Beg for mercy, demon. Oh, how I dreamt of slaughtering you … I have a thousand ideas of how to kill you … it's a pity that, in the end, I can only use one.'

John managed to rise to his feet, only slightly increasing his movement.

Odin looked towards the Huon. 'Fascinating. Not as much as I thought, but it shall be sufficient …. You realise that no matter how much of it *you* can steal, it won't prevent me from ending your terror.'

'Likewise for you, King,' yelled Zero down the hole made by John's body. He dropped into the artificial cavern, cloak fluttering like ragged black feathers. As soon as the black-cloaked Senior landed, he flew towards Odin, who had no time to react before the Senior tackled him to the ground.

With the distraction, John continued to the pool, wincing as pain slithered up his legs with each step he took.

Zero, like an eagle holding its prey, trapped Odin face-first onto the floor with his talon-like hands around his neck.

Odin rammed his elbows into Zero's ribs with little result. 'Get off me, you decrepit freak!' he roared. His protruding spinal columns extended swiftly and punctured straight through Zero's torso.

Zero grunted in shock as the spinal spikes retracted, and then he was knocked away by Odin's arm.

Odin stood and then hatefully kicked the prone, wheezing, black-clad Senior. Odin scowled at John.

The boy was separated by mere metres from the Huon.

Odin growled while breaking into a sprint, desperately racing to close the gap between himself and John.

Zero coughed and then darted up to pursue the king of Valhalla.

Odin was an arm's length from catching John; however, Zero sweep-kicked his legs, causing him to fall onto his hands.

Zero crushed Odin's neck between his left knee and right elbow.

Odin choked as shock and agony were carved into his expression.

Zero grasped Odin's light-grey hair, and then he slammed Odin's face against the brick floor. He fervently punched Odin's back to keep him from rising again.

Odin then rammed his right elbow, repeatedly, into Zero's already punctured rib cage.

The black-cloaked Senior ceased his strikes because he was knocked back.

Rising to his knees, Odin used his metallic right fist to punch Zero's left cheek; there was so much force in the strike that Zero was thrown a dozen metres back, and Odin's synthetic skin on his right arm fractured and then vaporised into minute platinum particles, revealing the arm's cable-mesh musculature.

John was a few paces from the Huon pool.

Odin glowered and roared, '*No. You. Don't!*' He punched through the air with his right arm; his arm unravelled, becoming tendril-like cables again. The cables shot through the air and then enveloped John's legs, pulling them from underneath the boy.

John fell onto his stomach, smacking his forehead against the mosaic floor. The cables, like a serpent, slithered around him to grasp his torso, while also tethering him to the floor below. The artificial vines around John compressed, cracking the ground it pierced and causing the boy to scream.

'I told you that Huon won't help,' said Odin. 'But even still, I won't let you take a single drop. My ambition needs *all* of it; I won't let an abomination contaminate this life source! Now, know my pain, know your weakness … at long last, feel your life end!'

The grey rough-textured cables that coated John tightened further—so much that his flesh started to seep blood through lacerations and his bones struggled to bend without breaking. With intense difficulty, John reached into his vest. In his left hand, he held his screwdriver.

Odin began to laugh cruelly. 'Do you think you can stop my designs with that?' he scoffed.

John gazed into Odin's mismatched eyes, to reply, 'You can. Please, stop yourself. This is your last chance.'

'My last chance!' Odin sneered, tightening his cables. 'Save your baseless confidence, you're at my mercy; what exactly can you do to stop me?'

John thrust the screwdriver onto the brick floor, causing its tip to snap off. Using this new blade, he stabbed into his own right forearm. He pulled the tool, incising the length of his forearm to the base of his wrist. He tossed the bloody broken screwdriver away from the pool; it bounced on the floor and then rolled, leaving a thin line of red.

John reached into his open forearm and retrieved the syringe that contained the fiery orange liquid. He gripped it in his left fist, and reaching the limit of his strength, he slammed the glass tube against the inner wall of the Huon-filled pool. The syringe shattered; the broken glass, as well as the metal needle and plunger, splashed into the purple fluid.

The Inferno solution oozed down the wall. It flowed into the Huon. Almost instantaneously, the entire pool, beginning from the point of the solution's entry, bubbled and hissed. The Huon turned a blue darker than the old night sky, and then it began to violently churn, appearing akin to a hurricane-stricken ocean. The darkened water, despite its lack of life, seemed to shriek.

Odin stood shocked.

John punched the already unstable, cracked ground, which collapsed, revealing that the pool extended further beneath the floor itself. The floor's fresh boulder, which was entangled by Odin's unfurled arm, fell into the bubbling pool.

The fluid stung John's wounds as he fell into it, and he felt himself becoming even weaker the longer he was submerged. The artificial boulder, which had dragged them both, crumbled, leaving Odin's tendrils loose enough for John to slip away.

Odin howled as he tried to surface from the churning pool; his thumping heart could be heard defiantly struggling against the cold grip that closed tighter and tighter around it.

'I'm sorry. I made you.' John gasped above the surface. 'So, I must unmake you.'

Odin roared angrily yet also miserably as his metallic body started to drag him below the liquid's unsteady surface and his organic material became stretched and taut from the Inferno's effect. Odin's nanites were trapped in a loop of trying to restore his falling flesh and solidifying the encompassing liquid; small diamonds were formed, but nothing to change the predominant liquid state, and metal followed where flesh retreated, but it was too slow to cease the decay.

Odin's midriff of metal and meat creaked as his flesh was ravaged by the Inferno; the amalgam unravelled. The distracted nanites lost focus on his spine, which splintered. The weight of the metal bones in Odin's legs dragged down until his spine cracked and the flesh split. His lower half continued to descend into the murk.

Dark violet blood spilled from Odin's eyes and mouth. He gurgled a roar through the liquid. His flesh blistered and began to wither—drying away, despite the submersion in liquid. His thick veins shrank into desiccated threads. Strands of his silver hair loosened and then drifted away as if on an underwater breeze.

John lay floating on the decreasingly churning water, kicking weakly to struggle afloat. A funnel erupted next to him as Odin's reassembled robotic arm wrapped around his throat; however, it lacked the strength it had prior, thus making it a contest of weakness rather than might.

'Do you think you'll get away with this, devil?' Odin hissed. 'I still have the strength to strangle the life out of you.'

John struggled to grab the pool's edge, while Odin's cybernetics weighed them both down, his flesh melting away from his metal frame. Light burns appeared along John's skin while Odin's skin grew thinner.

A shadow covered them both; a black-cloaked arm gripped John's, holding him above the shadowy fluid as Odin clung to him like a lamprey.

'Your current state is no less than you deserve, King,' announced the raspy-voiced Senior. 'By using such dangerous negative technology, you risked the occurrence of another Cataclysm. Your murder of two Seniors, attempted murder of the rest, and plot to ruin your old neighbours are utterly unforgivable. You are a monster.'

Odin groaned, wrinkled flesh peeling away from his metal skull, his heart erratically thundering behind his steel ribs.

'However, I share responsibility for your sins,' said Zero. He knelt at the pool's edge. 'Thus, I shall show you true revenge: we forgive you.'

'How dare you,' Odin gurgled. 'How dare you look down on me again.'

Zero reached his free hand into his cloak, and then he retrieved a syringe; the contents were hidden, as the vessel was solid silver. Zero pierced Odin's withering neck with the needle. He pushed the plunger, sending a substance along the path into Odin's cerebral cortex …

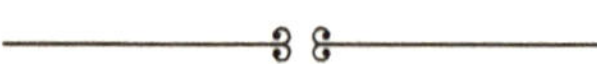

Odin examined his restored human body with astonishment while feeling his face and arms; the painful grip around his heart seemed to vanish ….

'Hurry up, Dad,' said a child's voice in his thoughts.

Ted looked up from his hands and saw two blonde children smiling—one was slightly younger than the other. 'Tommy? Connie?' Ted asked in a daze. 'You're all right?'

'Of course we are,' said Connie. 'Geez; relax, Dad.'

A woman with jet-black hair and alabaster skin walked up behind the children. 'Come on, Teddy,' said the woman in a dulcet voice. 'Let's go home.'

Ted smiled and replied simply, 'Home ... home together ... at last.' He laid an arm over his wife's shoulders, and they each held a hand of their young offspring. Consciousness faded into a bright yet soothing atmosphere ....

CHAPTER THIRTY-THREE

IF IT WORKED THE FIRST TIME ...

Zero stared at Odin; the withering man smiled, despite bloody tears streaming from his eyes. He clawed onto Odin's cybernetic right eye, and then he pulled it out with little resistance—its red aura faded to darkness.

Odin relinquished his hold on John, vanishing beneath the black water.

Zero lifted John away from the pool, leaving him to lie on the concrete beside it. He tapped the exile with his boot toe. 'Boy, are you still alive?' asked the Senior, with a lack of concern clear in his oration.

'Y-yes … I'm alive,' John responded meekly.

'I thought I told you to never return here.'

John smiled with what little strength he had left. 'I'm sorry about the … the Huon, Zero.'

'The Huon? Do not concern yourself,' said Zero. 'While it is exceedingly tedious, we can concoct more.' He walked to a section of the smoothed cavern wall. He then placed his palm against it; a pair of lift doors was unveiled, and under Zero's palm, an intercom-like device appeared. 'My fellow saviours, Artesano and Diamante,' he said, 'I require your immediate assistance.'

'Directly, Senior Zero,' a slightly gruff voice responded through the intercom.

Zero walked back to John; as soon as he reached the boy's side, the lift doors slid open.

Two Seniors emerged, both wearing dark blue cloaks of subtly different shades.

'Carry this boy,' ordered Zero.

The two Seniors nodded, and then they rushed towards John. They lifted John up; the dark water and his own blood formed small puddles around his feet. They allowed him to lean on their shoulders.

'Now, follow me to the surface,' said Zero while walking towards the waiting lift. 'There are a few unalive that we can use.'

Zero quickly tread down the silver ramp that extended out of Sevenite, with Artesano and Diamante carrying John in tow.

On the now-calm battleground, Murray and Richie sat next to the decapitated bodies of Howie and Leo. The green-clad Radar was attempting to console Lux, who sat weeping on Odin's crumbling glass throne, and finally, Váli lay silently where he had collapsed.

Lux looked up at Zero and the Seniors carrying John. She stood and marched towards them. 'You little bastard!' she cried. 'Odin nearly killed everyone because of you. You ruin everything that you touch. You drove him insane, but he was right about one thing: you are a monster!'

As Lux charged towards John, Zero caught her arm and then flipped her until her back hit the ground, dust covering her white attire.

Artesano and Diamante lay John next to Murray and Richie.

Artesano pulled back their hood, revealing sideburns and a friendly smile.

John looked up to smile meekly at Wally, who winked before restoring his hood and identity as Artesano.

'Get her back inside,' Zero ordered.

The dark-blue-cloaked Seniors grabbed Lux's arms. 'Fellow saviour, put aside this irrational rage; have you completely forgotten about your son?'

Lux's face appeared pale from shock. 'But my obligation to the Order.'

'To be a Senior requires sacrifice,' said Zero. 'However, the Seniors are not so callous to forever forbid a parent from their child.'

Lux was pulled to her feet and then dragged back up the silver ramp by the midnight-blue-clad Senior knights Diamante and John's now-respectable friend Artesano.

'What are you going to do to Herr Smith—that is to John?' asked Toat as his image materialised.

'Nothing. Normally I would just let him die because of all the trouble,' responded Zero. 'However, he has earnt some of my clemency, and his path is not yet complete. Now you, the embodiment of negative technology, are going to restore him.'

'That comment was uncalled for,' said Toat, then he sighed. 'Okay, very well. I'll help him yet again.' Toat turned to Richie. 'Sorge model fifty-one Alpha, my central control core is in Smith's vest; please retrieve it and momentarily meld it into your mind.'

Richie nodded solemnly; he fished through John's vest until he found the pocket that cradled the core. He placed the cubic core against his right temple. It sank as if his skin were quicksand. Richie's eyes emitted a blue glow.

'Okay, commencing process Deus Ex Machina,' said Richie-Toat.

Richie-Toat placed a hand on the backs of the headless androids. Some false flesh of the android bodies was pulled into Richie-Toat's hands, leaving hollow gaps in the backs of the deactivated beings. The possessed android then lifted his hands from the torsos; in each of his hands were small spinning balls of silver. He pushed his hands together, merging the objects into a single light blue sphere.

Richie-Toat pressed the sphere into John's chest. The harvested nanites instantly identified with the few that remained functional in John's body, and then they hurriedly mended their host's wounds.

John sat upright on his own, breathing deeply, although mostly unfazed by the pain caused by rapid and extensive regeneration; the burns along his skin were gradually fading away.

'I save you so many times that I'm going to have to start charging you, Herr Smith,' said Richie-Toat.

'Yeah … thanks,' John replied.

'You are fortunate, Herr Smith,' said Richie-Toat. 'Submersion in the Inferno reaction stripped away your Huon, but you had enough nanites left to keep you alive.'

'Yeah, that's me,' John said with a solemn look in his dull grey eyes. 'Always lucky.'

A small dark silver cube slid out of Richie's left temple. Richie grabbed it and then placed it back into John's vest pocket.

John shook his head as his perception of reality cleared, and Toat's holographic visage reappeared next to him. 'Richie, I'm so sorry about Howie and Leo,' he consoled.

'Don't worry, my man,' reassured Richie. 'This is reversible.'

'It's a real shame … Wait, what?'

Richie knelt between his deactivated brethren. He then grasped the bodies.

The dead sorges twitched, their crushed heads sliding back together and dismembered necks re-forming. Sand from the ground vanished into the bodies as they repaired seemingly fatal damage.

'That's one of many reasons I hate the unalive,' said Zero.

John was aghast at the revived duo adjacent to Richie. 'So, we were worried for nothing?'

'I wouldn't say nothing,' Leo said with a cough.

'Yeah, gettin' your head ripped off hurts like hell,' added Howie. 'But, as long as one of us survives, the rest of us can regenerate from most damage.'

'Okay … good.' John was confused but wholly relieved. He then turned to Murray. 'Are you feeling okay?'

'Physically? Yeah, I've survived worse,' responded Murray. 'But I feel pretty far from okay …' Clearly wanting to change the subject, he then said, 'By the way, thanks for taking good care of my coat.'

John examined his attire: it was far more battered than from his first confrontation with the king of Valhalla. Holes littered his vest, shirt, and borrowed coat, and his dark pants were so tattered that most of his upper thigh—plus his knees and shins—was largely on display.

'Yeah … sorry about that,' John said unconvincingly.

Murray shrugged and then rested his head on his knees. The trio of sorges sat around him.

Toat examined John while adjusting his oval-framed glasses. He tutted and then said, 'Yes, you look like you're in no shape to meet Doctor Factorem.' He placed a hand on John's shoulder; John's clothing changed hues to a bright silver, and then all its damage was repaired as the clothing seemed to knit itself back into its original form. When the attire had repaired itself, its colouration also reverted to its original state.

'Huh? Thanks, I guess, Doctor Toat,' said John.

Toat grinned and graciously nodded once.

'Zero—sorry, Senior Zero, can Murray and the androids stay here for a while?' John asked the black-cloaked Senior.

Zero glared intently at John, his red eyes piercing through John's own grey. The Senior glanced at Murray and the sorge trio, who remained seated on the ground. Murray, still holding his knees, stared at the sand beneath him. Zero then turned back to John. 'You're testing your luck, boy,' he responded. 'But fine.'

'And before I go back to Valhalla, I need to know: am I still exiled?' asked John. 'I'm sorry for what I've done, and turns out, Connie is still alive, which, thanks for not telling me …. And be fair, you did toss me into the wastes without emphasising the danger of Odin.'

'Normally, I don't even give second chances,' said Zero. 'And you're on your third. However, you have done well preventing the so-called Odin from destroying everything the Senior Order tries to protect. Very well; consider yourself absolved … for the time being.'

'One more thing,' said John. 'Please help Connie get better. And for sanity's sake, don't put any more of your damn negative technology into him. Odin's dead; you don't need him as a weapon any longer.'

Zero sighed and then nodded to Radar.

The green-donned Senior lifted the unconscious Colonel onto his shoulder and began to carry him back up the silver ramp into Sevenite.

'I assume that you are going to Haven to retrieve Lux's descendent,' Zero said. After John nodded, he concluded. 'Then, take this to Haven's former leader.' He pulled a small black crystal ball from his cloak pocket. His talon-like hand dropped it onto John's open palm.

John realised that it had been Odin's right eye. The eye that had caused terror to grow within his heart now seemed no more threatening than a glass marble. 'You know, you were only half right about the wastes,' he said.

'Is that so?' Zero retorted.

'Yeah, there was a lot of danger,' continued John, 'but there are decent people still outside Sevenite, and they deserve help from you … saviours, too.'

'Brazen opinion, boy.' Zero chuckled. 'However, perhaps something worth further consideration.'

CHAPTER THIRTY-FOUR

SALVATION

John traversed dishevelled dunes that looked like ocean waves caught in time—they had been formed during the aftermath of Odin's antimatter bomb blasts.

He arrived at the base of the disturbed hills around the facility named for the gods. Although the hill itself had mostly been crumbled and dragged away, the slithering metallic pathway remained, as it was a ridge of the metallic mountain that had been hidden like plant roots.

As soon as John had arrived at the platform in the centre of the crater's own centre area, a plate large enough for five people to stand upon arose a centimetre above the floor.

John stood on the dark grey plate; it descended, lowering him deep into the superstructure.

The plate stopped at the corridor that had once ended in the lift through which John had fled. The boy ran down the high corridors that he had earlier entered ill-prepared for the danger that dwelt within.

The halls hadn't changed, although they remained slightly darker, as there was no light from the black dome eyes that Factorem used to communicate.

When he clunked across the metal grate atop the pit of the ravenous chimera, John noticed a difference; the gluttonous beast had been impaled by spikes that had grown out of the pit walls around it. Part of its flabby flesh was absent; it appeared that before perishing, the chimera, in its persistent starvation, had tried to consume itself.

In the pods where the deposed 'gods' were imprisoned, the silk-clothed individuals no longer wore pained faces, as life was returning to them rather being than stolen from them. Some slowly opened their eyes, returning to the conscious world for the first time in nearly a decade.

John arrived at the doors that guarded Odin's former throne room; the doors opened for him, welcoming him, albeit eerily. The throne room had been drastically altered: the wall-pod-held 'gods' showed contentment in their dreams rather than despair from nightmares. The cable-mesh throne had been absorbed back into the floor and ceiling, and the corpses and surgical tables were gone.

Of the two doors diagonally opposite the one John came through, the door on his right creaked open. He entered through the doorway; beyond it was a room significantly smaller than the throne room, although it was still quite spacious.

The room was dark grey, like a lot of Valhalla's interiors John had seen, although it was lit by a rich combination of various light sources.

The single curved wall was covered with tangled cables, computer screens, multiple switches and buttons of varying hue and light, and tubes of unknowable liquids and, opposite the doorway, an extension of the lowest quarter of the wall assumed the form of a wide chair.

Sitting upon the seat was an emaciated man. His skin was grey, causing him to slightly blend with the room. The figure's attire consisted of a long robe that was either gold or silver that had patterning that appeared like a map of genes and a galaxy; the splendour of the cloak was evident even in the darkness of the chamber.

From the back of the seat, parts of the wall formed tendrils; the tips of which were plugs that had been embedded into the figure's skull. They were planted into his temples and the back of his top cervical vertebra, therefore making him appear to be an extension of the facility itself.

The figure had no eyes; instead, there were hollow husks. The middle of his forehead was a cavity that could house a third eyeball.

Next to the figure's seat, a quasi-mattress made of lab coats and white silk robes had been compiled; upon it lay a boy dressed in a white shirt and red overalls. Mack lay there asleep.

John slowly approached the seated figure.

'John … John Smith?' asked a fatigued yet dark and metallic voice from the figure.

'Yes,' John acknowledged.

'Ah … excellent, I have been expecting you,' said the figure. 'I know you don't recognise me, especially since we've never met face to face. I am Doctor Adam Factorem.'

'Oh … hi … thanks for getting Mack out of that prison place, sir,' John said. 'And from the looks of it, keeping him safe.'

'I know you would have wanted him to be freed, so it was the least that I could do,' said Factorem. 'Particularly for you, who liberated me from my nightmare.'

'One of the Seniors of my village retrieved this off Odin,' John explained. He then displayed the black eyeball to the room.

'Good … there is a port in my forehead; would you please insert the eye?' asked Factorem.

John held the eye between his fingers like a vice, and then he pushed the eye into the cavity in Factorem's forehead.

Nanoscopic wires plugged into the eye, pulling it into place, and then held it securely. The black eye lit up—a red sclera with a white-rimmed red pupil.

The room became slightly brighter as light grew stronger through the shadows.

'I'm eternally grateful, John,' Factorem said. 'Now this facility is back under sane authority and thus is, once again, Haven.'

'What is that eye, anyway?' asked John.

'It's the supreme command module for the entire facility,' answered Toat.

'Yes. Without it, I nearly killed myself undoing all of Theodore's programming,' said Factorem without opening his mouth, instead speaking through the walls. 'Fortunately, I was able to reverse his modifications. The Uplifted who survived shall recover their full strength shortly; the surviving Sevenite assassins, while they cannot be wholly restored, shall recover sufficient semblance of life.'

'How did Odin even get the eye from you?' John asked.

'Simple … I gave it to him,' replied Factorem.

'What? You gave it to him?' asked John. 'But why would you do that?'

'He was supposed to be my successor,' responded Factorem. 'I was so weary of watching over the Uplifted and their over-pampered offspring; they had become arrogant and self-centred. I thought fresh blood would be able to change the facility's fundamental attitudes …. But I now realise that a successor is not one I choose but one that will rise to the challenge. I suppose one benefit from King's betrayal is that the children may get their heads out of the clouds.'

'I must confess, Doctor Factorem,' said John, 'it was my fault that King was exiled from Sevenite, and so it's my fault that he betrayed you.'

'Oh, I already knew that. Theodore retold the event to me many, many times,' Factorem admitted. 'Nevertheless, I do not care about that mistake; what matters is not the past but the fact you undid his malevolent machinations. And do not forget, you may have been a factor that uprooted his life, however, you did not force him to choose his new life of treachery and murder. And it was I who transformed him into a formidable god.'

John felt an inner conflict, as he still carried guilt over contributing to the transformation of Theodore King into Odin. A part of John needed to relinquish the misplaced responsibility, yet another part wanted to keep the guilt as penance for causing the madness of Tommy and the exile of adult witnesses, including his own father, who, due to Malik's mad schemes, was sent as a slave to Lunacity—a settlement through which John had passed, unaware of this transaction. While fighting with the remorse, John hoped that perhaps time could assuage his sense of obligation to atone for the misery he had wrought, even if it were pain caused unintentionally and unknowingly.

'Now I have a confession of my own: I also utilised deception upon our first meeting,' Factorem explained. 'I knew Theodore would not be reasonable to your audience, nor could he be defeated by you and this small child; I would have to be as insane as him to believe you could. I knew that, to gain the necessary power to win, you would need to undertake the Deus Ex Machina process, and I needed you to be in a position in which you could not refuse it.'

John furrowed his brows in confusion; he felt too exhausted to conjure any anger, thus he simply let Factorem continue.

'I am sorry that I allowed you to be subjected to such agony. As with King's tyranny, that is another shame I must carry.'

John was still, lacking any movement, even signs of breathing; he appeared to be a weary wax model. However, this facade broke quicker than it had arisen. 'I would be very, very upset over that revelation,' said John, 'but I can't be close to being someone that gets all "high and mighty" over miscalculated misfortune, even if you did have some understanding of what would happen. And it isn't like you didn't suffer from your resistance, too.' He knelt next to Mack and gently tapped the child's shoulder. 'Plus, you protected this kid from the dangers I dragged him into.'

Mack awoke and yawned wearily; he locked eyes with John next to him. Mack then punched John's right cheek, wincing from the consequence of hitting something stronger than his own small fist.

'Yeah … I probably deserved that for dragging you into this mess,' said John as he stood up. 'I know I can never be forgiven, but hopefully, an introduction with someone you know might change your mind.'

Mack looked at John, an eyebrow raised in puzzlement.

'He means we found your mother, *kleines Kind,*' explained Toat. 'She may seem cold at first; however, I believe she can become like the mother you wanted, or at least some such idealised nicety.'

Mack slightly smiled as John helped him to stand.

'Over the last eight years, I've been thinking, as it was the only thing in which I had freedom. With this boy, I also send a proposal with you, John,' said Factorem. 'Haven has been an isolationist society for far too long; I accepted outsiders but never encouraged the search for others in need, and those born here were allowed to feel superior to those who were not. Ergo, I have concluded that—to ensure the survival of the Uplifted and perhaps humanity itself—a closer, kinder allegiance must be established between Haven and all the settlements in the surrounding area, and perhaps one day, beyond to every surviving colony.'

'Are you sure about that, Doctor?' asked Toat.

'Yeah, well … I don't think the Seniors would agree with your decision.' John frowned. 'They're possibly more elitist than your people … so, I'm not sure it would work.'

'Nonetheless, I entrust you to deliver my first message,' said Factorem in his natural, dark-sounding voice. 'We shall see what, if anything, is discovered through it … so, go now. I still have much of King's damage to repair …. And once again, thank you for amending my failure.'

John nodded half-heartedly, and then he began to retrace his steps back out of Haven, leaving Factorem, who John assumed would now work busily to correct the myriad aberrations King introduced, all from within his own gigantic living sarcophagus; Mack and Toat followed by John's side.

'Are you feeling all right, Mack?' asked John. 'You didn't get hurt in any way?'

'Not really. I fell asleep sometime after I got caught … I dunno how,' responded Mack. 'But I might hit you again for bringing me here unless we get to my mum before I feel like it. All the guys, too … Richie, Leo, and Howie, and Murray; my whole family.'

'Yeah,' John said, briefly distracted by the thought of the androids' impressive resurrections. 'All of them …'

'I told you, Herr Smith,' said Toat, adjusting his glasses routinely again, 'that Mack would be completely safe, in spite of being trapped and all alone.'

'Yeah, yeah, I know you told me so,' said John as he laid a hand on Mack's shoulder. 'You know, for what it's worth, I am really sorry.'

Mack brushed his hand off casually. 'I know you are, John, but I'm still mad you brought me here,' he said. 'But I guess it's okay now, and I'm gonna finally meet my mum … I hope she didn't abandon me because she didn't love me.'

'In spite of the way she is now,' said John, 'your mother truly does care about you.'

Mack's smile became more genuine, and his steps increased in speed; a light of optimism was clearly beginning to emerge from within him.

'Do you think Adam's plan will work?' asked Toat. 'Collaboration of rival factions has had some fairly disastrous consequences in the past, since it usually mutates into imperialism; it could happen again … for the six- or seven-thousandth time.'

'Who knows?' responded John. 'But I suppose it might be worth the risk with the benefit of history's knowledge.'

'I hoped that you would say something like that,' said Toat, grinning while adjusting his glasses further up the bridge of his nose. 'In fact, I expected it. You have made this reality more amusing than I had experienced, since I was actually among the so-called living.'

'Glad to be useful.' John half-smiled.

The dark blue halls of inner Haven changed slowly and moderately to a lighter shade as the restored master of Haven organised his superstructure.

The Uplifted—who had survived the absorption by the spheres that clung to them—were gently lowered out of the capsules in which they had been imprisoned.

The survivors were, ironically, clearer in their hearts and minds than before the false god had created his dominion. Their fundamental improvement elevated them closer to the roles that they had arrogantly assumed were rightfully theirs before their fall.

John Smith had hated almost everything about his existence; however, once he had lost everything, his presence in the world became significant, and most importantly, an unexpectedly more positive influence on the chain of causality.

Although John did cherish the memories he held of his friends, most of his recollections were buried in crushing boredom and a feeling of perpetual isolation. He was trepidatious while also optimistic that Connie would receive proper care, enough to recover his old self, so that, one day, he could pursue his dreams of renewal. John was surprised—and yet reassured—that Wally had been appointed a Senior—a group of ambiguity, albeit also with promise to reform into something more charitable.

As the cacophony of his enmity against Odin faded to memory, John felt the phantom pain caused by his father's disappearance. Whether John Salt was still held by lunar-dependent cultists or was somewhere else out in the world, John Smith tried to find solace in knowing that his search for his father wouldn't be alone.

John would remain alive and free, which enabled him to remember his nostalgia without being drowned in further monotony. Peril may threaten his sanity or life, and thereby his memories, yet it would never truly be able to destroy them; as long as his efforts survived in him, or others, John Smith would leave a legacy more compassionate.